Broken Lives

Book One of the Barrington Family Series

Chris Taylor

LCT Productions Pty Limited

LCT Productions Pty Limited

18364 Kamilaroi Highway, Narrabri NSW 2390

ISBN: 9781925119992 (eBook)

ISBN: 9781925441000 (Print)

Other books by Chris Taylor

The Munro Family Series (in order)

The Profiler
The Investigator
The Predator
The Betrayal
The Deception
The Negotiator
The Christmas Vigil (A novella)
The Ransom
The Defendant
The Shooting
The Maker

The Sydney Harbour Hospital Series
(in order)

The Perfect Husband
The Body Thief
The Baby Snatchers
The Final Bullet
The Debt Collector
The Lab Test
The Stolen Identity
The Cliff-top Killer
The Likeable Fraudster

The Sydney Legal Series
(in order)

An Accidental Murderer
At the Hand of her Father
A Woman Scorned
Lies and Deception
Ordinary Evil
The Ties that Bind
The Perfect Crime
A Toxic Inheritance
Malicious Love

The Craigdon Family Series
(in order)

Callum
Joel
Isabella
Nicholas
Sophia
Flynn
Noah
Logan
Elizabeth

The Barrington Family Series (in order)
Broken Lives
Broken Promises
Broken Bonds
Broken Spirits
Broken Minds
Broken Vows
Broken Hearts
Broken Dreams
Broken Homes

The Fairfax Family Series (in order)

A Cattleman in Disguise
A Cattleman's Quest

A Cattleman's Daughter
A Cattleman's Secret Baby
To Catch a Cattleman
The Doctor and the Cattleman
To Rescue a Cattleman
A Cattleman's Heart
For the Love of a Cattleman

Bachelors and Brides Series
(in order)

Matilda
Austin
Farrah
Benjamin
Verity
Denver
Ebony
Tyrone
Willow

Books by Chris Taylor
Writing as Bella Christian

This Is Where It Ends Series
(in order)

Jessie's Story

Ryan's Story
Holly's Story
Sarah's Story
Veronica's Story
Love audiobooks? Check out Chris Taylor Books on audio
iTunes   Amazon   Audible

Join Chris Taylor's Facebook reader group/fan page and be among the first to receive news of book releases, cover reveals and other amazing offers.

Join Now!

This book is dedicated to my daughter, Millie Taylor. Happy Birthday, sweet sixteen! You bring such love and laughter into our home. I'm so proud of the young woman you're becoming. I love you.

And as always, to my husband, Linden. My best friend, my soul mate. I love you to the moon and back.

Chapter One

Christopher Barrington leaned back against the richly upholstered, dark cherry-colored leather armchair and took a sip of single malt scotch. He took a moment to savor the rich, warm taste of the whiskey on his tongue before swallowing. His stepfather, Frank Barrington, sat in the matching armchair opposite. The sun had long since set on the balmy April evening and the usual frenetic energy that permeated the busy office had dissipated.

The secretaries, the receptionist and Frank Barrington's personal executive and her assistant had left for the night. The phones had fallen silent. Christopher and Frank had the spacious office suite to themselves. They'd taken advantage of it to indulge in one of the many bottles of fine aged whiskey standing tall and straight on the glass shelving that lined part of one wall of the suite behind them.

The CEO of Barrington Mining lifted his glass. The downlights overhead glinted off Frank's thick, snowy white hair. Though he'd turned sixty-five on his last birthday, his tanned skin glowed with good health and vitality and his trim frame was evidence that he paid close attention to his diet and exercised regularly. Christopher was sure his stepfather was fitter than most men half his age. The only giveaway of aging was the myriad of wrinkles that creased his eyes and the corners of his mouth—and those had more to do with the countless hours he'd spent out in the sun at mine sites than anything else.

"Here's cheers," Frank murmured.

Christopher obliged by leaning forward to clink his glass with his stepfather's. They both took a sip.

"What are we celebrating?" Christopher asked.

"Your coming of age, of course."

Christopher grunted. "I'm forty-one, Frank. Hardly a coming of age."

Frank had invited Christopher to call him "Dad" on the day Christopher's adoption became official, but Christopher had always resisted. He'd been twelve years old and angry at the world. Scrap that, he'd been angry at the world for most of his life.

Good old Henry Craigdon… My biological father… A man who had a lot to answer for…

"I didn't mean it in the literal sense son," Frank continued. His gaze settled purposefully on the white sling Christopher wore to support his right arm and shoulder. "You performed an act of heroism, saving Archie Craigdon from that fire last week. The old Christopher would have seen the smoke and flames coming from Archie's house and driven right on by. It wouldn't have occurred to *that* Christopher to stop. But not only did you stop and call for help, you entered a burning building and put your own life at risk in order to save someone else. Like I said, heroic."

Christopher squirmed. The action pulled his injured shoulder. He clenched his teeth against a wave of pain. He'd broken his collarbone and torn a few ligaments during his rescue of Archie from the house fire. The fact he'd suffered injuries didn't make him anyone special. Frank made him sound like some superhero. They both knew darn well he was as far from a superhero as he could get. Until recently, he'd been a selfish prick, living his life for no one but himself. It was strange how events had worked to change him into... *What?*

He didn't know. But Frank was right. He *was* different. He felt different. Better about himself. Hopefully the years he'd spent feeling bitter and twisted over a father who'd refused to recognize him, even on his death bed, were over.

Henry Craigdon…

They shared blood, but Henry refused to even acknowledge that. Even after the DNA tests proved it beyond doubt.

The prick.

Familiar feelings of anger and hopelessness welled up inside him. He forced the bitter memories away. He was done with feeling like that. Done with allowing those thoughts to stunt his life. Negativity would no longer be part of his life moving forward. Christopher's close brush with death in the fire had made him realize how much of his life had been spent getting nowhere. And wasting further effort on being angry with a dead man was an exercise in futility. He had so much time to make up. Starting now.

He took another sip of his whiskey and stared past Frank's shoulder to the floor-to-ceiling glass windows that perfectly framed the city skyline, including a glimpse of the iconic Sydney Opera House. Careful not to spill his drink, Christopher stood awkwardly. The sling made things a little difficult to balance. Steadying himself, he wandered closer to the glass.

He looked down to the streets far below. The occasional car and tram moved slowly along the road. He saw pedestrians walking along the footpaths, in singles and twos and threes. Heading home. Meeting friends for dinner. Going about their lives. It seemed they all had somewhere to go, someone to be with.

He felt a pang of loneliness and swallowed a sigh. It was no good feeling sorry for himself. He had no one but himself to blame for reaching the ripe old age of forty-one with nothing to show for it. In an effort to distract his attention from such maudlin thoughts, he turned back to face his stepfather.

"Have you heard from Vaughan?" he asked, referring to his adopted brother, the second of Frank's nine children.

"No," Frank said.

Christopher frowned. "It's like he's dropped off the face of the earth. I haven't heard from him for three days. I was meant to catch up with him for a drink in the city last night, but he didn't show. I've tried calling him. It just goes straight to voicemail. Where the hell is he?"

"It's only been three days," Frank replied. "I don't think we should be worried just yet."

"But it isn't like Vaughan to disappear like this. At the very least, I'd expect him to call me back. I waited for him to show up in that bar for over an hour and nothing. He didn't even bother to phone me to explain."

"Have you spoken to any of the others? Perhaps one of your brothers or sisters knows where he is?"

Christopher dropped back into the armchair and sighed. "I've called everyone. No one's heard from him since the party."

Frank nodded. "Ah, the party. Well, he did turn forty. Perhaps it hit him hard. Some people are like that. They don't cope well with getting old."

"You're right, but I never thought Vaughan was one of them. He certainly didn't act like that at the party. I spoke to him for quite a while and he seemed to be having a good time. He was surrounded by women as always, dancing and kicking up his heels. He seemed to be celebrating the fact he'd turned forty, not hiding in the shadows trying to pretend it wasn't happening."

"Maybe he's having a delayed reaction? I'm sure he's all right," Frank said.

Christopher compressed his lips and nodded, suddenly feeling the need to look on the positive side. "You're right. Maybe he's just gone somewhere to come to terms with the realization he's getting old."

Frank raised a single white eyebrow in silent query. "Is that what you did?"

Christopher grimaced. "Something like that. I wasn't at all happy to leave my thirties behind. In fact, I did my best not to acknowledge it. I got myself good and drunk for three days. By the time I'd sobered up, I'd accepted the fact I was forty, but I still didn't like it. Now I'm forty-one and I don't feel any more cheery about it. No wife, no kids. No job. I've wasted so much time."

"I wouldn't call it a waste of time. You spent years working for McClintock's. You gained a lot of experience along the way. You worked your way up into a position of authority. That's something to be proud of."

Christopher merely shrugged, unconvinced. He'd never told his family he'd been fired from McClintock's. Even now, the memory of that humiliation had the power to fill him with shame. Of course, it had been his own fault.

"Well, I can't do anything about a wife and kids, but I can fix the job thing," Frank said with a smile.

Christopher blinked away the unhappy memories and focused on what his stepfather had said. "A job? Here? At Barrington Mining?"

Frank shrugged and sipped from his whiskey. "Why not?"

Christopher slowly shook his head. "I mean no offense, Frank. But you've always known I have no interest in a career in mining. All that red dirt and heat in the Pilbara. All that coal dust in the Hunter Valley. I'm sorry. You're going to have to leave the mining to Hannah. I'm not cut out for that kind of job."

Frank gave him a wry smile. "Your sister didn't think she'd enjoy it, either, and look at her? She loves running that mine in the Hunter Valley."

"That might be so, Frank, but I'm not Hannah. She's twenty-three with her head still in the clouds. She's still full of optimism for her future. She doesn't have a clue who she is or what she really wants to do with her life. I'm glad running a mine has given her some direction, but it's not for me."

Frank shrugged and sipped from his whiskey. A companionable silence fell between them as they both became lost in their thoughts. A while later, Frank spoke again. "I bought some land around Badgery's Creek a few years back."

"The site of the new airport?"

"Yes."

"Smart. You always were a forward thinker. Now with the government finally developing the area that land's probably doubled in value."

Frank chuckled. "Quadrupled, in fact. I could make an indecent profit on it if I sold."

"Is that your plan?"

"No. I want to branch out, diversify. I want to invest in something other than mining."

"You're going to develop the land?"

"Yes. I have thirty acres. There are a few existing houses on the land. I bought all but one of the owners out a decade ago and have leased the properties back to them. Of course, they've all been given notice their current leases won't be renewed. As soon as the last one expires and we get the go ahead from the local council, those houses will be demolished."

"What are you looking to build?"

"Office buildings, apartment blocks, maybe even a hotel."

"Sounds ambitious. Who are you partnering with?"

Frank gave a wry grin. "Craigdon Enterprises. Does that matter to you?"

Eighteen months ago, Christopher would have been outraged that his stepfather had chosen to go into business with Christopher's biological father—the very same father who had caused Christopher so much pain. But Henry had died more than a year ago, leaving the company to a son he'd fathered with one of his mistresses and Christopher had finally learned to set his hurt and bitter disappointment aside.

"I've been in talks with Nicholas Craigdon," Frank continued. "He seems like a decent young man. He's keen to come on board with the Badgery's Creek development."

Christopher nodded. "Nick's a good bloke. A straight shooter. Honest. Good at his job. He's in charge there now since Logan Craigdon transferred his interest in the company over to him. He's a good man to have on your side."

"So you're okay about me getting involved with them?"

"Yes, Frank. I've come to terms with my feelings for the Craigdon family. We're good."

Frank's expression flooded with relief. "I'm glad you feel like that. I think a business relationship between the Barringtons and the Craigdons will be fruitful for many years to come."

"So, what's the time frame on this new development? Do you have a start date?"

"No, but soon. Hopefully within the next month or so. With the state government on board and pushing full steam ahead with the new airport, the local council's also decided to play ball. It will mean millions of dollars in development fees for them. Not just from us, but from all the other developers who are doing the same thing." Frank paused and then added, "The only possible cause for delay goes by the name of Lexi Greenaway."

Christopher quirked a single dark eyebrow. "Who's Lexi Greenaway?"

Frank sighed. "Right now she's a pain in my ass."

"How so?"

"Remember I said I'd bought all but one of the existing properties?"

Christopher nodded.

Frank continued. "Yeah, well Lexi Greenaway is a tenant in the one property I couldn't secure ten years ago. I approached the owners, of course, but they refused to sell. Back then, the new airport was still a pipe dream, so I let things lie. About eight months ago we started negotiations again. I was finally able to strike a deal. We completed the sale six months ago. I sent Lexi Greenaway a notice to vacate but so far she's proving difficult."

"Does she have a current lease?"

"No. Her lease with the previous owner had expired. That's if she even had one. I didn't see any evidence of it in the contract. I didn't see the need to go to the trouble of entering into a new lease. I knew it wasn't going to be that long before we'd be moving her out."

"Then she hasn't a leg to stand on. Without a lease, you're only required to give her ninety days' notice."

"Yes. And I've given her more notice than that. But she's refusing to accept the validity of my claim to the property."

Christopher frowned. "Why would she do that?"

"Beats me. I negotiated with the owners in good faith. Contracts were signed and the money was paid over. I assumed the owners would give their tenant some indication that the property had been sold, but perhaps they didn't. It's not my problem, but of course, it's become my problem because every time I send another letter informing her of the date she'll be required to vacate, she writes me a very curt response in return—to the effect that she's not going anywhere. I haven't worried about it too much because we were still a ways off from a start date, but that date's drawing closer and I need to resolve this outstanding issue."

Christopher compressed his lips. "Is there anything I can do to help?"

His father smiled. "As a matter of fact, yes."

Christopher shrugged. "Hit me."

"I need you to go and pay her a visit."

"You want me to rough her up?" Christopher asked jokingly.

Frank laughed and rolled his eyes. "Of course not. I just want you to introduce yourself. Explain the situation. Soften her up with your charm. We have the law on our side as far as evicting her goes, but I'd rather not have to go down that path."

Christopher smiled. For too long he'd resorted to dirty tactics to get his way, but that was the old Christopher. He'd vowed to change his ways, to turn over a new leaf. He could be charming when he put his mind to it.

"Leave her to me. What else do you know about her?"

"There's not much I can tell you. I haven't met the woman. My dealings were only with the owners and then, after the initial contact, everything else was conducted through the lawyers. The house she lives in isn't anything special. In fact, it's falling down around her ears. It's an old homestead that must be nearly a hundred years old and it hasn't seen any repairs in the time I've owned it. The land's the only thing of value."

"I wonder why she's so attached to it then," Christopher mused.

"From what I understand from my lawyer, she's lived there for quite a few years. She grows vegetables. Has a couple of sheep, some cows, a chicken run, some ducks and geese. An orchard too, I believe," he said dryly.

"Perhaps that's why she's so reluctant to leave? Finding acreage like that for rent anywhere near Sydney won't be easy."

Frank shrugged. Irritation filled his face. "That could be true, but that's not my problem. The house sits smack bang in the middle of my proposed development."

"She has to know she's not going to be left with much choice, especially when the excavators move in."

Frank sighed. "I've explained all of that in my letters. Nothing seems to get through to her. That's where I was hoping you might help."

Christopher shot Frank a wry look. "You already asked me to pay her a visit, remember?"

"Yes. But I'm hoping for more from you."

"Oh?"

"You just said you were looking for a job, something to keep you busy. How would you feel about heading up my end of the development project?"

Christopher sat up in his chair and gave a half-laugh of disbelief. "You're joking, right? It's one thing to visit an irritating tenant and convince them to move on. What do I know about construction management?"

"You've worked for developers before. The experience you gained at McClintock's should hold you in good stead. As for the rest, you can learn it on the run."

"I worked in the contracts department. Not exactly hands-on."

Frank merely shrugged as if Christopher's lack of experience was of no consequence. Christopher wished he had his stepfather's confidence in him. Still, the idea of heading a project on the scale this one promised to be held a certain appeal. It would be exciting, challenging and would no doubt consume his days for a long time to come.

"I need someone I can trust at the helm," Frank continued. "This is a long-term project. There's no guarantee a project manager won't leave before the job's done. You're family. I can count on you to hang around."

Christopher smiled. "Gee, thanks. And here I thought it was my expertise in construction you were attracted to."

Frank waved his comment away. "Don't worry about your lack of experience. You have something far more important: life experience. Plus, you're a good-looking bloke with plenty of charm to throw around when you choose. I need someone like you to convince Ms Greenaway to move out without giving us any further trouble. That's the first order of priority. Until she vacates that house, we're limited in what we can do."

Christopher nodded slowly. "Okay. I accept the challenge. What do I get if I convince this woman to move?"

"Half a million dollars," Frank replied.

Christopher whistled. "That's a nice chunk of change."

"It's chicken feed compared to what we anticipate we can make on this deal. You get that tenant out of there and it's yours. This woman's been a thorn in my side for the past four or five months. I'll be more than pleased to have the problem resolved."

"Leave it with me. I'll find out why she's playing such hard ball and explain to her that we hold all the cards."

Frank tapped his finger against his temple. "Maybe she's lost her marbles? Who knows?"

Christopher grimaced. "How old is she? Hell, if she's suffering from dementia or is just plain senile, that could cause a problem. The newspapers just love that kind of story: *Billon-dollar development company forces senile granny off her land.* Even if she's only a tenant, we need to keep this very quiet," Christopher continued. "If the media get wind of it, things could become extremely uncomfortable for us. If she *is* old and senile, are you prepared to offer her alternative accommodation, or are you going to go as far as eviction? You may need to have a backup strategy."

Frank's eyes gleamed with satisfaction. "Does this mean you're going to take on the job?"

Christopher smiled. "I think it does."

Frank grinned. "Well, great. As for your other question, I haven't asked the lawyers her age or her circumstances. All I've been focused on is the need for her to be gone. I guess if she's old and senile... We'll talk about other possibilities then."

"What's the time frame?"

"As soon as you can. A week or two at the most. I'm expecting a decision out of the Liverpool council any day."

"Consider it done." Christopher pushed away from his chair and stood. Frank did the same. He held out his hand to Christopher, who shook it with his good hand and then pulled his stepfather in for a quick hug. He felt Frank tense in surprise.

"Thanks for believing in me," Christopher said, his voice suddenly husky with emotion.

"I've always believed in you," Frank said quietly.

Christopher swallowed the lump in his throat and nodded. What Frank said was true. Even when Christopher had been consumed with anger and self-pity over the refusal of his biological father to acknowledge him, Frank had been there for him.

Determination flooded through him. Not for the first time, Christopher made a silent vow to put his anger and bitterness over Henry behind him and focus on a more positive future. The truth was, Henry had never deserved him as a son. Frank had been a real father to him. He alone deserved that honor.

"I'll text you this woman's details," Frank said. "No time like the present to make her acquaintance."

Christopher eyed him somberly. "I promise I won't let you down, Dad."

Frank's eyes flared wide with surprise and then filled with tears. Christopher felt an answering emotional response inside him. In all the years since Frank had come into Christopher's life, he'd never once called him "Dad." The significance of the moment wasn't lost on the man who'd been the only father figure Christopher had known.

When Frank finally responded, his voice was husky and low. "You take care, son. I'll speak to you soon."

Chapter Two

Lexi Greenaway tucked a loose strand of hair behind her ears and stared down at the letter in her hands. She'd read over the few short typewritten lines three times, but the contents remained the same. She was being evicted.

Like the previous letters she'd received over the past few months, this one filled her with a mixture of anger and foreboding. The dark bold letterhead seemed to mock her.

Barrington Developments.

She'd done some research on the Internet. Barrington Developments was a wholly owned subsidiary of Barrington Mining, a king in the resources sector. They had a limitless budget to throw at the fight, while she had next to nothing. What chance did she have against them? It wasn't fair. This was her home. The home she'd created with her husband. They'd moved in on their wedding day. And even though it had been four years since Ronnie had died, she'd continued to live there. And why wouldn't she? It was perfect for her needs and the needs of her children. Besides, she loved the place.

The farmhouse was set on two acres and surrounded by natural bushland. Lexi loved the wide open spaces. There was enough land to have a couple of dogs and a cat, some goats, a cow and some chickens.

Years earlier, Ronnie had dug up a sizeable vegetable patch and she'd taken delight in planting seasonal vegetables. Ronnie had also planted an orchard— orange trees, nectarines, apricots, mandarins. It took a few years, but finally the trees were big enough to bear fruit which was particularly handy now, when she had so many mouths to feed and money was short.

The place was also a reasonable distance from the hustle and bustle of the city of Sydney and that was another reason why she loved it. Though the roof leaked and wind rustled in under the eaves, filling the rooms with cold air on frosty winter nights, there was nowhere else she'd rather be.

The old house held so many memories and now that Ronnie was gone, those memories were even more poignant. She'd done her best to make the place cozy, adding colorful rugs on the wooden floorboards and bright throws and cushions on the couch. The curtains had faded, but they still served their purpose and added a stylish touch to each room. More importantly, her children loved living there too. It was the only home most of them had known.

How can I tell them our life here is over? How can I tell them we're being forced out? It isn't fair and it isn't right and I'm not giving in without a fight. This is Australia. A free and democratic country. They can't push me off my land. They have no right, no matter what they say. I don't care about their letters. Send me fifty letters, a thousand. I'm never going to change my mind. Barrington Developments can go to hell…

Lexi smiled at her burst of stubborn determination. It made her feel better, even for a little bit. She wished it were that easy; that she could merely tell Mr Barrington that thank you, but no. She wasn't going anywhere. Of course, she'd already done this in her two previous responses. Polite letters explaining to Barrington Developments that she had rights and she wasn't going anywhere. They obviously didn't agree because in return she'd received another letter, this one much more hostile.

She felt like David facing Goliath. The Christians squaring off against the lions. She might have the law on her side, but she was under no illusions. This was going to get messy and it was going to cost a lot of money. Money she didn't have. This wasn't a battle for the faint-hearted.

But what choice do I have? I'm not going to sit by and let them march all over me and take my home!

But underneath the anger and feelings of injustice was a cold lump of dread she'd refused to acknowledge. She'd dismissed the first two letters out of hand, but after the third one, she couldn't help but wonder if there was more to their claim they owned her land than she'd believed. Ronnie's parents had given them the land as a wedding present, but she'd discovered at the reading of Ronnie's will that the title had never been transferred to them. Her parents-in-law had muttered something in response to her question about that; the gist of what Lexi understood was that they agreed to attend to the oversight, but what if they hadn't?

Fear trickled through her veins. She couldn't deny that was a possibility. So far, she'd seen no evidence that the title was now in her name. It had been more than a year since she'd last brought it up with her parents-in-law.

Oh, God. What if the claims being made by Barrington Developments are legitimate?

The weight of her predicament suddenly felt overwhelming. Though she still missed Ronnie when she least expected to, it was at times like this that she really wished he was still around. Someone to talk to about it, someone to share the burden. Someone to help her fight, or at the very least, help her make the best decision.

Not that Ronnie had been strong in that area. He'd always been a risk-taker, had always lived life on the edge and to the fullest, despite the responsibilities he had. She'd despaired that he'd ever learn to grow up. And though she loved his free spirit, sometimes his lack of maturity had been exasperating. She'd joked more than once that his behavior was like having another child in her household.

But Ronnie was gone forever and over the years, lost in grief and the need to care for eight children, she'd lost touch with most of her friends. She still had Ronnie's parents. They lived a couple of suburbs away. But though they were good people, they always avoided confrontation—like they'd done each time she'd raised the issue of her property...

Once again, doubts assailed her. She couldn't shake the feeling that something was dreadfully wrong. Either Barrington Developments was mistaken and had no claim to her land... Or George and Dorothy had done something so terrible Lexi couldn't bear contemplate it.

She stared down at the letter. It was dated three weeks earlier. The third such letter she'd received. Like all the others, this letter talked about how the owner, Barrington Developments, was giving her notice to vacate.

She'd dismissed the earlier letters out of hand and had written back politely but firmly to the sender. They were mistaken. Her home wasn't owned by Barrington Developments. It had been a wedding gift from her late husband's parents. But it seemed whoever was in charge at Barrington Developments wasn't listening—or else they knew something she didn't. The thought filled her with a fresh wave of dread.

From somewhere deep inside her the stirrings of misgivings grew stronger. Three formal letters from Barrington Developments. Three letters, all purporting to have the legal right to ask her to vacate. Of course it could all be a hoax, but why would they be so persistent? It was time to speak to someone and get things sorted out, once and for all.

With fingers that weren't quite steady, she reached for her phone and dialed the number listed in the address details on the letterhead. It rang out twice and was answered by a pleasant-sounding woman.

"I-I'd like to speak with Frank Barrington," Lexi stammered.

"One moment."

The sound of music filled her ear. A few minutes later, the call was picked up.

"Barrington Mining. This is Casey."

"Oh, um... I was wondering if I could speak with Frank Barrington."

"May I ask who's calling?"

"It's Lexi Greenaway."

"Please hold."

Once again, music sounded in Lexi's ear. While she waited, she drew in a deep breath and tried to get control of the nerves that flip-flopped in her stomach.

"Ms Greenaway. It's Frank Barrington."

The smooth, deep voice jolted her. A fresh wave of anxiety surged through her. She drew in another breath and clung to her courage. "Mr Barrington. Thank you for taking my call."

"I'm glad you made contact. I take it you've received my latest letter?"

"Yes." Lexi swallowed against a lump of nerves. "The thing is, you don't seem to understand. It's like I pointed out in my previous responses. This land belongs to me. You have no right to force me to vacate it."

Lexi bit her lip and waited for him to respond. She didn't have to wait long.

"I'm afraid that's where you're wrong, Ms Greenaway," the smooth voice continued. "Barrington Developments acquired that land six months ago. It was purchased from George and Dorothy Greenaway. Your landlords, no doubt. I'm sorry that they didn't see fit to inform you. They were the property owners and I have no understanding why you are under the impression the land is yours. Nevertheless we purchased it fair and square, so your misunderstanding is with the previous owners and is really not my problem."

Lexi gaped as the shock of his announcement ricocheted through her. "No! No! You're wrong! George and Dorothy gave the land to me and my husband ten years ago!"

Frank Barrington sighed. "I don't know anything about that. What I do know is that Barrington Developments is not in the habit of committing illegal acts. Everything was researched, reviewed, negotiated in good faith. That land was purchased for a fair price. It belongs to me. I can send you a copy of the title deed to prove it. We are well within our rights to ask you to leave."

Over the noise in her head, Lexi strained to hear his words. In a panic, she stabbed her finger at the screen and ended the call. Her heart beat so hard she thought she might be having a heart attack. She forced several deep breaths in through her nose and out through her mouth before she felt calm enough to sort through her tumultuous thoughts.

It can't be true… It can't be true…

George and Dorothy Greenaway were the nicest in-laws a new bride could have hoped for. They'd sympathized with the fact she had no family of her own and had welcomed her with open arms. She'd been overwhelmed by their kindness, their love, their acceptance. They'd gifted the house to her and Ronnie as a wedding present. The house had been old and rundown even then, but it was theirs. A place for them to call home. A place to raise their family.

She'd always loved the thought of having a big family. It was something she and Ronnie had spent hours talking about when they were first married. But the years came and went and still she didn't fall pregnant. Eventually they went for tests. Ronnie was infertile. No one could explain why, but the doctors were all certain he'd never father a child. After spending a few weeks feeling sad and sorry for themselves, they decided to go down the path of adoption.

It was harder than they'd imagined. The waiting lists were long. It would be years before they qualified. So Lexi suggested they become foster parents. It was something she had firsthand experience with. Fortunately, Ronnie was thrilled with the idea and there was no end to the number of needy kids. They'd started with only one, but that had soon grown to four. Before she knew it, there were six and then seven. When she approached Ronnie with the thought of adopting some of them, he readily agreed.

Generally foster kids came and went as their family circumstances changed. It was always hard to see them leave, but Lexi understood that's the way it had to be. And then Ronnie had been killed and her world had been thrown into chaos. She'd never been more grateful to be surrounded by their kids. They'd helped her through what had been an immensely difficult time. Without them, she didn't know what she would have done.

She was just as thankful for the large old farmhouse that made it possible for her to have so many children under one roof. Four of the five bedrooms were filled with bunk beds. In her room was a double bed and enough room for a cot. Though most of the children she fostered were old enough to sleep in a bed, she occasionally took in a baby.

The big farm kitchen sported a large wooden slab that served as a dining table. Two long wooden benches ran the length of the table, giving everyone a seat. Meal times were always crowded, loud and noisy, but Lexi wouldn't have it any other way. She loved the fact the old home provided safety and security for so many vulnerable kids. That in some small way, she was helping them to have a better life.

But now that was all under threat and unless Frank Barrington was lying, it seemed like her in-laws were responsible. With nerves and nausea swirling inside her stomach, she reached for her phone once again and scrolled through her contacts until she found her mother-in-law's number. George and Dorothy had some explaining to do.

Chapter Three

Christopher checked the address his stepfather had given him. According to the GPS, Lexi Greenaway's place was only a few more miles ahead. A faded white wooden mailbox with the words "Serenity" painted in graying black was the only sign he'd arrived. Flicking on his indicator, he made the turn. His Mercedes bounced along a rutted dirt track toward a rundown house. With each bounce, he winced at the pain in his shoulder.

The injury to his collarbone and ligaments had happened a little over a week earlier. The fire that destroyed Archie Craigdon's house had happened the night of Vaughan's fortieth birthday celebration. Though the doctors assured Christopher it was healing well, it still hurt, especially at times like this when he was being jostled all over the place. Thankfully, the track ended about a hundred yards along and Christopher brought the car to an abrupt stop in front of the dilapidated house.

A century ago, no doubt the farmhouse had been charming, with a high pitched roof, large windows and surrounded by wide bullnose verandas on three sides. An equally ancient gum tree filled one corner of the front yard, providing shade for two red kelpies who were asleep in the sun. As he pulled up they came to their feet slowly and studied him with a lethargic kind of curiosity.

Their tongues hung out of their mouth and they both panted. He understood how they felt. It was mid-autumn, but the noonday sun was still hot on his bare head as he made his way across the yard. He climbed the four weathered steps that led to the veranda and then crossed over the creaking boards. He looked around him and noted the state of disrepair that was even more obvious up close.

Why wouldn't the woman jump at the chance to get away from this? The place is damn-near in ruins…

The thought gave him confidence. This should be like taking candy from a baby. Frank had told him about the call he'd received from Lexi Greenaway. She was still in denial about the ownership of the property. No matter. Christopher had the solution for that. He would produce the title deed and wave it under her nose. Legal title to the property trounced everything. His pocket held a copy of the deed and he was ready to produce it. Senile or not, there was no argument the old lady could mount against that kind of evidence.

Play nice, Christopher… You're not that prick anymore… remember?

He'd raised his hand to knock but before he could, the front door swung open. An attractive woman with sky-blue eyes stared back at him. She held a phone in her hand and looked both distracted and surprised. Her generous mouth was full and plump—just ripe for kissing.

That thought came from nowhere. Christopher cursed under his breath.

What the hell…? Surely this isn't the difficult tenant…?

He forced his gaze away from the temptation that stood before him. It had been way too long since he'd been with a woman. That's all this instant attraction was. A normal reaction of a hot-blooded man to an incredibly attractive woman.

A frown marked the smooth skin of her forehead. He guessed she was in her mid-thirties, though the rich chestnut hair that hung in thick waves around her shoulders and her slim shapely figure made her appear much younger. She put the phone back up to her ear and spoke into it.

"I'm sorry, Dorothy. I have a visitor. I'm going to have to call you back."

She ended the call. Her gaze swept over him from head to toe. Her eyes flared wide with momentary surprise at the sight of the sling supporting his right arm, but she quickly hid her reaction behind a polite mask.

"I'm sorry, but whatever you're trying to sell, I'm not buying. Please leave the way you came."

Christopher blinked away his surprise and offered her a smile. He'd learned a long time ago that his charm could get him most places. He was sure Lexi Greenaway was no exception.

"Oh, I'm not a traveling salesman. I'm looking for Miss Lexi Greenaway."

The woman folded her arms across her chest. "I'm Lexi Greenaway. And it's *Mrs*," she corrected defiantly.

Christopher hid his surprise and surreptitiously swiped at the sweat that trickled down his neck. This April day was uncharacteristically hot weather for autumn, even by Sydney standards. He looked at Lexi again. Frank had made no mention of a husband. Not that Christopher had asked, either. For some reason, he'd assumed the recalcitrant tenant was elderly and on her own. In fact, he'd assumed a lot of things.

For one, when Frank had talked about the woman who lived in a run-down farmhouse with a motley collection of animals, he'd envisaged a woman in her seventies or eighties, tottering around on a walking stick, tending to her four-legged friends. He even contemplated the possibility she'd lost her marbles and that was the reason she'd failed to comprehend that the property she occupied had been sold and she had to leave.

The woman in front of him couldn't be further from those imaginings. It took him a moment to recalibrate.

He belatedly held out his hand. "Mrs Greenaway, I'm Christopher Barrington."

She looked down at his hand and pointedly ignored it. Heat crept up Christopher's neck. Self-consciously, he dropped his hand to his side and gave her another beguiling smile.

"Lovely place you have here."

Her expression remained unforgiving. "Barrington? As in Barrington Developments?"

To Christopher's consternation, the heat spread across his face. He tried valiantly to hold her gaze, but only managed a few seconds before he lowered it. "Yes."

"*Hmph.*" She sniffed. "Are you related to Frank? The one who keeps sending me letters?"

"Um, yes. He's my stepfather. I'm here as his representative."

The dogs had come up to investigate and were now sniffing around Christopher's legs. One of them jumped up at him, getting a claw caught in the fabric of his five thousand-dollar suit. Christopher cursed under his breath and took a step back. The woman continued to glare at him.

A fresh trickle of sweat ran down his face. "Do you mind if we go inside, out of the heat, Mrs Greenaway?"

Her expression darkened. "Why should I let you inside? The people you work for are liars and thieves."

"I'm sorry you feel that way, Mrs Greenaway. I can assure you, that isn't true."

Her scowl deepened. She glared at him with eyes that glittered like sapphires. Right now they stared at him coldly.

"Get off my land."

Christopher reflexively held up his hands in a sign of surrender and then audibly groaned as his injured shoulder protested the movement. The pain was sharp and swift and left him gasping. From the look of alarm on the woman's face, he looked as bad as he felt.

"Are you all right? You've gone very pale."

He gritted his teeth and managed a tight nod. "I'm fine."

"What happened to your arm?"

"Broken collarbone."

"Did you get into a fight?"

Christopher gave a wry grin. "Not quite."

When he didn't bother to elaborate, curiosity burned behind her eyes. He deliberately waited her out. She didn't disappoint.

"So, are you going to tell me what happened?"

With his left hand, he swiped at the sweat on his brow. "Do you mind if I go inside, where it's cooler? I could use a drink of water."

He watched with barely concealed amusement as concern for his welfare warred with her instinctive dislike of him and all that he stood for. The battle played out on her face. And then, after a long moment and with obvious reluctance revealed in every tense line of her body, she turned away, leaving him to follow after her.

The long corridor was lined with floorboards that had no doubt once been polished to a shine. They now looked worn and dull. Doors opened on either side. In one room, two sets of bunk beds stood against the walls. Clothes spilled out of old wardrobes and shoes were scattered across the floor. He continued forward. Photographs in cheap wooden frames lined the walls on both sides of the hallway. Christopher glanced at them as he passed and then frowned. The photographs were all of children, of various ages and ethnicity, although the majority appeared indigenous.

Perhaps her husband's indigenous?

The woman turned and caught him staring at the photographs and seemed to pick up on his confusion. Though she didn't owe him an explanation, she opened her mouth and said, "My children."

He heard the pride in her voice and then the meaning behind her words penetrated. His eyes went wide. "*All* of them?"

"Yes. All twenty-seven of them." She eyed him defiantly as if daring him to question her.

Christopher wasn't often lost for words, but this time he couldn't have formed a reply if he'd tried. He opened his mouth and closed it again, and opened it yet again, before snapping his mouth closed. He felt like a barramundi on the end of a hook—mouth open, gaping and struggling for breath.

A tinkle of laughter filled his ears and he stared at Lexi Greenaway in astonishment. She covered her mouth with her hand in an effort to hold in her laughter, but humor continued to shine in her eyes.

"Oh, Mr Barrington! The look on your face!" She laughed again.

Christopher compressed his lips and scowled. He wasn't used to being the brunt of a joke. He didn't appreciate being the brunt of one now.

"Obviously they're not all your biological children," he bit out.

She chuckled. "How astute of you. You're right, of course. None of them are my biological children. Most of them are my foster kids. I've had so many over the years. Some of them are now grown and have gone out into the world. Others are still living here with me. Along with my adopted children."

Christopher was once again taken by surprise. Before he could formulate a response, the woman turned away again and walked down the hallway. With his head still buzzing, he followed her to the end of the corridor which opened up into a large and airy kitchen. She went immediately to an old fridge that stood in one corner. Reaching inside, she withdrew a tall pitcher of cold water and poured him a glass.

"Thank you," he murmured as she handed it to him. Their fingers brushed and he blinked at the arc of electricity that sparked at the contact. He snuck a glance in her direction, but she appeared completely indifferent.

What the hell? This is ridiculous! She's married for God's sake! I might be a reprobate, but I've always drawn the line at making a play for a married woman...

He drank greedily from the glass, emptying it in one go.

She quirked a silky, dark eyebrow. "You weren't joking when you said you were thirsty."

He set the glass down on the counter and resisted the urge to wipe the back of his hand across his mouth. "Yes. It's pretty darn hot outside."

It wasn't much cooler in the house. He looked around him. The windows in the kitchen were both open, but there wasn't much of a breeze. No ceiling fan, no air-conditioning. It was like stepping back in time. And yet Lexi Greenaway looked fresh and unruffled, completely unbothered by the heat. No doubt she was used to it.

"Would you like another?"

Given her earlier standoffishness, he was a little surprised by her courtesy, but accepted nonetheless.

"Thank you."

Once again, she filled the glass from the pitcher and handed it back to him. This time he made sure to avoid contact with her fingers. He muttered his thanks and took another couple of mouthfuls, his thirst now mostly slaked.

"So, are you going to tell me how you broke your collarbone?"

He eyed her steadily, calculating that it wouldn't do his case any harm by creating some kind of connection with her. Already some of her earlier aggression toward him had dissipated. What better way to build rapport than by sharing something personal? He half-grimaced and did a good job at feigning reluctance.

"I'm sure you're not really interested."

"I wouldn't have asked if I didn't want to know."

He grinned. "Okay, but don't forget, you asked."

A pretty flush turned her cheeks pink. She looked flustered. Satisfaction poured through him. He concealed it behind another charming grin.

It looks like you've still got it, old boy…

This was going exactly the way he'd planned. He let a couple of more beats pass before he spoke again in a deliberately offhand way. "I broke it while trying to rescue someone from a burning house."

She stepped back and her eyes flared wide with surprise. It was obvious that was the last thing she'd expected him to say.

"Are you for real?"

He shrugged and then winced as the movement sent pain arcing through his shoulder. "Yes. I assure you. That's exactly how it happened."

She regarded him with barely restrained curiosity. "And did you rescue them?"

Christopher nodded and gave her a lopsided grin. "Yes. I did. He got out of hospital a few days ago and is now recuperating at home. According to all reports, he's going to be fine."

Her eyes were still wide with surprise and there was now a gleam of admiration lighting the blue orbs. "Wow. So you... You saved his life."

Once again, Christopher went to shrug and then pulled himself up just in time. "I'm no hero."

She looked like she wanted to disagree, and then she seemed to remember the reason behind his visit and her expression turned circumspect. Her arms came up and folded across her chest.

"Why are you here, Mr Barrington?"

"You mentioned you'd received several letters from Barrington Developments. Do you happen to recall what they said?"

Anger flared hotly in her face. "Of course I do. That's how I know you work for a pack of liars."

"I take it you're referring to the fact the letters state your property is now owned by Barrington Developments and you're required to vacate."

Her expression turned hard. Her eyes were now shards of blue ice. "Yes, Mr Barrington. That's exactly what they say. Only, it's not true."

Christopher quirked an eyebrow and tried for some levity. "Which part, Mrs Greenaway? The fact we own your house, or that you're required to leave?"

Her gaze narrowed. "Is this a joke to you, Mr Barrington? Is the thought that I might lose my home— the only real home most of my children have ever known—something you find humorous?"

Something in the pureness of her expression and the directness of her gaze made Christopher uncomfortable. He flushed and hastened to reassure her. "No, of course not. I understand how upsetting this must be for you, but that doesn't change anything. This property was sold to Barrington Developments six months ago and the demolition team are on their way in. You need to leave and that's the end of it."

She stared at him for a moment and then shook her head from side to side. "No! You're wrong! I don't believe it! There's no way this place was sold! You're lying! You're just as deceitful as your stepfather!"

And then she placed both hands flat on the counter and leaned toward him with murder in her eyes.

"Get out. Get out and get off my property before I call the police!"

Christopher opened his mouth to argue, but decided to let things lie for now. Her face was flushed with anger. Her chest rose and fell from the force of it. There was no way she was open to hearing reason. Instead, he took the copy of the title deed from his pocket and set it on the counter. She didn't even glance at it.

"Momma? What's going on? Who's this?"

Christopher looked down in time to see a young boy of about three or four years old wander in from outside. His dark, golden skin and wide, flat nose were evidence of his indigenous heritage. His T-shirt was stained with mud, along with his face and hands.

Lexi's expression immediately changed to one of tenderness. She dropped to her knee and despite the fact he was filthy, drew the boy in for a quick hug.

"Michael! What have you been doing?"

The boy shrugged. "Nothing. Just playing." He turned his gaze toward Christopher. "Who's that?"

"No one you need to worry about," Lexi reassured him. "Mr Barrington was just leaving." She turned the boy to face the direction of the door. "Now, go and wash up so you can have something to eat. I have fresh nectarines and a nice glass of milk."

The boy's face broke into a smile and he happily rushed from the room. Lexi turned her attention back to Christopher. She scowled.

"Why are you *still here*, Mr Barrington?"

"Okay, okay. I'm going. But this isn't the last you'll see of me, Mrs Greenaway. I suggest you speak to your husband and work out where you're going to live. Because, make no mistake, you're going to leave. All of you."

With that, he turned on his heel, retraced his steps along the corridor then quietly let himself out.

Chapter Four

Lexi stared at the empty space across from her, where moments earlier Christopher Barrington had stood and told her the land she had believed was hers now belonged to someone else. Even though this wasn't the first time she'd been so advised, she still felt frozen with disbelief. The sinking sensation in the pit of her stomach had grown increasingly harder to ignore.

Lexi hadn't pressed her in-laws about transferring the title to her after Ronnie's death. After all, they'd just buried their only child. As the months passed and she heard nothing, she forced herself to be patient. The last time she'd raised it with them, they'd brushed her question away.

It had been just after Christmas lunch more than a year ago. Dorothy and George had hosted her and her eight children. They'd even given each child a present which had been extremely generous. Though they weren't struggling to put food on the table, Lexi's in-laws were certainly not well off. Besides, it was Christmas. Lexi didn't feel right questioning them further about the title to the property at that time.

She'd been in the middle of speaking with Dorothy when Christopher Barrington had turned up. Now she had to summon up her courage all over again. She couldn't put it off any longer. She had to know the truth.

Ignoring the lump of ice-cold dread lodged in her belly, with a hand that wasn't quite steady, Lexi reached for her phone and called her mother-in-law. Dorothy answered on the second ring.

"Lexi, how did things go with your visitor?"

Lexi got straight to the point. "He was from Barrington Developments, Dorothy."

There was a moment of shocked silence on the other end of the phone. Then Lexi heard a sob of anguish.

"They offered us a million dollars, Lexi. A million dollars! How could we say no to that?"

The lump of dread in Lexi's stomach morphed into a block of concrete. "When did this happen?" she asked numbly.

"I don't know. Six months ago, maybe."

"Why didn't you tell me?" she cried.

"We wanted to. We really did. But we didn't know how. We're so sorry, Lexi. But we had no choice. A million dollars! It seemed like a huge windfall at the time. You would have done the same thing."

"No, Dorothy. That's where you're wrong. My house might be nothing more than weatherboards and roofing iron to you, but to me it's our home. The home I shared with Ronnie. The home where I'm raising our kids. What are we going to do, Dorothy? There are nine of us! Where are we going to live?"

"I'm sorry Lexi," Dorothy sobbed. "I'm so sorry. Please believe me. The money... We couldn't turn it down."

"I'm your son's wife! Your daughter-in-law! These children are your grandchildren! Surely you don't want to see us put out on the street! We need your help!"

"I'm sorry, Lexi. But I can't help."

"Of course you can. You just got handed a million dollars."

"The thing is," Dorothy said hesitantly, "there's not much left."

It was the final insult. There was no way Lexi's in-laws had spent a million dollars in six months. What Dorothy must mean is that she didn't *want* to help them. It was as simple as that. Still, Lexi refused to give up. The safety and security of her children was at stake. She drew in a deep steadying breath and tried again.

"If you could see your way to giving us a small portion of the sale proceeds, we could buy something further out. Maybe move to the country. We don't need a million dollars. Just enough to give us another start."

"I'm sorry, Lexi. I just can't."

Lexi bit her lip against a surge of desperation and quietly ended the call. It would do no one any good to prolong the conversation. She was sure Dorothy and George hadn't acted with malice when they'd sold her house out from under her. Lexi knew what a million dollars could buy and how tempting such an offer would have been to a couple who lived simply.

So she understood their decision to sell. What she was terribly sad about and what she didn't understand was why Ronnie's parents hadn't found the courage to tell her. And now she knew—they weren't prepared to do anything to help her. She was now practically homeless. A mother with eight children and nowhere to live.

What are we going to do?

A wave of desperation washed over her. She jammed her fist against her mouth and stifled a sob. Not only was the old house filled with memories of her late husband, it was also the only real home her children had ever known. For the five she'd adopted and the other three who lived there.

Over the years, there had been many more. Foster kids in desperate need of love and security. A roof over their heads. Food in their bellies, a tender look, a comforting hug to get them through another night. Most had faced trauma no child should have to, and yet they were fighters. Their resilience continued to amaze her. Perhaps because at their ages, she'd been exactly the same.

A surge of determination rushed through her. She pulled back her shoulders and straightened her spine. Her gaze snagged on a sheet of paper on the counter. She picked it up. It was the title deed to her property. Sure enough, it showed the registered proprietor as Barrington Development Corporation.

Christopher Barrington must have left it there. He hadn't been able to convince her with his words, but they both knew a title deed didn't lie. Beside it was the latest letter she'd received from his stepfather. With a muffled oath, she grabbed both pieces of paper and crushed them in her hand.

Anger surged through her. With clenched fists, she screamed aloud her frustration, her anger, her hurt. This whole sorry mess might have come about because of her in-laws' actions, but she was in no doubt who the real enemy was.

Barrington Developments.

She wasn't going to take this without a fight. If Christopher Barrington thought he could come in and demolish her home without her doing all she could to stop him, he had another think coming. She looked forward to showing him just how badly he'd underestimated her.

Elizabeth Craigdon adjusted her sunglasses and stretched out on the pool lounger. She was taking advantage of the unseasonably warm autumn day. The sun sparkled like diamonds off the crystal-clear water. She glanced at Archie who lay stretched out beside her and felt a rush of love

I came so close to losing him. If it hadn't been for Christopher…

She resolutely pushed the traumatic thoughts away and focused on something more positive. For one, Archie was home now and doing just fine. The doctor had urged him to take things slowly, but expected a full recovery.

Thank God…

Her thoughts drifted to the letter she'd recently composed to the son she'd given up for adoption over forty years ago: Vaughan Barrington. She'd written him a letter before she'd discovered he was none other than the adopted brother of her stepson.

She'd intended to sit on the information for a while, to mull it over, taking her time to decide what to do with it, but then she'd grown impatient. Life was too short to spend wasting time. She wanted her son to know the truth. She wanted to meet with him, hold him, tell him how much she loved him.

She knew of Frank Barrington, even though they'd never met. He was the man Christopher's mother had married, the same man who'd adopted Christopher when he was twelve. Though Christopher didn't speak much about his other family, she knew they'd been good to him. It filled her with gladness that Vaughan had been raised in a good and decent home. About that, at least, she could finally put her mind at ease.

She hadn't told any of her six children that Vaughan Barrington was her biological son. She hadn't even told Christopher. In fact, the only other person who knew was Archie. After having so many secrets come between them in the past, they'd both agreed not to keep secrets from each other again. She'd honored that request, but the telling didn't extend to her children. All they knew was that she'd given up a baby for adoption years before she'd met their father. She wanted to wait until she'd spoken to Vaughan before she disclosed such important details.

As if privy to her thoughts, Archie turned to her and said, "So have you received a response to your letter yet?"

She grimaced and shook her head. "No. I posted it nearly a week ago. He should have received it by now." Her stomach clenched with a familiar anxiety. "What if he doesn't want to meet me?"

"Did you make it easy for him to contact you?"

"Of course. I included my home address, my email address and my phone number. I've made it as easy for him as I can. If he only wants to talk over the phone, that's fine. Or even write to me. I don't care. I just want to know he's okay with me being his mother."

Archie shot her a tender look. "Why wouldn't he be okay with that?"

She shrugged. "I gave him up for adoption. I'm sure he's wondered why. Maybe he thinks I didn't love him enough to keep him? Who knows?" She clutched at her hair with her fingers as her anxiety got the upper hand. "I jump every time there's a knock on the door or when my phone rings, thinking it might be him. My nerves are shot. I'm a wreck." She smiled wryly. "I know not much time has passed, but I hope Vaughan doesn't take too long to get in contact. I don't know that my nerves can stand it."

Archie leaned closer and patted her arm. "Don't worry so much about it, Lizzie. I'm sure he'll be in contact. But it might take some time. You have no idea what he was told about his birth parents. He might not have even known he was adopted. If that's the case, it might take him a lot more time to come to terms with the idea. You need to be patient and accept that whatever happens, happens. You've done all you can to connect with him. It's now beyond your control."

A surge of anguish nearly stole her breath. She blinked back a sudden rush of hot tears and turned her gaze on Archie. "But what if he doesn't *want* to talk? What if he wants nothing to do with me?"

"Then that's a decision you'll have to accept."

Archie's quiet response almost paralyzed her with an overwhelming feeling of devastation. Though the counselor from the adoption office had warned her that sometimes happened, she refused to believe it would happen to *her*. After all, she knew who Vaughan was and where he lived. The address provided to her was in Bondi. An affluent suburb on the beach and only fifteen minutes' drive east of the city.

She'd give it another week and then she might take things in hand. After all, it would be a simple matter to turn up outside his home. It had worked for Ashton Walker. The fact Ashton had turned out to be a con artist who only pretended to be her son was beside the point. At the time she'd accepted him and his story without question.

She sighed, hoping it didn't come to that. She'd much rather Vaughan be the one to make contact. That way she'd know for sure he wanted to meet her. Another option would be an ambush. That might work against her, but if her son didn't come to her, she'd be left with no other choice. She was damned if she'd let another forty years pass by without having him in her life.

It was late afternoon when Christopher made his way back to the offices of Barrington Mining. The last rays of sunlight glinted off the glass building, painting them in hues of crimson and orange. Christopher took the lift to his stepfather's suite, waving perfunctorily to Frank's executive assistant, Casey, who sat behind her desk.

He shot her a friendly grin. "Is he free?"

"Yes, Christopher."

Nodding in acknowledgement, Christopher continued down the corridor, past the boardroom and knocked on the open door to his stepfather's office. Frank spied him immediately and waved him inside.

"Christopher. Take a seat. I've been dying to hear how it went with Lexi Greenaway."

Christopher dropped into the upright chair that stood opposite Frank's desk. "You didn't tell me she was married."

Frank shrugged. "I didn't know. Like I told you before, I only dealt with the owners. An elderly couple. George and Dorothy Greenaway, if memory serves me right."

Christopher frowned. "Greenaway? Do you think they're related?"

"Maybe."

"That could explain why Lexi didn't know about the sale. Maybe they deliberately didn't tell her. If she's related to the previous owners, there's a good chance she would have objected to the sale of her house, especially given it's filled to overflowing with kids."

Frank's bushy white eyebrow quirked upwards. "How many are you talking?"

"I don't know, but she's a foster mother. She has photographs of twenty-seven children on her walls."

Frank's jaw dropped. "Twenty-seven? Are you kidding? Hell, the woman's a saint."

"I only saw one during my visit, but I passed several bedrooms that were wall to wall with beds. From the look of the place, she still has a fair number living there."

"What does the husband do?"

"I don't know. He wasn't there."

"So how did the meeting go? Were you able to convince her to leave?"

Christopher squirmed in his chair. "Not exactly."

Frank grinned. "What does that mean?"

"I told her our claim to the property is legitimate. That it was purchased six months ago from the owners. She called me a liar and...threw me out."

Frank burst into laughter. "Oh, and here you were so sure of the fabled Barrington charm. I'm disappointed in you."

Christopher held his jaw at a stubborn angle and waited out his father's mirth. "I'm not going to be beaten. She's chosen the wrong man to pick a fight with. We have the law on our side. I left her a copy of the title deed. It's only a matter of time before she sees sense and concedes defeat. Don't worry, Dad. I'll get her out of there."

"By fair means or foul?" Frank questioned softly.

Christopher scowled. "Fair, of course. I'm not that other man anymore. I've vowed to put all that trickery and nonsense behind me. I'm determined to only do what's right."

His stepfather nodded approvingly. "Fair enough. What's your next move?"

Christopher thought of the delectable Lexi Greenaway and narrowed his eyes. Though it gave him no pleasure to evict her and her houseful of children, he had no choice. That land belonged to Barrington Developments and nothing was going to change that.

Still, there was an old saying that one caught more bees with honey than vinegar and that surely applied in this situation. Lexi Greenaway obviously had a heart of gold. She'd fostered twenty-seven children. And she'd been concerned for him when he'd been in pain. She'd invited him inside, albeit grudgingly, and had offered him a glass of water, knowing full well he was the enemy. It showed him that underneath that anger and distrust, she was a decent person.

He was sure she'd eventually see reason and accept the way things were, especially if he plied her with some good old-fashioned charm. She might not have responded to it the first time, but he was sure that was only a minor setback, caused when she'd been taken by surprise.

No, all hope wasn't lost when he was dealing with someone as decent as Lexi Greenaway. He'd bet money on the fact she was related to the previous owners and for whatever reason, they hadn't seen fit to tell them about the sale. Well, that wasn't his problem, even if he was a tad curious about why they'd do such a thing. Keeping silent about the deal seemed unnecessarily heartless, cruel even. Particularly when they must know it wouldn't be easy finding another place large enough to house all those children.

Christopher thought about the absent husband. He hoped for their sake Mr Greenaway earned a sizeable income, although if he did, he certainly hadn't spent it on the house. The place was bordering on derelict. Looking after so many children was expensive. Relocating was also expensive. Yes, he hoped Lexi's husband earned a fortune.

They were going to need every penny.

Chapter Five

Lexi tossed the ball in Michael's direction and laughed when he caught it and in the same smooth motion, did a somersault over the lawn in the front yard.

"Way to go Michael!" she cheered.

Michael stood and brandished the ball high over his head, his grin splitting wide his face. Lexi's heart tightened at the sight of his joy and exuberance. He'd been living with her since he was a baby. He hadn't always smiled like that. She knew only the barest of details about his past, but none of them had been nice.

His mother had been a drug addict. Michael had been born with learning difficulties as a result. His father had disappeared before he was born, leaving Michael's mother to raise him alone. She'd done her best, but by the time child services had stepped in, he'd been in bad shape. Severely undernourished and living in squalor, three-month-old Michael had been removed from his mother's care. Enquires had been made about other relatives, but it seemed baby Michael had no one who cared enough to come forward.

Lexi and Ronnie were already registered foster carers. Though they had five others living with them at the time, Lexi had been only too happy to offer the baby a home. She and Ronnie had instantly fallen in love with him. When his mother died of a drug overdose a couple of months later, they had applied for adoption. The court papers had come through a week before Ronnie's death.

Lexi blinked in an effort to banish the sad memories. Ronnie was in heaven. She was determined to carry on the legacy they'd started together and to continue offering her home to needy and vulnerable children.

If only George and Dorothy hadn't sold our home…

That thought was immediately followed by another, more determined one. She'd find a solution. Something that didn't involve uprooting her or her children. She wasn't sure what that might be, but she'd work out something.

"Catch, Momma!" Patrice yelled.

Lexi's attention was dragged back to the game. The ball hurtled toward her and she caught it easily and then tossed it back. Patrice caught it with a triumphant shout and then tossed it toward her three-year-old foster brother.

"Catch, Leroy!" Patrice shouted.

Leroy moved forward on chubby legs, but fell over on the grass. Lexi's heart skipped a beat, but she smiled again when her youngest sat up, grinning. Patrice ran over to him and knocked him over again with a boisterous hug.

"I told you to catch, Leroy!" She pressed kisses over his sweet face. The toddler giggled.

Lexi's heart turned over with love. She couldn't imagine her life without her babies. All eight of them. Only five of them had been adopted. The other three were foster kids. Though she would have gladly adopted each and every one of them, there were rules and regulations about that kind of thing. Mainly, the biological parents had to agree. Some were willing and that had enabled Lexi and Ronnie to adopt five of the children, but others, like the biological parents of Patrice, Kishaya and Denzil were reluctant, and the system allowed them to have the final say.

No matter that they couldn't care for their children, or that the children would be better off in a safe, secure and loving home—not all biological parents were prepared to relinquish their rights and Lexi respected that. In the meantime, she ensured the children had contact with their biological parents as often as was practicable and encouraged their relationships. She would have given anything to have had the same opportunity when she was young.

That didn't stop her from longing for them to become legally hers. The thought that one day any of the three, or all of them, could be lost to her, saddened Lexi, but there was nothing she could do about that. While Denzil and Kishaya, at fourteen and fifteen respectively, understood how these things worked, five-year-old Patrice didn't quite understand. Every time Patrice told her how much she wanted to stay with her forever, Lexi was filled with a combination of overwhelming love and pain.

That's what made fostering so difficult; that any moment, a child could be taken away, returned to its biological parents, never to be seen by the foster carer again. Still, it was a risk Lexi was willing to take and there was always the chance she'd be given the go-ahead to adopt them. That's what kept her going. That, and the fact she knew without a doubt she was making a difference in that child's life. She was just so grateful the department had agreed she could continue to foster them and had remained supportive of her adoption plans.

As if sensing the direction of Lexi's thoughts, Patrice abandoned Leroy and ran across the yard. She threw herself against Lexi and hugged her hard. Lexi crouched lower until she was eye to eye with her foster daughter. Framing her little face with her hands, she kissed her.

"I love you, Patrice."

Patrice grinned and tightened her hold. "I love you too, Momma."

Patrice had turned five only a week earlier. Lexi could have sent her to school, but she preferred to wait until they were turning six. She firmly believed a child had a better start to learning if they were just that little bit older and the law backed her in this.

"Someone's coming!" Michael shouted.

Lexi stood and turned in time to see a dark gray Mercedes turn into her driveway. It slowly made its way up to the house. The kids ran to gather around her, not used to strangers. As the car drew closer, Lexi's heart sank. She'd been expecting him but hadn't been sure when he'd arrive. But now he was here. Her nemesis. Christopher Barrington.

This time he wore an Akubra pulled low over his dark head to shade him from the midday sun. His eyes were concealed behind designer sunglasses. His suit jacket had been removed and his tie had been loosened. He still wore the white sling.

She watched as he climbed awkwardly out of his car. She'd asked for this meeting, but that didn't make this any easier. She'd spent the past few days praying for a solution. The property had been sold, but perhaps she could appeal to his sense of decency to leave her house alone.

Failing that, she was hoping she could buy it off him. Though she didn't have much in the way of savings, she'd managed to set aside a bit. The money she'd received from Ronnie's life insurance had been invested and remained untouched. She'd set it aside to help fund her children through university when the time came, but maybe a greater need had just presented itself...

Christopher lifted his hand in acknowledgement. "Hello. How are you all?"

The kids broke ranks at his friendly smile and gathered curiously around him.

"You were here before," Michael stated.

"Yes, I was. You're Michael, aren't you?"

Michael nodded, looking pleased he'd remembered.

"What's your name?" Leroy demanded around the thumb he'd stuck in his mouth.

Christopher squatted on his haunches until he was at eye level with her three-year-old. "My name's Christopher. What's yours?"

"I'm Leroy. What happened to your arm?" Leroy pointed to the sling and then promptly returned his thumb to his mouth.

"I broke my collarbone," Christopher explained.

"What's a collarbone?" Leroy asked, his blue eyes dancing with curiosity.

"It's your shoulder silly," Patrice said with an eye roll.

Christopher stood slowly and regained his former height. Lexi could see he was trying hard not to smile.

"You're right," he said to Patrice, his expression perfectly serious. "It's one of the bones that joins up to my shoulder. Right here." His finger traced his clavicle. "You're so smart for someone so young. What's your name?"

"Patrice. I'm five."

"Five, wow." His gaze flicked to Lexi. She saw the question in his eyes.

"She turned five last week. The day after you were here."

"Shouldn't she be in school?"

Lexi stiffened. When it came to her kids, she didn't care for nosiness or any kind of criticism, implied or otherwise.

She stared at Christopher coldly. "Like I said, she's only just turned five. It's my legal right as a parent to hold her back from school until her sixth year. I've exercised that right because I believe it's in the best interests of my child. Do you have a problem with that?"

Christopher looked taken aback at her ferocity. He held up his good arm in a sign of surrender. "Whoa! Easy now. I didn't mean it as a criticism."

"Well that's what it felt like."

"I'm sorry. I don't know the first thing about kids. I just thought they were in school by age five."

"Some of them are. In fact, in this state you're allowed to send your kids to school as long as they turn five by July of that year. July! Can you believe it! They're still babies! At that age, they should be out running around, playing, being kids. Not stuck in a classroom expected to sit still and concentrate for hours on end. And people wonder why there are so many kindergartners who get distracted and cause disruptions. It's not because they're naughty. It's just that they need a little more time to mature. A year is a long time in the life of a child."

By the time she'd finished, her breath came fast. Embarrassment heated her cheeks. She always got worked up when it came to her children, and in particular, their education, and she knew not everyone felt as strongly as she did. Christopher appeared to be one of those. Then she recalled he'd told her he didn't know anything about children. That figured.

Forcing a few deep breaths into her lungs, she made a concerted effort to relax. And then she remembered the reason for his visit and she got tense all over again.

"I thought you might call ahead, instead of just turning up. You could have given me some warning," she admonished.

"So you could do what? Disappear? You were the one who asked for this meeting, remember?"

She grimaced. "Of course I do. It's just that…"

She glanced at the children who had returned to her side after satisfying their initial curiosity. He shrugged, as if it were of no consequence to him. And of course it wasn't. What did he care if her kids heard every word they were about to say? He wouldn't have to deal with their questions, their fear and concern for the future.

"Do you mind if we go inside?" he asked. "It's kind of hot out here."

With a nonchalance she was far from feeling, Lexi lifted her shoulder in a half-shrug and turned her back on him. The children scampered along beside her, plying Christopher with questions.

Lexi barely listened. Her mind had already turned to the upcoming conversation and the various possibilities of how he'd react.

What if he disregards my proposal and decides to throw us out anyway?

The fear associated with that weighty thought centered in her stomach and turned her feet to lead. He might be kind and do it with all the care and concern and sincerity she saw in his eyes, but the result would be the same. They'd be evicted. Homeless. She'd be forced to delve into Ronnie's insurance payout and she'd been hoping to avoid that.

Reluctantly climbing up the wooden stairs and across the veranda, she pulled open the front door. Not waiting to see if he followed, she made her way down the long hallway to the kitchen. Operating on autopilot, she opened the fridge door and pulled out a large pitcher of freshly squeezed lemonade made from the lemons she'd picked from their orchard.

She busied herself gathering enough glasses for the children and added a plate of homemade chocolate biscuits to the tray. She filled the glasses and then took the tray to the screened-in veranda that was off the back of the kitchen. It was a room they used as a play area during inclement weather and close enough that she could keep an ear out for any trouble, but far enough away that they wouldn't overhear the conversation she would have with Christopher Barrington.

So far, she'd managed to keep the dark specter that loomed on their horizon a secret from her children. Even the older ones, the teenagers—Denzil and Kishaya—were oblivious to the growing realization that the safest home they'd known was about to be bulldozed to the ground. That's if Christopher Barrington had his way.

He came into the kitchen carrying Patrice who clung to him like a monkey. The smug expression on her dark little face told Lexi all she needed to know. No doubt she'd begged and pleaded with Christopher to carry her and it seemed he'd fallen for her charms. Perhaps he wasn't as heartless as he appeared. The thought gave her hope.

Patrice was a precocious, confident child who'd come a long way from the quiet and withdrawn two-year-old Lexi had first welcomed into her home. It had taken a lot of patience and love to have the child set aside her instinctive fear of adults and to coax the toddler out of her shell. Little by little, Patrice was learning to trust her. Change didn't just happen and Lexi had cried the first time the little girl had spontaneously hugged her.

Like Michael and Leroy, Lexi had only been given the barest of details about the little girl's family life, but she'd been around kids like her long enough to know Patrice was now in a much better place. The case worker who regularly visited Patrice, agreed. Lexi prayed she'd be able to keep the child for as long as possible.

Christopher set Patrice down on the floor and she scampered off in the direction of the playroom. Lexi could hear her children chattering away together and decided to get the difficult conversation she was about to have with Christopher over with as quickly as she could.

"Can I get you a tea or coffee? Or maybe a cold drink?"

"A cold drink sounds great." He pointed toward the jug of lemonade. "That looks good."

She poured him a glass and handed it to him. He murmured his thanks and took a sip. As much as she wanted to get this over with, she wasn't about to forget her manners. She waited.

"*Mm*, this tastes great."

She suppressed the shiver of delight that reflexively pebbled her skin. He was her enemy and having his approval wasn't something she'd planned for. She needed to remember that. He might have the law on his side, but that didn't mean she had to like him, no matter how polite and engaging he was to her and her children.

"It's homemade," she forced herself to reply. "I picked the lemons myself."

His dark eyebrows rose in response. She could tell he was considering the implications of her answer. It was his stepfather's company who was moving the bulldozers in, not only to destroy her house, but no doubt the orchard, too. There would be no more freshly squeezed lemonade coming from these trees in the future.

He made a non-committal sound and took another sip. Lexi moved sideways until the counter separated them. She needed to put some distance between them, both literally and figuratively. Though she'd been forced to concede Barrington Developments was the legal owner of her home and land, she still hadn't given up hope of reaching a compromise. An agreement whereby she was able to purchase the land back from them at a reasonable price would be ideal. After watching Christopher interact with her children, she was confident he might just be decent enough to give serious consideration to her proposal.

Lexi poured herself a glass of lemonade and kept one ear out for her kids. Though they weren't capable of fully understanding the conversation she was about to have with Christopher, she still didn't want them listening in and asking awkward questions, or even worse, grasping enough meaning to realize their home was under threat. Her children had faced too much instability and insecurity in their short lives. She wasn't going to contribute to it if she could avoid it.

"So," she said, plastering a fake smile on her face, "let's get this over with."

Chapter Six

Christopher carefully set his glass down and pushed it to one side. Today Lexi was dressed in a T-shirt and denim cut-offs. Christopher couldn't help but notice how they emphasized the long, tanned length of her legs. He dragged his gaze upwards and concentrated on her face.

Her big blue eyes reminded him of the summer sky. Framed with thick, dark lashes, they regarded him with an air of vulnerability and innocence that made him want to take her in his arms and reassure her that he wouldn't let anything bad happen to her. Ever.

At the same time, he wanted to run a mile. He was there on business and it wasn't going to end well for her family. The last time they were together, she'd refused to accept his father's company had any claim to her land. Given that she'd been the one to call him and suggest another meeting, he could only assume she'd finally come around.

She cleared her throat, interrupting his musings. "Firstly, I'd like to offer you an apology. You were right. This property was sold six months ago to Barrington Developments by my husband's parents. It was done without my knowledge."

"What about your husband? Did he have any idea?"

She stared down at the counter and swallowed. At last, she looked up at him. "My husband's dead. He was killed in a motorbike accident four years ago." She blew out her breath and shook her head. "Four years. It feels like only yesterday."

Christopher didn't bother to conceal his surprise. At the same time, he felt secretly relieved the husband was out of the picture. He was immediately disappointed in himself for his uncharitable thought. He was trying so hard to put the old, selfish Christopher behind him. He'd turned a new leaf.

Before he could offer a suitable response, she continued, "I have some money set aside from Ronnie's life insurance payout—seven hundred and fifty thousand dollars, to be exact. It's a decent amount. I was... I was wondering if you'd consider allowing me to buy this property back."

Christopher started in surprise. It was the last thing he'd expected. "Buy it back? For seven hundred and fifty thousand dollars?"

"I understand it's less than you paid for it, but... That's all I have."

Christopher shook his head back and forth, still trying to get his head around her proposal. She didn't seem to understand this was business. Nobody sold a property for less than they'd paid for it. Not unless they were desperate and without any other options. Which they weren't—on either score.

"Surely you can't be serious?" he asked, unable to keep the incredulity from his voice.

She bit her lip and lowered her gaze. He could tell from the way she kept clenching and unclenching her fists that she was trying hard to stop herself from losing it. But then she appeared to call on some inner strength. He saw her shoulders go back and her spine straighten and her hands relax. She eyed him defiantly.

"It's a good offer, nevertheless I... I was hoping to appeal to your sense of decency. Your intention is to evict my family from our house. I have eight children, no husband and no family who can help us. Don't you care that you're as good as putting us out on the street?"

"I thought you just said you had seven hundred and fifty thousand?"

She made an impatient sound in the back of her throat. "I do. But that's for my kids' education. I didn't expect to have to use it just to keep a roof over our heads."

"What about your husband's parents? They banked a million dollars from the sale. Surely they're willing to share some of it with you, or at least give you an interest-free loan?"

She averted her gaze and shook her head. "I'm afraid not. They've made it clear they're not willing to help me. Besides, they've told me they've spent most of it."

"A million dollars?"

She shrugged. "So my mother-in-law says. It appears their familial obligation ended when their son died."

"They sound like real gems," Christopher said dryly.

"Don't judge them," she snapped. "They're good people most of the time. Salt of the earth. We don't quite see eye to eye about my children, but they were so supportive in the early days of our marriage. Though they didn't have a lot, they gave us this house as a wedding present. Well, I thought it was ours. Turns out it was only on loan. Now it's been sold out from underneath us."

Her voice cracked with emotion and tears glinted in her eyes. His gut twisted with guilt. He hated to see her so distressed—and over something his family was partially responsible for. He made a silent vow to pay a visit to her in-laws. It sounded to him that they needed a reminder of their daughter-in-law's existence, along with her kids. And he was just the person to do the reminding. The thought brought a grim smile to his lips.

Misunderstanding the cause for his mirth, Lexi's brow furrowed with anger. "What are you smiling about? Do you find my situation amusing?"

He quickly sobered. "No, no. Of course not. Nothing about this is funny."

He didn't elaborate any further. There was no reason for her to know his plans. In fact, it would be best if she were kept completely in the dark about what he intended to do. He thought about what she was doing—and all on her own. She appeared to have devoted her life to helping the vulnerable children thrown away by their own families and most of society. It was a noble cause. He wondered what had drawn her down that path.

He decided to appease his curiosity. "How did you become a foster mother?"

She flashed him a look of surprise, but in a halting voice that grew increasingly stronger, Lexi told him about her husband's fertility issues and how they'd turned to adoption but when that seemed an impossible dream, they decided to foster instead.

"Of course, I was on my own much of the time. Ronnie worked long hours on building sites. He usually came home late, often well after most of the kids had gone to bed. I didn't mind. I loved being a foster mom, knowing I was helping to give a vulnerable child a better life, even for a short time.

"Over the years, kids came and went, some more quickly than others. You might recall there have been twenty-seven so far. I've adopted as many as I can. I'd adopt all of them if I could. Of course, the final decision's not up to me."

Christopher stared at her, filled with reluctant admiration. He didn't want to like this woman, but it was proving hard to remain unaffected. Of course, it could all be a ruse. She might only be in it for the money. She wouldn't be the first foster carer to cash in on the generous government allowances paid to them. It was a cynical attitude, but then again, cynicism was his fallback position. And while he'd promised himself that he'd try to change, the habits of a lifetime were hard to shake.

Christopher prided himself on being able to sniff out bullshit from miles away and he wasn't getting that kind of vibe from this woman. She appeared to be as good and decent as she made herself out to be. In fact, compared to most of the people he came into contact with she was damn near Mother Teresa.

"There are not too many people who are willing to take on troubled kids," he said.

She looked appalled. "They're not troubled! They come from troubled homes. There's a difference. Most of the time, all they need is some genuine love and attention and a safe and secure place to lay their head. The same kind of basic needs we all yearn for."

She said it so wistfully, he was moved into thinking she spoke from experience. He voiced the question.

"You're right. I've had personal experience in the foster care system."

She drew in a deep breath and eased it out on a heavy sigh. "My mother was a fifteen-year-old runaway. I lived with her in my early years, although I have no memory of that. I never met my grandparents. For all I know, they're dead now. I was eventually removed from my mother's care and put into a foster home."

"How old were you?" he asked softly.

"Three, or so I was told."

"What about your father?"

She shrugged, but there was a tension in her body that belied the casualness of her motion. "I never knew my father. He wasn't listed on my birth certificate."

"What about other family?"

"Again, no one came forward to claim me." She gave a sad little smile. "I've thought about that over and over. I guess I just wasn't that lovable. Over the years, I was passed from foster home to foster home. No one wanted to keep me. A few weeks here, a month or two there. It was endless and always the same. I grew up thinking there was something wrong with me; that I was someone no one could love."

Her voice was thick with emotion. Once again, he saw her struggle to hold back tears. He was surprised by an urge to go to her, to draw her into his arms, to offer her comfort, to reassure her she was the most amazing, lovable woman in the world.

But he did none of those things. He barely knew her. And it had been so long since he'd been in a relationship, he felt rusty and out of practice. Almost awkward. His instincts to offer comfort couldn't be trusted.

What if she rejects me?

So he stayed where he was and waited quietly for her to regain her self-control. Looking around, he realized how much this house must mean to her. It wasn't just weatherboards and nails; it was her *home*. As she had said, it was the place where she'd planned to raise her children, a place where they all felt safe and loved.

Christopher suddenly realized how lucky he was to have a mother who loved him, and even though his biological father had refused to recognize him, he'd had the love of his stepfather and had known safety and security for most of his life. He'd been dealt a much better hand than Lexi, even though he hadn't fully appreciated that until now.

He and his brother, Vaughan, had always known they were adopted. Of course, neither of them had been babies when their adoptions had taken place. And Christopher still had his mother. Frank had married his mother, Evelyn, when Christopher was eleven. Christopher had lived with them. Frank could have let Christopher remain as his stepson, but he hadn't. He'd gone the extra mile and legally adopted him.

Christopher felt ashamed that he'd never given Frank any credit for all he'd done and tried to do for him. Frank hadn't been forced to offer his name, his protection. And yet he had.

Christopher made a mental note to thank the man. It was well overdue.

And then Christopher's thoughts turned to Vaughan. His brother had been out of touch, missing for more than a week now.

Why isn't he answering his phone? What's he running from?

Christopher had tried calling Vaughan a number of times and the calls always went through to voicemail. He didn't even know if Vaughan was checking his messages. Still, Christopher was confident Vaughan would surface when the time was right, when he'd come to terms with whatever had caused him to leave. Christopher hoped it would be sooner rather than later. The family missed him.

Glancing back at Lexi, he passed her a box of tissues he saw on the counter and turned away to give her some privacy while she wiped her eyes, blew her nose and pulled herself together. He was almost overcome by a second, stronger urge to go to her and hold her close and promise her they'd find a way through, but once again, he resisted.

"I'm sorry," he said. "You've been through a lot. More than most." He drew in a deep breath and let out a weary sigh. "But I'm not sure I can help you. It's nothing personal, but this is a business deal. It's not just your house. My stepfather's company has purchased a number of properties adjoining yours. Acquisition of them all was part of a grander plan. He's building a large-scale development. Apartment blocks, hotels, office space. Your house sits smack in the middle of it all." He paused and then added, "So you see? It's not just a matter of negotiating a sale price. It's too late. The deal's been done."

The look she gave him was so filled with disappointment Christopher had to look away. He tamped down his guilt and frustration.

What the hell does she expect of me? I can't turn back time…

Her property had been sold and that was the end of it. There was nothing he could do.

Christopher left Lexi's place with his thoughts in turmoil. He'd told her the truth when he'd said it was impossible to reverse the decision to buy her place, but that didn't mean he didn't want to do something to help her. There was something about her story that touched him in a way he hadn't been touched in a long time.

For years, Christopher had allowed himself to be consumed daily by the hurt and bitterness he'd felt at the cruel rejection by his biological father. Henry Craigdon's brief fling with Christopher's mother more than four decades earlier had resulted in his birth, but in all those years, Henry refused to acknowledge him. Even after DNA tests proved beyond a doubt he was Henry's son, the recognition never came. He hadn't been happy, so he did his best to undermine other's happiness. In those days he'd taken great satisfaction by making others miserable.

When Henry died, Christopher had clung to the hope that in death, if not in life, Henry might have sought to make amends; that he might have seen fit to make mention of his first-born in his will. Alas, such hopes had been cruelly dashed once and for all. There hadn't been the slightest hint, the tiniest whisper that Christopher existed. In fact, Henry had gone out of his way to drive the blade in deeper. He'd explicitly referred to Jett Craigdon as his first-born. It had been the final insult.

Christopher had wasted almost a year wallowing in self-pity and hate against a dead man to the point where it obliterated everything else. Christopher's hurt and anger had for years dictated his every thought, his every action. It had been slowly destroying him, and if he were being truthful with himself, it had also had a lot to do with why he was still single, had no children, not even an ex-wife at the ripe old age of forty-one.

But slowly, with the love and understanding of Elizabeth Craigdon, his stepmother, and in more recent times, her children—Christopher's half-brothers and sisters—he'd begun to let the hurt and bitterness go. He didn't want to live like that anymore. He'd wasted so much time feeling bitter and twisted and allowing his darker feelings of resentment to affect everyone around him.

But no more. That was the old Christopher. The new Christopher was determined to live a better life. It wouldn't happen overnight. After all, he'd lived with the pain, the hurt, the bitterness for a long time. But he was determined to take small steps in the right direction and turn his life around. He might not be able to prevent the sale and destruction of Lexi's home, but he could pay a visit to her in-laws and find out why they weren't more supportive of their late son's wife. Not to mention her children. They must know how difficult it would be for her to find alternative accommodation, particularly with limited means.

Okay, so seven hundred and fifty thousand dollars wasn't to be sneezed at, but that was all Lexi had and she'd unselfishly set it aside for her children's education. She was that kind of person.

What did her in-laws do with their million dollar windfall?

He was determined to find out.

A phone call to his father's executive assistant provided him with the address details the Greenaways had listed on the contract of sale. They lived in a modest red-brick and tile house a couple of suburbs away from Lexi's acreage. As Christopher climbed awkwardly out of his car, he winced at the pain in his shoulder. It was getting better, but every now and then it let him know he wasn't completely healed. Still, there was no time for that now. He was on a mission.

The front yard was neat enough. The grass was freshly mowed and the flower beds were free from weeds. An ancient Toyota, with cracked and faded paintwork, sat in the driveway outside a garage. He walked up the concrete steps and across the veranda and then knocked with his left hand on the front door. He waited a few moments before it was answered.

The woman who stood on the other side of the screen door looked to be in her sixties, with short gray hair that curled around her ears. She wore a cheap, old-fashioned floral print dress that billowed out over her substantial frame. With narrowed eyes, she regarded Christopher with suspicion.

"I'm sorry. Whatever you're tryin' to sell me, I ain't buyin'. You're wastin' your time."

Christopher blinked in surprise. Lexi had said something similar when he'd first arrived at her place.

Must be a family mantra…

Either that, or they got more than their fair share of traveling salesmen. Christopher offered her his most charming smile.

"Oh, no! I'm not here to sell you anything. I'm a friend of Ronnie's."

Christopher was disappointed how smoothly the lie fell off his tongue. He was trying so hard to reform! Still, finding this out was important and sometimes the end justified the means.

The suspicion in the woman's eyes deepened. "I don't think so. My son's been dead four years."

"Yes. I know. I was at the funeral. You might not have seen me because I sat way in the back, but I was there." He paused and then added for good measure, "It was a beautiful service."

The woman sniffed. Some of the distrust in her eyes eased. "What did you say your name was?"

Christopher smiled again. "I didn't. Please excuse my bad manners. I'm Christopher Bar…Burrows." At the last moment, he modified his surname. It wouldn't do for the old lady to recognize it was the same last name as the purchaser of Lexi's property.

"Mr Burrows. I don't recall Ronnie mentionin' you. How did you know my son?"

"We worked together on numerous construction sites," Christopher improvised, recalling how Lexi had said her husband worked in construction. "He was a good bloke."

Tears glinted in Dorothy Greenaway's eyes. "Yes, he was. The best son a mother could hope for."

"It was tragic, the way he went... In a motorbike accident... Then again, he sure loved riding that thing."

Once again, Christopher offered her an understanding smile. She sniffed and smiled back at him.

"Oh, yes. That bike meant the world to him," she agreed.

Christopher tilted his head and smiled again. "Do you mind if I come in, Mrs Greenaway?"

She stepped back and allowed him to enter. The interior was dim and musty with age. If they'd spent all the money like they'd told Lexi, it sure as hell hadn't been put into the house. Still, the place was clean and tidy with a sofa and two matching armchairs arranged around a TV in the front room. They passed two bedrooms, both with the beds neatly made up and then the house opened up into a kitchen and adjoining dining room.

"Is Mr Greenaway home?" Christopher asked. It was best to say what he'd come there for in front of both of them. That way there would be no misunderstandings.

"I'm afraid not. Today's his golf day."

Christopher swallowed a snort. *Good old George. Out playing golf. How nice.*

"Can I get you a cup of coffee?" Dorothy asked, moving to stand by the window in the kitchen.

"No, thank you. This won't take long."

The woman's face registered her surprise. "Why are you here, Mr Burrows?"

Christopher eyed her steadily. "I wanted to talk to you about Lexi."

The woman's face shuttered. Her lips thinned. Undeterred, Christopher plowed on.

"You see, I wasn't just friends with Ronnie. I was friends with his wife, too. Surely you remember Lexi?"

An ugly blush stained the woman's cheeks. "Of course I do! She's my daughter-in-law. What do you think: I've lost my marbles?"

Christopher continued to regard her somberly. "How long's it been since you saw her? Or your grandchildren? Weeks? Months?" Christopher was only guessing, but something told him Ronnie's parents were no longer as devoted to Lexi and her family as they might have once been. They hadn't even found the time or wherewithal to tell her that they'd sold her home out from underneath her.

Twin spots of anger erupted on Dorothy's cheeks. "You have no right to ask me that!"

"Of course I do. Lexi's struggling. She needs help. How would you feel having to raise all those children on your own? On top of that, she's grieving her husband and the only family she has can't even be bothered to call on her, to ask if she's okay. To give her a helping hand."

Dorothy's eyes flashed. "This is about the sale, isn't it? Did Lexi put you up to this? I bet she did."

"Lexi didn't put me up to anything," Christopher said coldly. "In fact, she doesn't even know I'm here."

"I don't believe you."

Christopher held her gaze. "I don't care what you believe. What I care about is Lexi. You sold her house with neither her permission nor knowledge. She's entitled to some of that money. At least half," he added for good measure.

Dorothy sputtered with anger and surprise. "*Half?* You have to be kiddin'. That property was ours. We owe her nothin'."

Christopher's anger swirled dangerously to the surface. "You gave her that property as a wedding present."

The woman's jaw jutted out at an obstinate angle. Her eyes narrowed. "No, we gave it to our *son*. Now Ronnie's dead. It was just fortunate we took good advice from our lawyer and didn't transfer the title back then. The property was rightfully ours and we are the rightful owners of the sale proceeds. *All* of the sale proceeds."

Christopher glared at her. He held onto his temper with his fingernails. "She's your daughter-in-law! Those kids are your grandchildren."

Dorothy scoffed. "She's not our daughter, our flesh and blood. As for her kids... They're not our grandchildren. They're not Ronnie's blood. They're...strays...castoffs... Even their real parents didn't want them."

Her callous attitude and the complete disregard she had for Lexi and her kids ignited Christopher's fury. His breath came fast. His hands clenched into fists. The pain in his shoulder reminded him he was in no condition to over-extend himself. As much as he wanted to get in the woman's face, he managed to control the urge. Pushing an old lady up against a wall and threatening her would get him nowhere and would put a serious dent in his efforts to reform.

"I see," Christopher replied in a deceptively mild tone. "And does your good husband feel the same way?"

"Yes. He tried to dissuade Ronnie from going down that path. Who wants someone else's castoffs? Troubled kids who'll never amount to anything? It was wrong. We told him that many times. But he wouldn't listen. *She* got in his ear. She made sure he didn't listen to a word we had to say on the subject."

Christopher stared at her with disgust. He'd never met a more selfish, uncharitable person. As far as he was concerned, Lexi and her children were well rid of them. All they wanted to do was bring them down. Selling their house right out from under their feet was an effective way to do so.

He continued to glare at Dorothy. She defiantly held his gaze. He wanted to make nastier threats, but decided against it, reminding himself that he wasn't that person anymore. Still, there might be something he could do. He still had friends in high places, after all. Everyone had an Achilles heel. He just needed to find theirs.

Deciding there was nothing more he could do at that time, he shot her a scathing look as he headed for the door. "Well, I hope that money keeps you warm at night and brings you comfort in your old age. I hope it visits you in the nursing home and shows up at your funeral because you're sure as hell doing all you can to ensure none of your family will be there. Because, like it or not, Lexi and her children are your family. The only family you're ever going to have. I would have thought you would put a higher value on that than you obviously do."

He narrowed his eyes at her. "Think hard before you turn your back on your family. I can tell you firsthand, when the chips are down, money is never enough. It's your family you want around you when times are tough, not your bank account."

With that, he left the house.

Still seething, he pulled out his phone and scrolled through his contacts. It didn't take him long to find the name he wanted. He dialed the number and waited for someone to pick up.

"Julian. It's Christopher Barrington."

"Christopher. Wow. It's been…five years."

"Really? That long. Time flies. Tell me, how's Angela?"

"She's… She's fine. She's out of rehab and well on the way to getting her life back together. I… I don't know how I can ever thank you."

"No thanks necessary. What are old friends for? I'm glad to hear she's back on track and that I was able to help out."

"You did. You definitely did. We could never afford the rehabilitation costs if it weren't for you. You saved my daughter's life."

Christopher waved off the praise. "Nonsense. All I did was help out a school mate. You would have done the same thing."

"You're too modest. Allison and I are just so grateful… If there's anything we can do to repay you… I don't mean in a financial way… Just… You know…"

Christopher smiled. It was just the invitation he needed. Though what he was about to propose was illegal, he was counting on Julian's gratitude to overlook that slight complication. "Funny you say that. There's a reason for my call. Tell me, do you still work for the bank?"

"Yes. I've been promoted since we last spoke. I now work in the Credit Department. I'm responsible for doing all the credit checks on loan applications to the "big four" banks."

Christopher's smile widened. "Great. I was wondering if you could do me a favor."

"Of course. Anything."

"I need you to look into the financial dealings of some people for me. A husband and wife. Dorothy and George Greenaway. They live out at Camden. I'll text you their address. I want you to look at their bank statements, term deposits, credit card bills and anything else you can find on them and let me know how they're doing financially."

"No problem. Give me a few days."

"Fantastic. Thank you, Julian. I really appreciate that."

Christopher gave the man his email address and after a few more minutes of social chitchat, he ended the call.

There. It's done. Let's see what the Greenaways have done with all that money, if anything. For all I know, they could have been lying to Lexi when they told her it was all gone...

With a bit of luck, he'd find the million dollars they were paid by his father's company tucked away in a little term deposit. Then Lexi could file a claim for at least part of that money and let the courts work out what was fair and just and to hell with her nasty in-laws.

Chapter Seven

Christopher turned onto the main road out of Camden that would take him back to the city. On impulse, he took the exit toward Richmond. It had been more than a week since he'd visited Elizabeth. Now that Archie was out of hospital, it would be nice to catch up with them both.

Elizabeth had always been supportive of Christopher, even during the times when he'd let himself down. She'd been instrumental in sparking his real desire to change. He owed her a great deal.

He turned into the wide sweeping driveway that led to the entrance of Craigdon Manor. The architecturally designed mansion had been inspired by the Art Deco era and though the three-story building was spectacular at night lit up like a Christmas tree, in the bright afternoon sun, the full grandeur of the place was on display.

Christopher parked his car at the top of the circular driveway and climbed out. His shoulder was aching and he thought absently about popping a couple of pain killers.

He walked up the wide stone steps that led to the front door and knocked. It wasn't long before the door opened. Elizabeth regarded him from the other side of the doorway, her face breaking into a wide smile.

"Christopher! What a lovely surprise! What are you doing here?"

"I was in the neighborhood. I thought I'd stop by and see how you and Archie were doing."

She pecked him on the cheek. "We're fine, and it's lovely to see you. Come in."

She stood back and allowed him to enter. He blinked his eyes to adjust to the sudden dimness.

"It's nice and cool in here," he said.

"Yes. I had Amy switch on the air conditioner. It's rather hot outside for April, isn't it?"

"Absolutely. I guess we should be grateful. Winter will be upon us all too soon."

Elizabeth grinned. "You're right about that."

She led him into her music room. It was filled with soft furnishings, comfortable sofas and in pride of place in one corner stood a shiny black baby grand piano.

"Have you been playing lately?" he asked as he seated himself on the three-seater.

"Yes, as a matter of fact. Archie likes to hear me play. It relaxes him."

Christopher looked around him. "Where is he? How's he been?"

"He's doing well. The doctors are pleased with his progress. Right now he's upstairs resting."

Christopher acknowledged her comments with a nod. "I'm glad he's on the mend."

Elizabeth sat in the armchair opposite. "Thanks in no small part to you."

Christopher shrugged self-consciously and then bit his lip against a surge of pain.

Elizabeth sat forward, looking concerned. "Are you all right? You've gone pale."

"I'm fine," he managed between clenched teeth. "Every now and then I forget that I'm not quite healed. You wouldn't happen to have some pain killers handy, would you?"

"Of course. I'll get some right away." She stood and disappeared in the direction of the kitchen, returning a short time later with a packet in one hand and a glass of water in the other.

"Here. Only take two. They'll work faster and you'll still be able to drive. I've also asked Amy to bring us in some coffee."

He took the white tablets she'd popped out of the packet and tossed them into his mouth which he followed with a mouthful of water.

"Thank you," he said.

"How often does it trouble you?" Elizabeth asked.

"Not often. In fact, it's feeling a lot better than it was a few days ago, but I've been out and about most of the day and I'm starting to feel it."

"What have you been up to?"

Before Christopher could answer, Amy came in bearing a tray laden with a shiny silver coffee pot, two fine china mugs and a plate of fresh pastries. The housekeeper had been with the Craigdons for longer than Christopher could remember. She was pretty much treated as one of the family.

Amy smiled. "Hello, Christopher. It's nice to see you again."

Christopher murmured a greeting in response.

"Thank you, Amy. This looks lovely." Elizabeth watched the housekeeper set the tray on the coffee table between them and quietly leave the room.

Elizabeth poured the coffee. Christopher took his black. She added milk and sugar to hers. Sipping from her mug, she sat back against her armchair and eyed him quizzically.

"You didn't answer my question. What have you been up to?"

"I've taken a job at Barrington Mining. Well, not on the mining side of things. We've set up another company—Barrington Developments. I'm overseeing a large-scale property development out near Badgery's Creek."

Elizabeth nodded. "The site of the new airport?"

"Yes. In fact, we've partnered with Craigdon Enterprises. After all, Nick's the one with all the property development experience."

"Good for you. I'm so pleased you've found some direction at last. And I'm even more thrilled that you're working closely with family."

Christopher's laughter was self-deprecating. "Yes. So am I."

"Well, that sounds like it's going to keep you busy. Are you involved in anything specific?"

"Yes. In fact, that's part of the reason I stopped by. I need your advice."

Elizabeth continued to regard him steadily, her expression calm and relaxed. "Ask away."

Christopher paused. Now the moment was on him, he wasn't sure how to proceed. "It's... It's about a woman. She's like no other woman I've ever met. She's...amazing."

Elizabeth smiled softly. "I see. And does she have a name?"

"Yes. It's Lexi. Lexi Greenaway."

"Tell me about her."

Christopher relaxed back against the sofa and began talking about Lexi. Once he started, he couldn't stop. He told Elizabeth about Lexi's husband being unable to have children, and how they began fostering kids. "They adopted five of them. And then her husband was killed in a motorbike accident. It happened four years ago. But Lexi has continued to foster children. A total of twenty-seven, so far."

Elizabeth's eyes were wide with surprise. "Wow. That's quite a story and you're right. She sounds amazing."

Christopher sat forward. "That's why this is so hard. The situation. The thing is, the house she lives in has been bought by Barrington Developments and is earmarked for demolition. She can't afford to buy something of similar size in the same general location. But Dad's adamant the whole development project relies on having her land. It's smack bang in the middle of the whole thing."

Elizabeth quirked an eyebrow and regarded him with a gentle smile. "Dad? You mean, Frank?"

Christopher blushed. "Yes. Frank. Sorry, it's still pretty new to me, too. You'll be pleased to know I've finally made my peace with...Henry...and with Frank. He's been more of a father to me than the one who provided his DNA to give me life. Frank deserves the honor."

Elizabeth nodded approvingly. "Yes, he certainly does. I'm happy for you, Christopher." Her gaze roved over him. "Despite this present predicament, you appear calmer, happier. More settled. Am I right?"

"Yes, but this thing with Lexi is driving me insane! I want to help, to find an equitable solution that will work for everyone, but no matter which way I look at it, there doesn't seem to be one at hand." He paused and shot her a look that bordered on desperation. "I was hoping you might have a suggestion."

Elizabeth pursed her lips in thought. "So she can't afford to buy the property off you?"

"No, and even if she could, it wouldn't be a solution. Like I said, all of Dad's plans for this development include her property. The projects pivot around that, and without hers they would have to be re-configured. Dad's in the final stages of approval through the local council. There's no way we can change those plans now."

"Then perhaps Barrington Developments can help her get into something else? Is Frank willing to pay her some additional compensation for the loss of her home? Surely a fair sale price was negotiated?"

Christopher grimaced. "See, it was never *her* home, even though she thought it was. She says her in-laws gave it to them as a wedding present. She's lived there all this time, but the property was owned by her husband's parents. They're the ones who sold it to Dad's company. They pocketed the cash."

"Are they prepared to give her some financial assistance to get into another place?"

"No. They've flatly refused to do that."

"Wow. That sounds harsh. Surely she deserves something? Maybe you could talk to Flynn. His specialty is in family law, but he might be willing to give her some pro bono legal advice on this property matter."

Christopher nodded. "That's a good idea. And even if he won't do it for free, I'd be happy to pay for it."

Elizabeth looked across at Christopher and nodded approvingly. He'd come a long way from the troubled, bitter man she'd counseled on and off for a lot of his life. Her gaze moved over him. It was true. He looked calmer, less angst-ridden than he had for the best part of a year. Whoever this woman was, she was having a positive effect on Christopher and that was a good thing.

The woman's problem certainly presented a dilemma. If the parents-in-law were the rightful owners of the property, there might not be any legal recourse open to her. Then again, it was worth a try. From what Christopher had said, she had nothing to lose.

Elizabeth stirred restlessly. She'd always been a problem solver. That was the reason so many people came to her for advice, including her children. Though Christopher was her stepson, she'd never treated him any differently than her other children. He'd come to her for advice. She wouldn't send him away empty handed.

But what can I do about the situation? I can't force Frank to hand the property back. It was a deal done in good conscience and it's obvious too much relies on it going through.No, the solution didn't lie in that direction. Better to think of some way the poor woman could get enough money to make a new start. How could she help?

In her mind Elizabeth began to consider and tick off the possibilities: sponsorships, a fundraising event, partnerships, call for donations, grants... But there wasn't much time. *What could be done most easily and quickly?*

Another thought intruded. She still hadn't heard from Vaughan.

Why hasn't he contacted me? Not a single letter, an email. Not even a phone call. It was killing her not knowing how he'd reacted to her news.

An idea began to form around a fundraising event... What better way to force him into action than by inviting him to her house under the guise of a charity do?

Christopher took a sip from his coffee. Elizabeth did the same and then set the mug carefully down. In order to allay suspicion, she waved her hand around in a casual manner, as if the thought had just occurred to her.

"Well, perhaps I can help... A charity do... I could hold a fundraiser for Lexi—a dinner with a silent auction—and raise funds for a new home for her and her charges. I'm sure if I called around to a few of my friends, they'd be only too happy to donate to such a worthy cause."

Christopher stared at her with amazement. "You'd do that?"

"Yes, of course. Unless you think she wouldn't be open to the idea?"

Christopher frowned. "Why wouldn't she be open to the idea?"

Elizabeth shrugged. "Some people get offended at the thought they might be considered a charity case."

"Why would she think that? This isn't about her being a charity case. She has huge responsibilities and is strapped for cash and she knows as well as I do she's fast running out of options."

"That might be right, but just go gently, won't you? Even someone who is all out of options has their pride. Trust me, she won't thank you if you trample all over hers."

Christopher's brow furrowed in thought. "I guess I could come at it from the angle that we're raising money to put toward the needs of her foster kids. That should get her over the line."

Elizabeth nodded. "That's something, at least." She sat forward. Now for the most important part. "You could invite all of your family. Frank and your mother, your brothers and sisters. They could all come. The more the merrier. There are quite a few of them, aren't there?"

"Yes. Nine of us, in fact. Although no one's seen or heard from my stepbrother Vaughan for more than a week. He seems to have disappeared off the face of the earth."

Elizabeth's stomach sank. She did her best to rearrange her features into something bland, but it was difficult.

"Disappeared? What do you mean?"

"Just that. We celebrated his fortieth birthday the same evening of Archie's fire and all seemed well, but not long after that he just up and left. We haven't heard from him since."

Elizabeth was filled with consternation. "Do you know where he is?"

"No, he didn't say, but I dropped around to his apartment yesterday. There was no one home."

"Did he say how long he'd be gone?"

Christopher shook his head and frowned. "No. We're all kind of hoping he'll show up in the next day or so." His expression cleared and he reached for Elizabeth's hand.

"Did you really mean it when you said you'd be happy to host a fundraising gala for Lexi?"

Elizabeth forced a smile. "Yes, of course. How about next Saturday night?"

Christopher grinned. "Thank you, Elizabeth! You don't know how much that means to me! I knew I could count on you! You always know how to solve the most difficult situation! I can't wait to tell Lexi!"

Chapter Eight

The sun was low in the sky when Christopher left Craigdon Manor. Elizabeth had invited him to stay for dinner, but Christopher was keen to visit Frank and bring him up to date. What he really wanted to do was see Lexi and tell her about Elizabeth's suggestion, but he knew that she'd be busy this time of evening with the children and he didn't want to intrude on that, especially when she'd made it clear that the children didn't know about their situation.

He still wasn't quite sure how she managed to take care of eight children. Okay, so five of them were in school all day, but what about when they weren't? Just the thought of cooking for nine gave Christopher the horrors. He was a passable cook, but the most he'd ever catered was for three or four, when he invited friends over and that was normally for a barbeque where the cooking skills required were minimal. He couldn't imagine cooking and serving up three meals a day for eight children.

She certainly appeared to be a strong and determined woman. And to be doing it all on her own... Admiration for her flooded through his veins, along with something else he tried to ignore... Desire.

As he drove through the city streets, he gave himself a moment to think about how much Lexi Greenaway turned him on. It was more than her overt sexiness—her shiny chestnut hair that had been loose both times he'd seen her; the smile that lit up her blue eyes in those one or two moments in which she'd allowed herself to do so; her long tanned legs, her generous breasts. All of those things had sent the blood rushing straight to his cock. But it was more than her physical appeal. It was her innate goodness reflected in the way in which she spoke to her children and interacted with them. The way she'd still tried to speak kindly about her in-laws in spite of knowing what they'd done to her and their refusal to help.

Based on his own brief meeting with her mother-in-law, it was obvious her in-laws had never really accepted her. Dorothy had made it clear the wedding gift had been given to their son. She'd deliberately bypassed any mention of his wife. And for them to have sought and taken legal advice to the effect that they should keep the title to the property in their own names—he assumed on the off chance the marriage didn't survive—seemed so cold.

Then there was their disgusting attitude toward the children. Some of them had been legally adopted by Lexi and their son. It was like Christopher had told Dorothy—they were her grandchildren. What did it matter if they weren't her flesh and blood? They'd seemed happy, lovable kids.

He thought of his brief meeting with a few of them. The precocious Patrice, with her giggles and cheeky laugh. Leroy, with the adorable smile. And Michael. Full of curiosity and questions. Christopher had barely known them five minutes and he'd been captivated by their easy acceptance and openness. Why couldn't Dorothy and George see what he did?

Truth be told, Christopher was surprised by his reaction to the children. He'd never felt inclined to spend time with children in the past. Though his Barrington brothers and sisters were single, some of his Craigdon siblings had children and Christopher had never felt the slightest inclination to engage with them and yet he was keen to reengage with Lexi and her entourage as soon as possible

So what makes these kids so special?

He knew the answer, of course. It was Lexi. Her simplicity and honesty and the genuine love she had for her kids had captivated him. He couldn't wait to meet up with them again to share the news about the charity event and convince her of its merits. Maybe his burgeoning feelings would dissipate on closer acquaintance, but he felt driven to find out.

Not that he'd act on them if they were real. Lexi had given no indication she was aware of him as a man. The only discussions they'd had were about her dire financial circumstances and the very real predicament she was in. Oh, and about her late husband and her kids. From her point of view, Christopher was the enemy who was working to leave her homeless.

Still, he'd never been deterred by a lack of encouragement. He was the kind of man who went after what he wanted and damn the consequences. He frowned. That was the old Christopher.

I'm trying hard not to be him, remember?

That meant changing his old ways. Being more thoughtful, kinder, considerate. And that meant staying clear of Lexi Greenaway's delectable body and instead focusing on helping her get back on her feet. He'd just have to try harder to shift his focus away from the erotic fantasies that had kept him awake for the last few nights... At least for now.

Nicer, kinder, considerate...

If he repeated the mantra often enough, it just might just stick.

Christopher swung his Mercedes into his allocated parking spot beneath the building that housed the Barrington Mining headquarters. Traffic heading east toward the city had moved freely and he'd made good time. Even so, it was fully dark when he entered the lift and ascended to the top floor. He strode into his father's lavish office suite.

He'd phoned Frank on the drive, knowing he'd still be in the office, and had requested a meeting. Frank was happy to comply. He was keen for an update. He'd received the final approval from the Liverpool Council and the demolition equipment was on standby, ready to start. Lexi was the only tenant who hadn't vacated.

The offices outside his father's suite were quiet. The staff had long since gone home, including Frank's EA whose desk sat empty. Christopher walked past and headed down the corridor to the corner office. He knocked perfunctorily on the half-open door and stepped inside.

"Christopher. Good. You're here. I just poured us both a scotch."

Christopher grinned. "Sounds good. Thanks."

The two men sat in the leather armchairs that stood off to one side of the suite and sipped at the amber liquid. After a few moments, Frank spoke.

"So, what's happening with our recalcitrant tenant? Have you made her see sense yet?"

Christopher savored the taste of whiskey a moment longer before responding. "She's not what I expected, that's for sure. Young, for one. Mid-thirties, at a guess." He grinned slightly. "Definitely not old, definitely not senile. In fact, far from it."

"I take it she's still putting up a fight?"

"You could say that. But at least she's accepted we have legal claim to the property."

"Well, that's progress."

"Yes. The thing is, I know there's nothing we can do to reverse the sale, but I want to try and help her out. She's a good person. A foster mother, remember? And get this: She'd believed that the house was a wedding gift from her husband's parents."

Frank raised a single white eyebrow. "And her husband was okay with them not transferring the title?"

"I don't know what he thought or if he even knew about that. He died four years ago in a motorbike accident. Another blow to the poor woman. But that hasn't stopped her. She's still fostering kids, only she's doing it all on her own. I tell you, Dad, she's the most incredible woman I've ever met."

"I sent you out there to evict her, not fall in love," Frank said dryly.

Christopher flushed. "Don't be ridiculous! But I'm not a complete bastard. She's a decent woman. Trying her best to make the world a better place."

Frank looked at him in disbelief. Christopher's flush deepened. He ducked his head and clenched his jaw and finally made eye contact again. "I get it. I'm the last person you'd expect to show even a modicum of empathy. But I'm trying to be a better person, remember?"

Frank nodded approvingly. "Good for you."

"Anyway," Christopher continued, "as I suspected, the property was sold by her in-laws who'd retained title to the property instead of transferring it to the newlyweds. They failed to tell her about it. I've met with them. Well, the mother-in-law, at least. To look at her, you'd think she was any other pensioner, doing the best she can to get by. They're living in a modest house. The car parked in the driveway is about a hundred years old and looks like it should have been turned into scrap. She dresses in the manner of a charity store shopper and yet they're sitting on a million dollars."

He shook his head. "And here comes the real kicker. I didn't have to scratch hard below the surface before Lexi's mother-in-law showed that she's as mean and nasty as they come. They're refusing to share any of the sale proceeds with their daughter-in-law though she's lived there for years, married to their son. It seems they weren't too keen on the whole adoption-foster-children thing and now that their son's dead, they don't see any need to support their daughter-in-law and her tribe of kids."

Frank looked at him, aghast. "But those kids are their grandchildren. At least, the adopted ones, and from what you've told me about Lexi, I can't imagine she treats her foster kids any different than her adopted children."

"You're right. She doesn't. And as far as those kids being Dorothy's grandchildren, which I pointed out to her, she doesn't care. Her flesh and blood is dead. She doesn't feel any obligation toward Lexi."

Frank made a sympathetic sound in the back of his throat and took refuge in his whiskey. Christopher did the same. The darkness outside closed in around them, cocooning them in a comfortable silence. Frank was the first to break it.

"I'm not sure what you want me to do here, Christopher. I commiserate with Lexi's difficult circumstances, but that doesn't change anything. I need that property. If Lexi's place is taken out of the equation, the whole grand plan comes crashing down and there are too many people who've already invested hundreds of thousands of dollars into getting this project off the ground—and that doesn't include the millions we've shelled out to acquire those properties." He compressed his lips and shook his head. "I'm sorry, Christopher. I wish I could help, but I can't."

Christopher grimaced and leaned forward. "I understand that. I told Lexi the same thing. But there must be something we can do."

Frank shrugged. "I'm open to suggestions, but I can't agree to anything that involves Barrington Developments selling back that property. I don't mean to sound heartless. She's in a terrible predicament. But this is business and I'm not the only one who's invested. You need to come up with a different solution. One that doesn't involve her staying where she is."

Christopher scrubbed a hand through his hair. "The only thing I can think of is to find some way of getting her a share of the sale proceeds from her in-laws. Okay, so her name might not have been on the title deeds, but from all intents and purposes, she'd believed she was the legal owner. Her in-laws did a right job on her. I can't imagine having family like that. The worst of it is, I bet they'd never have done it if their son was still alive."

A surge of anger washed over him, filling his face with heat. If there was one thing he hated it was injustice and Lexi had been treated unfairly and unjustly by her in-laws.

"I'm going to speak to Flynn and see if he has a legal angle we can take on against the Greenaways," he continued. "Failing that, I'm hoping Lexi might be able to buy something else, something that suits her needs as well as, if not better, than her current arrangement."

"Does she have the means?"

"No. That's the problem. She has some money from her husband's life insurance, but it's not enough. She'd have to take out a mortgage and even then, she'd have nothing left. She's been saving that money to put her kids through university. She has no other way of coming up with such a substantial lump sum."

Christopher took another sip of his drink and focused on the warm bite of the whiskey in an effort to distract himself. He was a problem solver. Being unable to find an immediate solution to Lexi's predicament was frustrating.

He sighed wearily and leaned back against his chair. "I stopped by to see Elizabeth Craigdon. I hadn't seen her since Archie was released from hospital."

Frank acknowledged the comment with a nod. "How's he doing?"

"Fine, I think."

"You did a very brave thing, rescuing him like that. You both could have died in that fire."

Christopher shrugged off the praise. "The thing is," he continued, "Elizabeth has offered to hold a fundraiser for Lexi—a dinner and a silent auction. I think it's a great idea. We might not raise all the funds we need, but it'll surely help."

Frank nodded in agreement. "Sounds like a good idea. It's certainly a step in the right direction. Will Lexi go for it? Some people are too proud to accept charity."

Christopher compressed his lips. "I think so. I'm going to appeal to the importance she places on helping her kids. Instead of this being a handout, I'm going to convince her it's about bringing like-minded donors together who wish to contribute to helping out needy and vulnerable children. How can she refuse that?"

Frank grinned. "Good idea. When's the dinner being held?"

"Next weekend. Saturday night. Elizabeth's extended an invitation to the entire Barrington family. I hope at least you and Mom can come."

"I'll speak to your mother. She's in charge of our social obligations. As far as I know, we aren't committed elsewhere."

Christopher nodded his thanks. "Have you heard from Vaughan?"

Frank frowned. "As a matter of fact, yes. He sent me an email."

Christopher grimaced. "At least we know he's still alive. What did he say?"

"Not much. Just that he's okay and he needed to get away for a while."

"Did he say for how long?"

"No, but I checked with the HR department. Apparently he submitted a last minute request for a leave of absence. He's taken six months off."

"Six months? Hell. I don't understand why he took off."

"That makes two of us." Frank sighed. "I guess we just have to trust he had a good reason and knows what he's doing. I'm trying to give him space."

"Fair enough." Christopher finished his drink and then set the crystal highball on the carved wooden coffee table between them. He stood and stretched his good arm up above his head, careful not to jostle his injured shoulder.

"How are your injuries healing? Shoulder still sore?" Frank asked.

"As good as can be expected. I'm impatient to get back to full use of my arm, but the doctor reassures me everything's healing as it should. It just takes time."

Frank stood and embraced him, careful to stay clear of Christopher's shoulder.

"Thanks for stopping by with the update. I look forward to hearing how you get on. Hopefully you'll come up with a solution that everyone can live with. In the meantime, take care of yourself."

Christopher nodded. "Thanks, Dad. You take care, too."

Though it was after seven when Christopher left the underground car park of Barrington Mining, he scrolled through his contacts and put in a call to his half-cousin, Flynn Craigdon. Flynn's father, Archie, and Christopher's biological father, Henry, had been brothers. It was Archie Craigdon whom Christopher had saved from the fire. Though some in the family saw his actions as heroic, Christopher dismissed the accolades.

He'd done what any decent person would have done when presented with a similar scenario. There wasn't anything heroic about it. Still, he felt certain Flynn would feel some kind of obligation to help him out with a favor if he could and Christopher was counting on that.

When Flynn answered, Christopher could hear the sounds of music and laughter in the background.

"Sorry about the noise. I'm with Jayde at Beaches Bar," Flynn explained, referring to the popular bar in Balmoral, the same bar Flynn's fiancée now ran in the absence of her father who was awaiting sentencing for serious drug offenses.

Christopher cut to the chase. "I need a favor."

"What is it?" Flynn shouted over the din.

Christopher began to explain Lexi's predicament. Flynn interrupted him.

"Hang on a minute, Christopher. I can barely hear you."

Christopher waited a few minutes before Flynn spoke again. This time, there was the crack of a door closing followed by muted background noise.

"That's better. Sorry about that. Do you mind starting from the beginning?"

Christopher bit down on a burst of irritation and forced himself to start again. He gave a brief rundown on Lexi and her predicament, including how her home had been sold to Barrington Developments.

"The purchase was all above board. We bought it off her in-laws. But here's the thing: During her marriage she'd understood the property was gifted to her and her late husband on their wedding day. She only found out recently that the legal title had never been transferred. Now her in-laws have sold the place right out from under her. It was a gift that hadn't really been gifted at all."

"Wow, that's tough," Flynn replied. "Still, in my line of work, I'm never surprised by what people who supposedly love each other can do to each other."

Flynn specialized in family law. Christopher could only imagine the kind of things he saw every day.

"Look," Flynn continued, "this isn't my area of expertise, but I can refer you to someone else in the firm who has experience handling challenging estates."

Christopher breathed a sigh of relief. "That would be great. Any advice would be appreciated."

"Leave it with me. I'll text you a name and some contact details."

"Thanks, Flynn. I owe you one."

"Not at all. After what you did for my father... You saved his life. We'll all be forever grateful."

Once again, Christopher brushed away the praise and muttered something unintelligible.

Flynn merely chuckled. "I'm intrigued. It's not like you to go out of your way to help someone less fortunate. Are you sure you didn't hit your head in that fire?"

"Ha, ha! Very funny."

"I'm serious. For as long as I've known you, you've been hell-bent on making life difficult for those around you, including those nearest and potentially dearest to you. What happened to change your attitude?"

Christopher grimaced. "Let's just say I woke up to myself."

"Well, whatever happened and whoever's responsible, I'm glad to see the changes. Life's too short to go around bearing grudges."

Christopher thanked Flynn again and ended the call. He thought about what Flynn had said. It was true. He *had* changed. And he felt all the better for it. He had a long way to go before he would feel worthy of the attentions of someone as good and kind and decent as Lexi Greenaway, but he was working on it. One day at a time.

A few minutes later, his phone beeped, indicating an incoming text. It was from Flynn and included the name and number of a Sydney Legal probate lawyer. After saving the contact details to his address book, Christopher sent Flynn a thumbs up. It was a shame the day was over. He was eager to talk to someone as soon as he could about Lexi's problem.

But first he had to run his ideas and suggestions by her. As much as he wanted to take charge and forge ahead by putting plans into actions that might see an end to her problems, he'd learned enough along the way to realize not everyone wanted someone to solve their problems. The old Christopher would have carried on regardless, without thought to how someone might react to his decisions, but the new Christopher was determined to be more sensitive to other people's needs. Starting with Lexi's.

Nicer…kinder…considerate…

He'd go and see her tomorrow and discuss his ideas with her: seeking legal advice about her position, and in case receiving a share of the million dollars was a pipe dream with no legal substance, his backup plan was the fundraiser. Regardless of the outcome of discussions with the lawyer, they could still raise funds for a worthy cause. If Lexi and her children happened to be that good cause, then there was nothing wrong with that.

Anticipation and excitement coursed through him. He grinned. He might not have been able to overturn the sale, but that didn't mean he hadn't come up with a viable solution. He just hoped Lexi would go for it. After all, what did she have to lose?

Chapter Nine

Lexi sat on the front veranda in one of the ancient rocking chairs and peered out at the gray morning. The rain had started in the early hours and looked like it had settled in for the day. It was one of those cool gray days that reminded everyone winter was just around the corner.

Leroy snuggled on her lap, a soft blanket tucked around him. His thumb was in his mouth, his eyes closed. He snored softly in the silence. She'd been reading to him—a Doctor Seuss book—one of his favorites. Somewhere between the fourth and fifth page he'd fallen asleep.

Carefully, she set the book down on the floor and adjusted Leroy in her lap. His silky blond curls lifted in the gentle breeze. She reached over and stroked the hair back off his face. He looked so peaceful. So different from the scared and fearful baby she'd taken in more than two years ago.

He hadn't spoken at all when she'd first met him. Now he had an impressive vocabulary that was growing every day. His confidence had blossomed under her gentle encouragement and slowly, but surely, he'd begun to feel safe. He now had brothers and sisters who cared about him, along with Lexi who adored him. She'd been over the moon last year when his seventeen-year-old biological mother had agreed he was better off with Lexi.

Lexi had met with the girl a number of times. Removing a child from its biological parents was always a last resort. But in the end, the department had stepped in. The child's safety was paramount and Leroy's caseworker had grave fears for him. Still, Lexi had done her best to facilitate get-togethers between Leroy and his mom. She believed it was important the two maintain some kind of relationship, even if his mom wasn't in a position to see to his daily needs.

But as the months went by, it became more and more obvious Leroy's mom was never going to be in a position to take care of him. Then she'd given birth to another child. Her new boyfriend wasn't interested in raising another man's child. They were living in less than ideal accommodations and the caseworker was certain Leroy's mom was using again.

In the end, Lexi had petitioned for adoption and Leroy's mom had signed the papers, seemingly without regrets. She'd urged Lexi to take care of her son and had told her he was much better off with her. It gave Lexi no pleasure to know the girl was right or that more than likely the new baby would also be removed from her care.

All Lexi cared about were the children, the scared, lost, lonely, unloved children who were often forgotten when the family unit broke down. She remembered what it was like to feel unloved and abandoned as a child. That was the reason she was so determined to do whatever she could to prevent the same happening to other children whenever she was able to do so.

She had so much love to give. Ronnie had been the same. Though she'd been the one to suggest becoming foster parents, he'd quickly warmed to the idea. And he'd been so good with them! Playing and skylarking and having fun. He'd been as big a kid as any of them. With his constant funny games and antics, he'd drawn out the most subdued of them. They'd loved him as much as she had.

And then Ronnie had died so suddenly and her world had caved in. Through sheer strength of will and determination, she'd pulled herself out of a dark place and vowed to continue to carry on the legacy she and Ronnie had started, fostering as many needy children as she could. Leroy was just one of them.

Of course, it wasn't easy on her own, but every time she thought about the challenges, she also thought about what it would be like for those children if she didn't keep on doing what needed to be done. Though she couldn't save all of them, she did what she could and she was okay with that.

She gave them her attention, her consideration, her love. She offered them a warm, safe, secure place to live. It made all the difference when trying to raise a strong, functional adult.

But now that essential foundation for her children was under threat. Christopher had made it clear it was a done deal and it wouldn't be long before the demolition team was at her door.

What will I do then? Where will we go?

The sound of tires crunching on the gravel driveway caught her attention. She looked up, recognizing Christopher's gray Mercedes as it pulled up outside her house. He climbed out and moved toward her.

He wore another tailored suit, this one in a shade that matched the gray sky. His tie, a navy-blue-and-white stripe, contrasted nicely with the crisp whiteness of his shirt. Though he still wore the sling, that didn't take away from the strength that emanated from his tall, muscular frame. The gray at his temples lent him a sophisticated air.

She greeted him with a wary smile. "Hi," she said softly, mindful of the toddler who slept in her lap.

Christopher glanced at Leroy and his expression softened, easing some of the lines on his face. He looked younger when he did that. For the first time, she allowed herself time to absorb his attractiveness. The dark hair that he wore a bit too long to be fashionable. The green eyes that were clear and direct. The tanned skin. The chiseled jaw that even this early in the day was shadowed with his beard. He swiped at the droplets of rain that clung to his jacket.

Indicating Leroy with a movement of her head, she looked up at Christopher. She pitched her voice low. "I'll be right back."

"Do you need a hand?" he whispered.

"No, I'm fine. But thanks."

Coming upright, she carried Leroy toward the door. Christopher beat her to it and held it open for her. She murmured her thanks and slipped inside. She went into the bedroom Leroy shared with two of his siblings and eased him down onto his bed. He murmured in his sleep and then rolled over onto his side and fell quiet. She pressed a kiss on his forehead, drew another blanket up around him and then left the room.

She found Christopher still out on the veranda. "Come in. Please."

He followed her into the kitchen. "Would you like a cup of coffee? It's not really lemonade weather."

"You're right. It's been raining all the way from the city. Good for your garden, I guess."

She grinned, pleased he'd remembered. "Absolutely. I just finished planting my winter crop. Strawberries, capsicum, snow peas..."

Her voice faded off. It didn't matter what she'd planted. Odds were, she wouldn't be here for the harvest. Neither would her vegetable garden.

Christopher appeared to follow her train of thought. His expression darkened. "I'm afraid I don't have good news. I met with my father. I always knew it was a long shot and I was right. There's nothing he can do about the sale."

A flash of anger burned through her. "You mean he doesn't *want* to do anything about it."

Christopher tensed. "I already told you. It isn't that easy."

"Of course it is. He's the developer, isn't he?"

"There are other people involved. Investors he's made promises to. Besides, even though he sympathizes, the project has gone too far for him to bring it to a halt."

She opened her mouth to argue further, but he held up his hand.

"Please, Lexi. I'm trying to help. I *want* to help."

She frowned, suddenly filled with suspicion. "Why? You don't even know me, or my children. You owe me nothing. Why would you want to help a stranger?"

He gave her a lopsided smile. "Is it so hard to believe I want to do it for no better reason than it feels right?"

She shrugged. "Most people couldn't care less about what feels right. It's all about what feels *good*. For *them*. And to hell with everyone else."

He winced and she could tell she'd struck a nerve. "I take it you know what I'm talking about."

He nodded. "I'm embarrassed to admit it, but I was exactly like that. Selfish, self-centered, in it only for myself. I was all that and more." He gave a self-deprecating laugh. "Just ask my family. They bore the brunt of it."

Lexi regarded him curiously. She'd never known a man to admit such flaws. It took courage to do so.

"What made you change?" she asked softly.

Christopher drew in a deep breath that expanded the width of his chest. "It didn't happen overnight. There were a number of things—and people—in my life who made me realize I needed to let go of past hurts, the resulting bitterness and get on with living my life. A few months ago, some of their words finally made sense and I started listening." He gave her a disarming smile. "And here I am."

The smile transformed his face. Her stomach somersaulted with nerves. She guessed he must have smiled before, but this was the first time she'd really *felt* it. No doubt she'd been too caught up in her own problems to pay him close attention. But that had just changed.

All of a sudden, the room was electric with awareness. Her nipples puckered. Her skin felt hot. She glanced at him, wondering if he felt it too. She couldn't interpret the look on his face. She turned away to hide her reaction to him.

"Tea or coffee?" she asked, keeping her back to him and taking refuge in filling the kettle over the sink.

"Coffee, please. Black, no sugar."

She nodded and began collecting mugs, the tin of instant coffee and then she rummaged in the pantry for some homemade cookies. Chocolate chip. Leroy's favorite. Baked fresh the day before. By the time she'd set a plate in front of Christopher, she was once again in control of her personal response to him, at least outwardly.

"So, why have you returned?" she asked.

The last time she'd seen him, she'd spilled her life story and while he'd shown some compassion toward her dire situation, he'd made no promises about being able to fix it. Not that she'd expected him to. Since Ronnie's death, she'd learned not to rely on anyone. Her past experiences had taught her if she trusted anyone, they most often let her down. Just look at her in-laws. She was still coming to terms with their betrayal. No, it was better to accept she only had herself to rely on. It was easier that way.

"I've been thinking about your predicament," he said. "I've come up with a couple of ideas."

She looked at him, surprised. After making it clear to her the last time she'd spoken with him that he wasn't in a position to overturn the sale, she hadn't expected him to give her situation another thought.

"Oh?"

"Yes." He fixed his gaze on the counter. A flush spread slowly up his neck and across his cheeks.

Lexi recalled him saying how not so long ago he'd been a selfish asshole. She wondered if his willingness to help her find a solution made him feel uncomfortable. He'd admitted that trying to be a nicer person had been a recent thing.

Perhaps he's still getting used to the idea?

The thought amused her. Still, she was anxious to know what he'd come up with. At this point, any idea was welcome. Having realized that viewing him as her enemy would be an exercise in futility, ironically, she thought talking to another adult would be nice.

Their conversation flowed easily. Surprisingly, he was a good listener. She knew nothing about his past, or why he'd felt the need to become a better person, but begrudgingly she was coming to like the man. In fact, if it wasn't for his role in her circumstances, she would probably like him a lot.

The realization surprised her. Since Ronnie's death, she hadn't been interested in men or new relationships. She'd been consumed with doing all she could to ensure her kids felt safe and secure and loved, despite the fact Ronnie was no longer there. It was only the older ones who remembered him now.

Leroy hadn't even been born when Ronnie had died and Michael had only been a baby. Patrice had yet to come into their lives. Still, Lexi had been left with five children to care for and the challenge of doing it all on her own. Four years down the track, that reality hadn't changed. It was a sobering thought.

Christopher watched Lexi busy herself in the kitchen. She spooned instant coffee into two mugs, added boiling water. She gave his a stir and added milk and sugar to hers. Her cheeks were still pink. He'd been intrigued by the blush that had stolen over her face when she looked at him. He wasn't sure what had brought about the sudden heightened awareness, but he wasn't unhappy that she'd become aware of him as a man.

Until now he didn't have a clue if she'd even noticed him. He'd arrived there representing the company she considered her enemy. She was so determined to hold her ground, to paint him as the cause of all her problems, he was certain if he'd turned up sprouting devil's horns she definitely wouldn't have been surprised.

But after she'd shared some of her most private memories, the air had shifted between them. He couldn't be happier. He'd been fighting his attraction to her from the moment they'd met. It gave him hope that she might finally be seeing him as more than her sworn enemy. A friend, or maybe even something more...

Careful, Christopher... Don't go getting your hopes up. Your stepfather's kicking her out of her home and she's likely still grieving her husband, or at least the memories of the life they shared in their soon to be demolished home. Don't rush her. You'll only screw things up...

She carried the coffee to the counter and set a mug in front of him. "Have a cookie," she urged, pushing the plate toward him.

He took one and bit into it. The buttery biscuit melted on his tongue, along with the rich taste of chocolate "*Mm*, this is good."

"Choc chip," she said. "My kids love them. Leroy, especially."

Christopher looked around him. "Where are the rest of them?"

"The older ones are at school. Michael and Patrice are doing jigsaws in their room. They'd prefer to be outside playing, but it's raining."

He winked. "I remember what that was like, being cooped up inside all day while it poured buckets outside. I used to get bored to tears. I didn't have any siblings back then to keep me company, either."

"Tell me about your ideas."

Her gentle smile illuminated the translucency of her skin. Her blue eyes sparkled. Up this close, he could see a smattering of tiny freckles that danced across her nose. He caught himself staring and hurriedly buried his face in his coffee mug. The hot liquid scorched his tongue. He cursed beneath his breath.

Lexi laughed. "Careful. It's hot."

Christopher flushed. He felt like an awkward school boy. He couldn't remember ever feeling like this. He'd grown up fast and tough. He'd always been the one lording it over people, always the one with the upper hand. It had been a defense mechanism: Get them before they get you. But with Lexi he felt off-kilter. He didn't know which way was up. For someone used to being in control of every situation, it was rather disconcerting and yet there was nothing he could do about it. Short of staying clear of her. Which he didn't want to do.

Christopher cleared his throat. "Yes, my ideas..." he finally said, focusing on their conversation. "Okay, firstly I think we should seek legal advice about your options regarding your in-laws. They gave you this property as a wedding gift and then pretty much stole it back. There must be some avenues we can pursue in the courts."

Lexi's face fell. "I can't afford to take legal action. It would cost thousands, maybe tens of thousands."

Christopher tamped down his irritation. "Don't let the money aspect deter you. There are always avenues around that."

"Easy for you to say," she scoffed. "I'm betting you haven't done without much in your life."

He let that comment pass and tried to remember Elizabeth's advice. *Go gently... Don't trample on her pride...*

Right.

He drew in a deep breath. "Let's put the cost issue aside for now. If you took your in-laws to court, you might be awarded a substantial sum of money. They were paid a million dollars for this land. Land that rightfully belonged to you."

Her expression remained stubbornly closed. "How can I put the cost issue aside? Besides, court cases can drag on for years. Even if I could manage to scrape together the money for the legal fees, what would we do in the meantime?"

"True," he conceded. "A court case wouldn't be resolved overnight. Still, maybe if you have a strong enough case, they might settle. It might not even go to court."

She opened her mouth to protest again, but Christopher held up his hand. "Okay, I know what you're going to say, but just hear me out. I have a cousin who's a lawyer. He specializes in family law so he can't help you himself, but he's given me the name of a probate lawyer. There's no harm in meeting this guy and seeking some advice. You don't have to take it. This is just a matter of exploring all options. What do you say?"

Her nod, when it finally came, was slow and filled with reluctance. "I suppose there's no harm in getting some advice..."

He breathed a sigh of relief.

Great. We're making progress. This is harder than I expected... Remember, go gently...

He drew in another deep, fortifying breath. "Now, for my next idea." He cleared his throat, more nervous about her reaction than he'd expected. Lexi hadn't reacted quite the way he'd expected to his first suggestion. The fundraiser was a little trickier. He needed to handle this with finesse. The last thing he wanted to do was insult her.

"See, I was talking about you to Elizabeth Craigdon. She was so moved by your plight. Right away, she wanted to do something to help. She—"

A frown had made its appearance on Lexi's forehead. Christopher stopped speaking. "Um, is something the matter?"

Her frown deepened. "That name sounds familiar. Elizabeth Craigdon. Who is she?"

"She's...um...the wife of the late Henry Craigdon. He was pretty well-known in Sydney. A property developer of some renown, among other things. He owned Craigdon Enterprises."

"Oh, yes. That's right. He and his wife were big supporters of several worthy charities."

Christopher nodded. "My stepmother has always spent a lot of time on various boards and she's renowned for her fundraisers. That's what I wanted to talk to—"

Lexi's eyes had grown wide. "Elizabeth Craigdon's your stepmother?"

"Yes. Henry Craigdon was my biological father."

Lexi shook her head with disbelief. "Wow."

Christopher shrugged, uncomfortable with the focus on his father. "It wasn't as good as you think. Henry... Well, he refused to recognize me as his son, despite DNA tests that proved I was. He went to his grave denouncing me."

Lexi looked appalled. "Oh, no! I can't imagine how that made you feel."

Though the admission was difficult, it didn't cut him the same way it used to. A rush of bad memories bombarded him, but to his surprise, he was able to keep them at bay. The usual tsunami of anger and bitterness was also miraculously absent. He was healing; finally setting those painful feelings aside. It was a good thing. It was progress.

"It was tough," he admitted softly, "but I always had my mom. And of course, I was adopted by Frank Barrington a year after he married my mother."

Lexi's expression now filled with compassion. "How old were you then?"

"Twelve."

"You were one of the lucky ones," she said wistfully.

He nodded. Until that moment, he'd never fully appreciated the fact. "Yes."

"So Elizabeth Craigdon's your stepmother."

"Yes."

"Is she as lovely as she appears in public?"

"Absolutely. Completely genuine. Honest. Kind. Like I said, she wants to help you. She's willing to hold a fundraiser."

Lexi's frown reappeared. "As in, a charity fundraiser?"

"Kind of. Not that you're a charity," Christopher hurriedly added. "She's approaching it more from the angle of foster kids. There are so many of them out there who need our help and you're right there amongst it. Taking these children into your home, showering them with love and kindness. Giving them safety and security. The kind of things many of them have never had. Elizabeth wants to help with that. She's someone who's always been willing to roll up her sleeves and do what needs to be done."

Lexi's frown had eased. She now regarded him with cautious curiosity. Christopher kept talking, making it up as he went.

"It's not just a matter of fundraising. Elizabeth also wants to raise awareness, not just of your plight, but of the plight of all foster kids caught up in a system that so often fails them. She thinks a fundraiser might achieve all of that."

Christopher stopped speaking. Lexi looked thoughtful. He held his breath.

"Elizabeth Craigdon would really throw her considerable influence behind a cause like mine?"

"Yes, she would. All you have to do is agree and she'll set the ball in motion. In fact, she already mentioned a date.

Next Saturday night."

Lexi's eyes widened in shock. "Next Saturday night? But... How can she pull something like that off so quickly? A fundraiser normally takes months to plan."

Christopher grinned. "You don't know my stepmother. When she puts her mind to something, she's a force to be reckoned with."

Lexi chewed on her lip and looked undecided. Christopher went in for the kill. "Think of the money we could raise for these kids, Lexi. Money you could put toward new accommodations. You could buy something bigger which would allow you to help even more needy kids."

"It would all have to be above board," Lexi said thoughtfully. "Properly accounted for. I wouldn't be comfortable merely accepting donations to alleviate my situation. It has to help more kids. I'll find a solution to that. I'm not sure what or how, but I'll think of something."

Christopher bit back a groan of frustration. The whole point of these machinations was to help Lexi and her children, but he was astute enough to realize she'd never accept the donations on that basis alone. He'd have to slowly coax her into the idea over time. He'd keep reminding her about her children, in particular her foster kids. That was key to getting her to capitulate. His agreeing to her vision then changing direction as he could... He only hoped it worked.

Christopher forced a grin. "So, can I tell Elizabeth to go ahead and start planning?"

Once again, Lexi chewed on her lip with indecision. Christopher could almost see the arguments for and against, running through her head.

"Think of the kids," Christopher prodded, playing his trump card.

Finally, Lexi's shoulders slumped on a defeated sigh. "You're right. This is a fabulous opportunity for exposure and for fundraising. It's nothing less than such kids deserve. As much as I don't want to feel indebted to anyone, I can't in all good conscience turn the offer down."

This time Christopher's grin was genuine. "Yes! That's the way to go." In his enthusiasm, Christopher threw his one good arm around her and gave her a spontaneous hug.

Lexi tensed with surprise, but then he felt her relax against him and she hugged him back. It felt so good to have her pressed against him, her softness, her curves. Her exotic perfume wafted toward his nostrils. He breathed it in.

And when she pulled away with her cheeks flaming, so were his. For a man who prided himself on his suave way with women, he couldn't feel any more awkward.

"I'm sorry, Lexi. That was out of line. I... I got carried away."

She grinned through her embarrassment, helping to ease his concern. "It's fine, Christopher. I hugged you, too. I guess I'm feeling just as excited as you. I can't believe someone with the standing of Elizabeth Craigdon wants to help my cause. It's... It's like a dream come true. A wonderful dream."

Christopher swallowed a sigh of relief. Though the feel of Lexi pressed against him was imprinted on his mind and body forever, he wasn't confident she felt more for him than she would a friend. He needed to take things slowly, gage her reaction, see where she stood. Maybe he could get a better read on her at the fundraiser. Or at the least, he could engage the help of his siblings to assess the situation and give him advice.

Images of his eight Barrington half-brothers and sisters ran through his head. On top of that, there were six half-siblings on the Craigdon side. That was one hell of a lot of people sticking their noses into his business. So... Maybe keeping this thing he had for Lexi quiet was a better idea. He was pretty sure he didn't want any of his meddlesome siblings having an inkling that he might very well be falling in love.

Love? Did I really just use that word? No, lust would be a more accurate description...wouldn't it?

Aware that Lexi was waiting for him to respond, he pushed away the new thoughts that clamored for attention and cleared his throat.

"I'll call Elizabeth right away so she can start planning. Is next Saturday night good for you?"

Lexi laughed. "Yes! Of course! Any night she wants to do this is good for me. The only thing is, I'll have to find a sitter..." Her enthusiasm faded. She sighed. "Actually, next Saturday night might be a problem. I might not be able to find someone on short notice."

"Bring the kids with you! I'm sure there will be other kids there! And I know for sure my brothers and sisters will only be too happy to help out with them."

Lexi looked surprised. "Really? They'd help out with someone else's kids? They don't even know me!"

"Of course they would! They're good people. Almost as good as you."

Christopher looked at her. Their gazes caught and held. His heart began to thump and nerves filled his gut. Lexi licked her lips. Christopher zeroed in on the action and watched like it was in slow motion. The tip of her pink tongue. The moistness of her lips. Slightly parted on a sharp intake of breath.

"Lexi…"

Unable to help himself, he reached out with his good hand and cupped her cheek. He lowered his head and gently brushed her lips with his.

Soft… So soft…

The kiss was over before it started, but neither of them moved away. It was like their gazes were joined together by some invisible silken thread. And then Lexi blinked and Christopher ducked his head and cleared his throat.

"I'm sorry, Lexi. That was out of line. It's too soon… I… The thing is, I couldn't help it."

Her cheeks were crimson. She wouldn't meet his gaze. "It's okay, Christopher. Let's not dwell on it."

He swallowed a sigh of relief. "Yes, good. Okay. Of course. I… I'll let you know when I've arranged an appointment with Flynn's colleague. You're still okay about meeting with a lawyer, aren't you?"

"Yes. I guess it can't hurt to explore my options."

"Good. And I'll call Elizabeth." He grinned. "I can't wait for you to meet her. She's going to love you."

Chapter Ten

Vaughan Barrington swiped the sweat off his brow and shoveled ice into a tall glass. He added a generous splash of vodka and topped it off with soda water and lime juice. He grinned as he handed it to the attractive twenty-something woman with her messy brown hair and twinkling eyes.

"Here you go."

She smiled back and handed over some money. "Keep the change," she quipped.

The invitation in her eyes was tempting, but he wouldn't get off work for another four hours. For now, he'd have to be content with flirting.

The bar where he'd taken a job was positioned in a popular part of Bali. Nusa Dua Beach stretched for more than a mile along Bali's southern coastline and was a haven for water sports. It was also an enclave of large five-star resorts and catered almost exclusively to cashed-up tourists looking for a good time.

That was what had attracted Vaughan when he'd spontaneously packed his bags two weeks earlier and boarded a plane. The only thing on his mind was a need to escape, to go somewhere no one knew him, somewhere he could hide out, have a good time and think.

Thanks to his well-paid job at Barrington Mining, he had plenty of money. It wasn't that he needed to work, but he didn't know how long he intended to stay in Bali and he knew he'd go mad if he sat around too long. He was still trying to get his head around the idea that his biological mother was Elizabeth Craigdon. Even more shocking, she was very much alive and wanted to meet him.

Vaughan had read her letter and all he'd felt was panic and disbelief. He'd grown up believing he'd been orphaned at birth. At least, that's what the various foster carers had told him. He'd always assumed they'd been given the information by the government officials and caseworkers who'd traipsed through the first eleven years of his life, before he'd been lucky enough to be adopted by Frank and Evelyn Barrington. But now he knew that wasn't the case. Someone had lied.

A tourist wearing a flamboyant red-and-white floral print shirt sidled up to the bar.

"What can I get you?" Vaughan asked with a smile.

"A beer thanks."

"You want to try the local brew?" he asked.

The man shrugged. "Why not."

Vaughan cracked open a can and handed it across the bar. The man slapped down a twenty and took his drink.

"Keep the change."

Vaughan smiled his thanks. "Cheers. Enjoy your beer."

Vaughan served several more customers. Mostly young, tanned, attractive. All having a good time. Many of them were on holiday and were staying at the resorts that lined the beach. He laughed and joked and took their money. It was mindless work, but it kept him from thinking too much about why he'd taken off without a word to hide out in Bali.

He took a moment to skip ahead a few songs on the playlist that belted out of cheap speakers above the bar. He found a song with a good strong beat and turned up the volume. Tapping his fingers in time to the rhythm, he flirted with the female customers and exchanged jokes with the men. It was his job to make sure everyone was having a good time, so they'd keep coming back. Of course the mixer drinks were watered down like crazy, especially in the last half of the night. But by then most people were too drunk to notice, so it worked out all right.

He moved to the counter behind him to check his phone. No messages. No texts. Of course, nobody had his number, so what did he expect? He'd left his old phone in his apartment in Bondi and had purchased a cheap disposable one at the airport.

He didn't want his family calling him, asking him where he was, badgering him for answers. He'd sent his father an email reassuring him he was okay. That's it. As far as he was aware, none of his family knew the truth of his recently discovered past.

The fact that he'd been adopted had never been a secret, but he was sure his family, like him, had assumed his biological mother was dead. Now it appeared that wasn't true. No, far from being dead, she was alive and well and had been married to one of the wealthiest men in the country.

Vaughan recalled hearing from Christopher that Henry Craigdon had died from a heart attack a little over a year ago, so Elizabeth Craigdon was now a widow.

Is that why she's finally reached out to me after four decades? Because her husband's dead? Has she kept me a secret from him, from her family, all these years? Had she been too ashamed to tell them?

That's what it felt like. That she'd been ashamed of him. Hadn't wanted her family to know. Especially her husband. But now Henry had died she was free to reveal her shameful secret. Why else would she come looking for him after so long? Nothing else made sense.

It was late when Vaughan's shift finally ended. He hopped on his moped and left for home. He'd reconnected with a couple of university friends who were living in cheap accommodation a fifteen-minute ride away. Brent and Marty had been living and working in Bali as engineers for the past few years. The three of them had kept in touch. When Vaughan decided to up and leave Sydney, Bali was the first place to pop into his mind.

Switching off the ignition, he kicked down the stand and climbed off the bike. He pulled off his helmet. Helmets weren't compulsory in Bali, but they were in Australia. Old habits died hard, he guessed. Besides, there were thousands of bikes in Bali. They crowded every inch of the road. They recklessly wove in and out among the cars; accidents were common. While he was looking to escape, that didn't mean he had a death wish.

Tucking the helmet under his arm, he let himself into the first-floor apartment. It was small and cramped, but it had a stove and a microwave and a fridge. Best of all, it had three bedrooms. At forty, he was a little too old to be sleeping on someone's couch.

The house was dark and quiet. His roommates were either still out or had gone to bed. Probably the latter. They left early for work and didn't return until dark. Vaughan had once questioned them about the point of being in Bali if they didn't get time to enjoy it, but both of them had laughed and told him they wouldn't want to live anywhere else.

Vaughan could understand their attitude. Bali had a laid-back feel to it that couldn't be replicated back home. The locals were relaxed and friendly, always smiling, despite the hardships of trying to eke out a living in a developing country.

They were a very accepting people when it came to the life they'd been given. He supposed it had something to do with the fact the Balinese were predominantly Hindu. He'd read that while less than two percent of Indonesians practiced Hinduism, almost eighty-seven percent of Balinese did. They truly believed the difficulties they experienced in their life on earth would turn into pleasures in the next life. He didn't know for sure, but he guessed that's why they appeared so happy.

Shrugging off his backpack, he set his helmet on the kitchen counter and toed off his loafers. Then he opened the fridge and grabbed a beer. Cracking open the tab, he swallowed most of the contents before pausing to drag in a lungful of moist air.

It appeared the air conditioner had again gone on the blink and the apartment was stifling. A single ceiling fan stirred the hot air in desultory waves, but with little noticeable effect. Vaughan's Hawaiian shirt stuck to his skin—hot, sticky and uncomfortable.

The humidity had taken some getting used to. In fact, he still hadn't acclimatized. His flat mates assured him he wouldn't even notice it after another month, but Vaughan wasn't so sure he could last that long. First thing in the morning, he was going to call their landlord and see what the man could do about the air conditioning. It was one thing to be roughing it on the cheap in Bali, but that didn't mean he was prepared to do without air conditioning.

Finishing his beer, he tossed the can into the garbage bin that stood under the sink and then padded through the silent house to the bathroom. Stripping off his clothes, he stepped into the shower and began to soap himself up.

He'd kept himself fit since arriving in Bali with regular gym sessions on the beach. An early morning jog before the humidity got too bad was also part of his daily schedule. Though it wasn't quite the punishing gym sessions he'd endured when he lived in Bondi, it was enough for him to maintain his toned and muscular physique.

He ran a razor over his cheeks and scraped at the whiskers on his chin. Plenty of hot Bali sun had bronzed his skin to a dark golden color, contrasting with the caramel-gold shade of his hair. He didn't know why he'd bothered to continue to shave. Force of habit, no doubt. It wasn't like he'd be fronting a boardroom any time soon.

Drying off, he tied his towel loosely around his waist and then left the bathroom. He dropped the towel on the floor of his room and threw himself naked across his bed. The illuminated dials on the clock radio on his bedside table told him it was almost two.

No wonder I feel wrecked...

With a sigh, he stacked his hands behind his head and thought about the letter in the bottom of his suitcase. The one he'd received from Elizabeth Craigdon. His mother. Apparently. And just like the first time he'd stared, incredulous, at the contents, with a muffled curse, he forced their import from his mind.

Christopher watched from his position on the footpath as Lexi climbed out of the taxi. She wore her hair loose around her shoulders. It made her look younger. A peach-colored lipstick the same shade as her sundress drew his attention to her luscious mouth and he was suddenly reminded of their kiss. It had been nothing more than a brief meeting of lips, lasting no more than a few seconds, but the memory of it was burned into his mind. He wanted to taste her again.

But right now they had an appointment with Grayson Thorpe, the probate lawyer Flynn had recommended. Christopher had done a little research. Grayson Thorpe had an impressive list of credentials. In addition to specializing in probate law, he was also a litigation expert.

Lexi had agreed to meet outside the offices of Sydney Legal. And here she was. Along with three of her children.

Christopher hadn't given any thought to the logistics of her meeting him in the city. Of course, the older children were at school, which meant she had no choice but to bring the younger ones with her.

The challenges of being a single mother…

As he waited, he saw Michael, Leroy and Patrice slide out of the back seat of the taxi and stand uncertainly on the curb. Lexi grabbed the hands of the two youngest and instructed Patrice to hold onto Leroy's other hand. She turned and saw him and her face broke into a nervous smile. His heart skipped a beat.

She's so beautiful… So open and sweet… So genuine…

So unlike him… Bored, jaded and not above stirring the trouble pot for his own amusement.

We're so different, she and I. She's far too good for me…

Before he could contemplate his musings further, she approached, greeting him with another smile.

"Hi, Christopher. Sorry, I hope you don't mind I brought the children. I didn't have anyone to leave them with."

He managed a grin. "Of course not. I'm sorry I didn't think of that when I arranged the meeting." Crouching at eye level, he greeted the children by name.

Lexi looked pleased he'd remembered. "Say hello to Mr Barrington," she told them.

"Hello, Mr Barrington" they duly chimed.

He ruffled Michael's hair. "Enough of this Mr Barrington. Please, call me Christopher. How was your trip to the city?"

While they began regaling him with stories of the different people on the train and the strange cloth on their taxi driver's head, Christopher took hold of Michael's free hand

and steered the five of them through Martin Place toward the offices of Sydney Legal. It was crowded with shoppers and workers hurrying to get to their destination. The kids chatted excitedly, their eyes wide with wonder. He wasn't sure if Lexi took them into the city much, but he guessed, if she did, it wasn't too often.

Not that he blamed her. With so many people around, he was nervous they might lose someone. He glanced at Lexi. She looked calm and happy. A smile played around her lips. She didn't look concerned that one of the kids would run off. He drew in a deep breath and reined in his burgeoning panic.

They reached the glass doors that led inside the building that housed Sydney Legal. Inside, out of the noise, the kids fell silent. Or maybe they were a bit awed by the marble and tile foyer. Or the colorful artworks that lined the walls. The huge abstract sculpture that dominated the area near the lifts was also rather impressive.

Christopher approached the bearded man in a smart suit who sat behind the reception desk. "Hi. I'm Christopher Barrington. We're here to see Grayson Thorpe."

The man nodded and picked up a phone. Christopher moved away. A few minutes later the man called to him.

"Mr Thorpe's secretary will be down in a minute."

"Thank you."

Christopher went to stand beside Lexi who had her hands full answering questions from the kids about the paintings, the building, the sculpture.

"What are we doing here, Momma?" Patrice asked.

"We're visiting a friend," Lexi asked. "He's going to help us with some information."

"Does he live here?" Michael asked, his eyes wide.

"No. He works here," Lexi answered.

"So this isn't his house?" Leroy sought clarification.

"No, honey. It's an office building."

"What's an office building?" Michael asked.

Just then, the doors to one of the lifts slid open and a tall, slim woman in her twenties, wearing a navy-blue suit and incredibly high heels, strode toward them. Christopher heard Lexi's quiet sigh of relief.

"Mr Barrington?" the woman asked.

"Yes. I'm Mr Barrington," he replied, stepping forward.

She held out her hand and he shook it. "I'm Anne Howarth. I work for Mr Grayson. He asked me to come and get you." Her gaze took in his entourage. "Are all these people with you?"

"Yes," he said hurriedly. "This is Lexi Greenaway. And her three children. Patrice, Michael and Leroy."

The young woman did a credible job of hiding her surprise. Obviously her boss hadn't alerted her to the fact there would be two of them, and a number of children besides.

"Okay, well, come with me." She turned on her heel. Her straight, shoulder-length brown hair flared out behind her.

Christopher and Lexi herded the children toward the lift. Anne held the door open for them, waiting patiently. The doors slid silently closed behind them and the lift began its ascent.

The children *oohed* and *ahhed*, looking both apprehensive and curious. Lexi was quick to reassure them. They touched the shiny silver walls and watched the movement of lights that indicated the different floors, all the time chattering between themselves. Their excitement was contagious. No doubt it was their first time riding in a lift. From the corner of his eye, Christopher could see both Anne and Lexi were trying hard to hold back a smile.

The lift came to a stop and the doors slid open. Once again, the children fell silent. They stepped out onto thick carpet and followed Anne down a long corridor. She punched a security code into a pad on the wall and then opened the door and ushered them inside.

"I'll just go and find some more chairs," she said. "Mr Grayson won't be too long." With that, she disappeared.

Christopher looked around him. This wasn't his first visit to the offices of Sydney Legal but he'd never been there with a pile of kids in tow. Michael and Leroy were already perched up on two of the plush velvet seats. Patrice was going through the pile of glossy magazines, running her fingers over the covers.

"Why don't you sit down?" Christopher suggested to Lexi, pointing to the only other available chair.

"Are you sure?"

"Yes, of course. I can stand."

"But what about your arm?"

"It's fine. Thanks."

A moment later, Anne reappeared, carrying another chair. She set it down beside Lexi.

"There. I'm sorry, that's the only one I can find."

"It's fine," Lexi said, pulling Leroy onto her lap. Patrice promptly plopped herself on the recently vacated seat and began thumbing through a magazine.

Christopher heard the sound of a door opening and looked down the corridor in time to see a good-looking man in a designer suit striding toward him. Late twenties with short blond hair, green eyes and the kind of muscular body that indicated hours spent in the gym.

"Christopher? I'm Grayson Thorpe."

The two men shook hands, Christopher using his left. Grayson didn't say anything about the sling. Instead, he turned his attention to Lexi.

"Hello. I'm Grayson Thorpe."

"Lexi Greenaway."

Christopher watched her, noting her calm expression and polite smile. Whether she'd taken note of the lawyer's good looks or not, no reaction registered on her face. She merely introduced her children and apologized for having to bring them along. To Grayson's credit, he appeared unperturbed by the extra visitors.

"If it's all right with you, Mrs Greenaway, I'll have Anne keep an eye on your children out here. That way we can talk without interruption. Anne's great with kids. She has younger siblings. Right, Anne?"

Anne smiled. "Absolutely. In fact, I might even have some crayons in my desk drawer for them to borrow." She turned to the children. "You could each draw me a picture. What do you say?"

"Yay!" Patrice cheered. "I love drawing."

"A picture! A picture!" Leroy chortled with delight.

Michael appeared equally content with the arrangements.

Lexi set Leroy on the seat and crouched low, gathering the children around her. "Okay, so Momma has to go and talk with Mr Grayson for a few minutes. I promise I won't be long. Anne has very kindly agreed to keep an eye out for you and she's going to give you some crayons and paper to draw with. I want you to be on your best behavior, okay?"

There was a chorus of agreement. Lexi stood and spoke to Anne. "Thank you, I really appreciate this."

The young woman smiled. She had the kind of girl-next-door look about her that inspired confidence.

"No problem. I'll give you a shout if they need anything."

"Please do that," Lexi said. She looked over at Christopher. "Okay. Let's do this."

Chapter Eleven

Grayson ushered them into his office. While he didn't have a view of the harbor or the Botanical Gardens, the office was spacious and nicely furnished with matching leather chairs, a walnut desk and a carved coat rack that held an Akubra hat and an umbrella.

Christopher and Lexi took a seat. Grayson settled himself behind his desk and stacked his hands beneath his chin. He looked from Christopher to Lexi.

"So, Flynn gave me a brief rundown of your situation, Mrs Greenaway, but would you mind going over it again in your own words?"

"Yes, of course."

Lexi cleared her throat and went through the details that led up to the point that she discovered her home had been sold out from underneath her. As he listened, Thorpe took notes. Occasionally, he'd interject with a question. Finally, Lexi's story came to an end.

Grayson looked thoughtful. "Did your in-laws ever actually *say* the property was yours?"

Lexi shook her head. "It was a wedding gift. I believed ownership was implied."

"Did you ever ask for the title deed?"

"No."

"Why not?"

Lexi bit her lip. "It didn't occur to me. Besides, the gift came from Ronnie's parents. I left the details up to him."

"Did you pay rent?"

"No, of course not. We thought the place was ours."

"What about local council rates? Did you attend to payment of those over the years?"

"No."

"So you assumed they were being paid by your in-laws."

"To tell you the truth, I didn't think about it. Ronnie looked after our finances. He took it upon himself to pay bills, negotiate contracts with our telephone and electricity providers, that kind of thing. I had my hands full with the children.

"Of course. And from what I hear, you've been doing a remarkable job," Grayson said smoothly.

"She's fostered twenty-seven children so far," Christopher said. He glanced at Lexi, unable to keep the pride from his voice.

She gave him a grateful smile. He wanted to reach out and squeeze her hand, but she was seated on his right and it was a bit too awkward to reach over with his left.

"When did you find out you and your husband weren't on the title?" Thorpe asked.

"When I explained the place was sold out from underneath her," Christopher replied. Anger tinged his voice.

Lexi shot him a calming look, for which he was grateful.

"Actually no," Lexi corrected.

Christopher started in surprise.

Lexi continued. "I first found out when Ronnie died. The family lawyer was going through Ronnie's will. There was no mention of the property. I asked the question. That's when I found out the legal title had never been transferred to us."

"How long ago was this?" Thorpe asked.

"Four years."

Thorpe's eyebrows rose in surprise. "Four years? And you hadn't taken steps to have the title transferred in all that time?"

Lexi flushed. Christopher could feel her discomfort. This time it was him giving her a reassuring smile.

"I tried to. I raised it once. It was during the reading of Ronnie's will. I asked George and Dorothy if they'd transfer the title to me, now that Ronnie had gone."

"What did they say?"

"Not much. They mumbled something in response. I thought it was along the lines that they'd attend to it, but I didn't press. They'd just buried their only child. I didn't want to appear insensitive."

"You didn't follow up?"

"I did one time. It was at Christmas. Again they avoided answering the question. They'd been very generous with the children's presents. I didn't want to seem ungrateful. It was... awkward."

Thorpe nodded, his lips compressed. "So they could argue that you knew you weren't the rightful owner and you did nothing about it. In fact, you'd known for four years. That's a long time."

Once again, a flush stained Lexi's cheeks. Christopher felt outraged, but he held his tongue. Thorpe was on their side. He was only pointing out the very same facts that would be used by Lexi's in-laws in the event this dispute went to court.

Thorpe sighed quietly and folded his arms in front of him. He regarded them somberly. Christopher could tell whatever the lawyer was about to say didn't bring him any pleasure.

"I'm sorry, Mrs Greenaway. From what you've told me, I don't think there's anything you can do. If you'd spent all these years truly believing you were the rightful owner, then maybe we might have a case. But the fact is, you've known for the past four years that the property hadn't been transferred to you and you did nothing about it. That's an argument for implied acceptance. I'm not confident if you took this to court that you'd win."

Outside the offices of Sydney Legal, Christopher did his best to revive Lexi's spirits. "Don't look so down. It was worth a shot."

She compressed her lips. "Yes. If only I'd—"

"Hey," he said gently. "Don't go there."

She threw up her hands in frustration. "I feel so stupid. I can't believe I never once gave any thought to things such as council rates and property tax notices. But it was like I said. Especially in the early days. I just assumed Ronnie had dealt with it. He'd always been the one to attend to the paperwork and pay the bills. Then, afterwards...

"To tell you the truth, I was in a daze for quite a few months. I couldn't believe Ronnie was dead. Taken from me, just like that. It was a shock. He was only thirty years old." Her expression became resigned. "I should have pushed harder. I should have demanded they transfer the title to me. And do you know what? They didn't even know about Ronnie's insurance money. That makes their attitude toward us so much harder to understand." She sighed. "Not that I blame them for any of this. It's my fault we've lost our home. I only have myself to blame."

Christopher glanced at the children who stood nearby. Patrice held Leroy's hand. Michael scuffed at the pavement with his shoe. Their mood was less jovial than it had been earlier. No doubt they sensed their mother's inner turmoil. Unable to fight his instincts any longer, Christopher surprised both of them by pulling her against him with his good arm and giving her an awkward hug. Just as quickly, he let her go.

His pulse raced at her nearness, at the feel of her warmth and softness pressed against him. Her eyes were wide, her cheeks flushed. Her chest rose and fell with the increased speed of her breaths.

"I'm sorry. I couldn't help myself," he explained. "I can't bear to see you looking so miserable. You shouldn't be so hard on yourself. You were going through a tough time. You had a lot going on. Besides, you had no reason to believe Ronnie's parents had done the wrong thing by you."

She drew in a shaky breath. "You're right. I thought they loved me like a daughter. They'd told me as much. I guess their feelings dissipated on Ronnie's death."

Christopher gave her a smile of reassurance. "Well, all is not lost. We still have the fundraiser to look forward to, remember? If I know anything about Elizabeth Craigdon it's that she throws herself wholeheartedly into whatever project she takes on. The night will be a success. I'm sure of it."

Lexi's smile in response was a little less confident. "I hope you're right."

"How about we go and get some lunch? The kids must be starving."

His suggestion was met with a chorus of cheers.

"I want ice cream!"

"I want pizza!"

"Milkshakes!"

Lexi threw up her hands and gave him a helpless smile. "I hope you understand what little monsters you've just unleashed."

He laughed, pleased to see the clouds had been chased from her eyes. His laughter was interrupted by the ringing of his phone. Checking the screen, he saw it was Julian. He turned to Lexi. "I'm sorry, I have to take this. Can you give me a minute?"

"Of course. We'll wait for you over there." She pointed to a bench a few yards away.

He nodded and turned away from her, answering the call. "Julian. That was faster than I expected."

"Yes. I got onto your request right away. There wasn't a whole lot to find. The only thing of interest is the exorbitant credit card bills. Seems like one or both of the Greenaways has an addiction to online shopping."

"What about their bank accounts? Did you find any money?"

"They deposited a million dollars into their account about six months ago. I haven't traced where the money came from. Perhaps they won the lottery?"

"Oh, yeah. They won the lottery all right," Christopher muttered. "Tell me, how much is left?"

"That's the thing. They've gone through almost all of it. A million dollars gone in the space of six months. I wouldn't believe it possible, except I saw the credit card statements."

Christopher gaped in surprise. "Almost all of it? What the hell did they buy?"

"Anything and everything. TVs, stereo equipment, white goods, holidays, handbags, rare first edition books. Hell, I lost count of the number of books."

"So it's all gone?"

"Yep. They have a total of thirteen thousand two hundred and fifty-six dollars in their account."

Christopher cursed under his breath. He'd been hoping there would be enough left that he could persuade the Greenaways to do the right thing and give some of the money to their daughter-in-law. It seemed that plan was now a non-starter. He was counting on Elizabeth's fundraiser to fare better.

Elizabeth added the final touches to the table decorations and then stood back to better view her handiwork. Fifty round tables, all seating ten people each, dotted the manicured front lawn of Craigdon Manor. The house was set well back from the street and surrounded by mature trees and tall hedges. Though the event had been set up in front of the house, privacy was guaranteed. Not so long ago, they'd held one of her children's engagement parties on that very lawn and she couldn't have been more pleased with how the party had turned out. Hopefully she would have similar success with Lexi's fundraiser.

She just hoped Vaughan would make an appearance. After all, he was the reason she'd offered to hold the dinner in the first place. Oh, it was true she'd been moved by Lexi's plight and Elizabeth had always tried hard to help out those less fortunate, but it was the thought of coming face to face with the son she'd given up for adoption forty years earlier that was her primary motivation.

Nervous anxiety washed over her. She hadn't received any form of communication from Vaughan, so she had no way of knowing how he'd reacted to her news.

Was he shocked? Of course he was. He would have had no inkling they were related. *Was he angry?* Maybe. No doubt he had a million questions running through his head about why she'd abandoned him. Even more pressing, why she'd taken forty years to find him. He'd certainly not told his family. If he had, she was sure Christopher at least would have confronted her.

It wasn't going to be easy, facing Vaughan and providing him with answers. The answers she gave might not even satisfy him. He might think she was lying.

But she'd lived through enough hurt and deceit to last a lifetime. She wouldn't wish that kind of pain on anyone. No, if and when her son came to her looking for answers, she'd tell him the full unvarnished truth.

She looked up as Archie approached, still looking handsome in a tuxedo, despite the advancing years. She smoothed out the skirt of her evening dress and went to him.

"You're looking beautiful as usual," he said and smiled.

She took a moment to straighten his bow tie and then kissed him on the cheek. "How are you feeling?"

"I'm fine."

"It's only been a bit over a couple of weeks since the fire. Are you sure—?"

He pressed a finger gently against her lips. "Yes, Lizzie. I'm sure. You can't keep me holed up in your bedroom forever." He winked. "At some stage, I need to get out and get some fresh air."

She rolled her eyes. Only that morning, he'd spent another hour relaxing on a lounger by the pool. She'd been pleased he'd been feeling well enough to do it.

He looked around at the circular tables decorated with crisp white linen tablecloths, silver candelabras, and fresh flowers. The color scheme Elizabeth had chosen was gold and white and hundreds of Chinese lanterns in such colors hung from the trees. There were also fairy lights and around the perimeter were tall bamboo torches throwing off golden-orange flames.

"They're to keep the mosquitoes at bay," Elizabeth explained, following the direction of his gaze.

"They look good too. Like a tropical island. We could be in Fiji."

She grinned. "Or Bali. Remember that trip we all took that year? Callum and Noah were stung by blue bottles. They nearly screamed the hotel down."

He laughed. "Yes, of course. How could I forget? I remember we managed to sneak away and spend some time alone on the beach. Just the two of us. We watched the moon rise over the water."

She smiled and cupped his beloved cheek. "It was a special time."

They shared a tender look and then Archie cleared his throat. "I'm sure I don't have to ask if you have everything under control, but do you need me to do anything?"

"No, my darling. You were right the first time. I have everything under control."

"So who is this Lexi Greenaway, anyway?"

Elizabeth gave him a brief history of what she knew. "The main thing is, she's become very important to Christopher. Though he hasn't said anything specifically and I wouldn't be surprised if he hasn't even realized this himself, he has feelings for this girl."

Archie's eyebrows rose with surprise. "Wow. Who would have thought?"

"What's that supposed to mean?"

Archie shrugged. "Well, Christopher hasn't exactly endeared himself to the family over the years. I'm surprised he's capable of thinking of anyone but himself."

"Of course he is. And you judge him too harshly. He's come a long way in recent months. Don't forget he was the one who saved you from the fire."

"Of course," Archie readily agreed. "And I'll be forever in his debt. The truth is, I wish him all the best. Life is immeasurably better with someone you love by your side."

Elizabeth's heart melted. She leaned in and kissed him properly on the lips.

"Don't mess up your makeup," Archie teased.

She winked. "Don't worry. It's smudge-proof."

Chapter Twelve

Lexi peered through the window of the taxi at the mansion that loomed just ahead. It was lit up like the Sydney Harbour Bridge on New Year's Eve. Luxury cars lined either side of the long paved driveway. She suddenly felt overwhelmed.

She'd never been in such grand surroundings. The thought of having to make conversation with Sydney's rich and famous left her feeling nauseous. But she had no choice. She was doing this for her kids and for other children in foster care who so desperately needed help.

She looked at the empty space beside her. In the end, she hadn't needed to arrange for a sitter. Her teenagers, Kishaya and Denzil, had been only too happy to look after the younger children while she was out. Lexi had left them with boxes of pizza and a movie, as a special treat. She hoped they didn't tear the house apart while she was gone.

Christopher had offered to collect her from home so they could arrive at the dinner together, but she'd turned him down. He lived on the lower north shore. She lived a long way south. He'd have to pass by Elizabeth's house and then drive back again. Though touched by his offer, she'd persuaded him she'd be fine to make her own way there. Now she wished she'd accepted.

The taxi reached the top of the driveway where the road curved around. A cobblestone pavement met wide stone steps that led up to a grand front door. Paying the driver, Lexi gathered her long skirt and climbed out, feeling a little self-conscious as she took in the lavish surroundings.

The grounds were immaculate. Wide swathes of perfectly manicured lawns were punctuated by neat, colorful flowerbeds. Shrubs and hedges were expertly pruned. Mature trees would no doubt provide plenty of shade. Not that shade was required tonight. The sky was velvety and clear, enabling a million tiny stars to shine through. The slight autumn breeze was balmy and the scent of orange blossoms from a murraya hedge filled the air. The very same trees that would provide generous shade had been decorated with gold and white Chinese lanterns and thousands of fairy lights.

The whole place had a magical feel to it. Lexi felt like she was stepping into a fairy garden. She felt transformed—like a princess, waiting for her prince. And then she spied Christopher coming toward her and her nerves soared.

Of course he wasn't her prince, but she couldn't deny he made her heart beat faster and her palms moisten. Her gaze roved over his muscular form resplendent in a black on black tuxedo. Clean-shaven and smelling like pine forest and damp earth, even with his sling, he stood tall, broad-shouldered, strong.

He was a reliable, solid presence. He'd never promised to solve her problems, but he was here just the same, wanting to help. And he barely knew her. Though he'd hinted that he hadn't always lived honorably, she could only judge him on the way he'd treated her and so far, he'd been her champion.

"Good evening," he said, leaning in to peck her cheek and take her hand as if it were the most natural thing in the world.

She blushed at the contact and regarded him shyly. "H-hello."

"You look beautiful," he said, his gaze roving over her long, royal blue dress.

"Thank you."

Lexi had agonized for hours over her wardrobe. Not that it was extensive, in fact far from it. Her busy life as a mom hadn't left time for socializing, much less attending formal events. She had two classic evening dresses dating back to her college days. A short, black, lacy cocktail dress and the blue satin one that now kissed her ankles.

The capped sleeves framed her narrow shoulders and the deep V-neck highlighted her generous décolletage. Though she wasn't as tall as some women, she was in proportion and the four-inch stilettos she'd dug out of her closet brought her up to eye level with the man who'd been consuming far too many of her thoughts and visiting her in her dreams.

She drew in a deep breath and let it out on a shaky sigh. Christopher, still holding her hand, gave it a squeeze.

"Don't be nervous. They're going to love you. And even though you might feel like every eye is on you, trust me, they're more interested in catching up on the gossip. These high society dos are a veritable pit of half-truths and stories.

It's like they can't get enough of hearing about the downfall of one or the other, the latest scandal, the most recent marriage break-up."

Lexi shook her head, appalled. "And these people are your friends?"

"No. They're not my friends. Make no mistake about that. What they are, are five hundred of the most wealthy and influential people in Sydney. They paid two hundred dollars a ticket just to walk in and then there's the silent auction."

Lexi gaped at him. "Two hundred dollars? For one dinner? Are they crazy?"

He laughed and drew her close. "That's chicken feed for these people. Besides, it makes them feel good about themselves to give to a worthy cause and if there's one thing they know about Elizabeth, it's that she only supports worthy causes. And of course there's Elizabeth herself. Being the widow of a wealthy and controversial Sydney-ite is also an attractive lure."

Lexi felt overwhelmed with emotion. "I still can't believe she wanted to do this for me, for the kids. She doesn't even know us. Her generosity... It... It blows me away."

"Come on. I'll introduce you. I'm sure she's dying to meet you."

Christopher tucked her hand in his and together they walked across the lawn. Lexi reveled in the feeling they were a real couple, not just partners for the night. Off to one side stood a makeshift bar, complete with rows of sparkling crystal classes and smartly uniformed waiters. A string quartet was set up on a temporary wooden platform, away from the tables. The classical strains of Strauss helped to calm her nerves.

"Can I get you a drink?" Christopher asked solicitously.

Lexi licked her dry lips and nodded. A drink would help take the edge off. "Yes, please."

"What's your pleasure?" Christopher asked as they came up to the bar.

"Champagne, please."

Christopher winked. "Coming right up."

He turned to the barman and gave him their order. Within minutes, Christopher handed her a glass of golden champagne and accepted a glass of beer.

"Cheers," he said and touched his glass to hers.

Lexi smiled. "Cheers."

Together, they moved away and then Christopher's face broke into a grin. "There's my stepmother, surrounded by people, as usual. Come on. I'll introduce you."

Once again, Lexi's stomach filled with butterflies. She took a hasty gulp of her champagne and a fortifying breath and walked steadily beside Christopher. He halted beside a regal-looking woman with perfectly coiffed, snowy-white hair. She wore a long, deep purple chiffon and satin dress that had a fitted bodice and was cinched in at the waist. The skirt fell in loose, elegant waves to her feet. As Christopher called out to her, she turned and smiled at him. And then her gaze shifted to Lexi.

"Elizabeth, I'd like you to meet Lexi Greenaway. Lexi, this is my stepmother."

Lexi was so full of nerves she was surprised to hear herself calmly respond, thanking Elizabeth for all she'd done in support.

"Don't be silly. It's nothing." Elizabeth dismissed her remark with a kind smile. "After Christopher told me about the circumstances you and your family were facing and how you help foster children, I wanted to do something to help." She spread her arms wide to indicate the large gathering. "And here we are."

"Thank you for your generosity. I'm ever so grateful," Lexi managed.

"You're welcome, but I'm happy to help. I've been more fortunate than most." Elizabeth smiled. "I believe in giving back and I receive as much pleasure from giving as most do from receiving. When Christopher spoke to me about you and your situation, I trusted his judgment in advocating for you to be able to continue your fostering work. Providing children with loving, stable environments creates a strong foundation vital to their success as fully functioning adults."

"Yes, absolutely. And I'll be forever in your debt," Lexi replied. "The generosity of the people you have gathered here tonight will be a tremendous help to many needy children."

Elizabeth chuckled, her eyes alight with good humor. "Starting with yours, I hope. I hear you have quite a brood."

Lexi blushed. "I do. Eight, in fact."

Elizabeth's eyes widened with surprise. "Eight. Wow. I thought six was enough to handle and I wasn't trying to raise them on my own." She paused and her expression grew serious. "I have nothing but admiration for what you're doing, Lexi. It takes a very special person to take on what you have and to be doing it on your own, without support..." Her voice faded. She shook her head, smiling gently.

Tears pricked Lexi's eyes. She'd never expected to be shown such support, such kindness and compassion from a woman of Elizabeth Craigdon's standing. It made the whole night even more surreal. And cemented her understanding that no matter what flaws Christopher identified in himself, he came from good stock. Of course, that had a lot to do with his adopted family, too.

Over his shoulder she saw three tall, broad-shouldered, impossibly good-looking men approach them. One of them slapped Christopher on the back. He winced.

"Sorry, old man. I forgot you were injured," the man said, looking completely unrepentant.

"Yeah, sure you did Trace," Christopher grumbled good naturedly.

Elizabeth nodded her hellos and smiling at Lexi and Christopher, murmured her goodbyes and moved off into the crowd. Christopher turned to Lexi.

"Lexi, I'd like you to meet some of my brothers. This one with the smart mouth is Trace."

Trace turned to Lexi with a comically somber expression on his face. He stuck out his hand. "It's lovely to meet you, Lexi." He followed his words with a cheeky wink.

Lexi couldn't help but smile.

"And this one is Wade."

Lexi turned her attention to the man who stood beside Trace. He looked slightly younger, but was every bit as good looking.

"Hi, Wade. It's nice to meet you."

"And you too, Lexi. Any friend of Christopher's is a friend of mine."

Christopher gave an exaggerated eye roll. The other two men burst into laughter.

"And for the final Barrington comedian, this is Zac," Christopher finished.

Once again, Lexi found herself being scrutinized by a good-looking man. Zac appeared to be the youngest. He gave her a broad smile and lifted an eyebrow at Christopher, which he ignored.

Christopher looked around. "Where's Lincoln?"

Wade shrugged. "Who knows? Probably at the bar, drowning his sorrows. You know how he is."

Christopher grimaced. He turned to Lexi and lowered his voice. "Lincoln did three tours of Afghanistan. This isn't really his thing. In fact, I'm surprised he came."

Lexi felt a stab of compassion. She couldn't imagine the kind of trauma, and no doubt nightmares, a soldier who'd experienced so much combat would be battling. The recent scrambled evacuation of the last of the Allied forces out of Afghanistan would also likely be playing on his mind. The Taliban were back in power and it seemed that twenty years had gone by and nothing had really changed there.

"Has anyone seen Vaughan?" Zac asked.

Christopher shook his head. "Not yet. Do we know if he's coming?"

There was a jumble of mumbled responses. As best Lexi could work out, no one knew where Vaughan was.

"Who's Vaughan?" she asked.

"Another brother," Christopher explained. "He's a year younger than me. We celebrated his fortieth just over a couple of weeks ago. Then he took off. We don't really know why. He emailed my father not long after he disappeared to let him know he was okay, but nobody has heard from him since. I sent him an invitation to the fundraiser, but I've no idea if he'll show."

"There you are! Where have you been hiding?"

Lexi turned just as a petite, stunning woman with long, dark, wavy hair and arresting blue eyes pounced on Christopher, grabbing his good arm and spilling his drink in the process.

"Charlotte! For heaven's sake! Take it easy," Christopher grumbled.

The woman named Charlotte grinned unrepentantly. "Everyone's talking about Lexi. I've been dying to meet her." Charlotte turned and focused her attention on Lexi.

"Hi. I'm Charlotte. Christopher's sister. I'm one of the triplets. Along with Trace and Molly. Have you met Molly, yet?"

Lexi barely had time to process the information before Charlotte had enveloped her in a boisterous hug.

"Oh, okay. It's... It's nice to meet you, Charlotte. And no, I haven't met Molly."

"Oh, you'll love Molly. Everyone does. She's just one of those lovable people, if you know what I mean?"

"Yes, I think so," Lexi answered uncertainly.

"What about Hannah? Have you met her?"

"Um, no. I don't think so." Bemused, she looked over Charlotte's shoulder at Christopher who merely smiled and shrugged. Though it was obvious he accepted his family members were unruly and a little overwhelming, she could also see the close bond they shared. There was a lot of love surrounding them. She instinctively knew that though they poked fun at each other, probably mercilessly at times, they'd have each other's backs when needed.

She felt a pang of yearning. She'd never had siblings; never known that kind of unbreakable bond. The kind of love and support you could always rely on. It was something she'd often longed for while she was growing up. Even one brother or sister would have been enough. Perhaps that's why she'd adopted so many children. She didn't want any child to ever feel that kind of loneliness.

"Oh, hey! There are Molly and Hannah now," Charlotte said. She cupped her hands around her mouth and yelled out over the crowd.

Two women dressed in glamorous designer dresses turned almost simultaneously. When they caught sight of Charlotte surrounded by her other siblings, both of them smiled and started heading toward them. Lexi braced herself to meet even more Barringtons.

Introductions were quickly made and the girls plied Lexi with questions. They kept looking from her to Christopher and back again. She could see the blatant curiosity in their eyes. No doubt they assumed she and Christopher were a couple. And then Charlotte confirmed that understanding.

"I hope you know how special you are. Christopher's never brought a date to a family function before."

Heat crept up Lexi's neck. She didn't dare glance at Christopher. "Oh. We-we're not dating," she stammered.

"Christopher's helping me out. That's all."

The women nodded as one, but looked totally unconvinced.

"Uh, uh," Molly said and linked her arm with Lexi's. "Whatever you say. That's cool. But just so you know, I think you're lovely. Christopher would do well to hang on to you."

Lexi's blush deepened. She tried to disentangle her arm, but Molly was having none of it. The girl looked nearly a decade younger than Lexi, but she appeared surprisingly determined to have her way.

"Come with me, Lexi. I want to introduce you around. There are so many people here for you to meet. Let's start with the Craigdons. They're a fine bunch of people. They're related to Christopher, you know."

"Yes, I met his stepmother," Lexi murmured as Molly dragged her away. Lexi threw another helpless glance over her shoulder in Christopher's direction. Once again, he merely smiled and shrugged. So no help from that quarter. She saw him mouth "good luck."

She smiled. As Molly chattered about the who's who at the party, Lexi felt herself relax. She took another sip of her champagne and made a silent vow to enjoy the night.

Nicholas Craigdon tightened his arms around his fiancée's waist and drew her in close. The party was in full swing. The place looked amazing. Trust his mother to pull off a grand do on short notice. There was no doubt about it; she knew how to put together a fabulous event. It boded well for his upcoming wedding.

At the thought of how soon he and Harper would be husband and wife, he pulled her in tighter. Her enlarged belly bumped against him. Though they hadn't planned a baby before the wedding, that's how things had worked out. It was the reason they'd moved the wedding date forward. Harper had insisted she wanted to be Mrs Nicholas Craigdon before their baby arrived.

"How are you feeling?" he murmured against the softness of her hair.

"Good. Although I'm glad we're dancing early. My feet will be killing me later in the night."

"I'm just glad for the opportunity to hold you in my arms," Nicholas replied with a smile.

Harper pulled back a little and grinned. "You don't need to dance with me to do that."

"Ah, but it's nice, don't you think? You and me and our bump? Enjoying some time together for a change."

Harper pulled a face. "Hey, it's not my fault you're working twelve hours a day. And you're the one who insisted I needed to take time off. I told you I was quite capable of continuing to work until the baby arrived."

Nicholas pretended mock horror. "What? And run the risk of the next Craigdon heir being born on the Craigdon Enterprises boardroom table?"

Harper giggled. "Why not? It would make for a pretty good story."

Nicholas chuckled and once again pulled her in as close as her protruding belly would allow. "I never said you couldn't come back, but you know what the doctor said. Your blood pressure's higher than he'd like. He suggested you cut back. The easiest way to do that is to stay at home and put your feet up. There'll be plenty of time later for you to do your bit at Craigdon Enterprises."

"Have you found my replacement yet? I hope she's at least fifty-five and completely without charm."

"Now why would I want to employ an executive assistant like that?" Nicholas teased. "I'll have you know, I culled every application that came in and cast aside anyone who was over twenty-five."

Harper looked momentarily outraged. She slapped Nicholas on his chest. "You did not!"

He grinned. "You're right. I didn't. I'll hire whoever is the most experienced. Nothing else will matter."

"I guess," Harper said grudgingly, but there was a sparkle in her eyes.

Nicholas gazed down at the woman who'd stolen his heart. He couldn't imagine life without her.

"I love you Harper Wyburn."

"I love you Nicholas. Always."

Chapter Thirteen

The multi-course dinner had been served and the plates cleared away when Elizabeth finally allowed herself to seek out Christopher once again. She'd wanted a private word with him all evening, but that had proven impossible. As the hostess, there had always been someone vying for her attention and then there had been the formal part of the evening—the reason for all of them being there and the need to appeal to the generosity of her guests. The few minutes she'd managed with him earlier in the night he'd been with Lexi. Elizabeth could hardly bring up Vaughan with Lexi standing there.

But now the official part of the night was over and she could afford to relax. She found Christopher seated on one of the garden benches.

"There you are, Christopher. How has your night been?"

Christopher smiled. "It's been absolutely wonderful, Elizabeth."

"Yes, it all seems to be going well. I checked on the silent auction. We've raised nearly one hundred thousand dollars there already. Of course, that's in addition to the hundred thousand raised from the sale of the tickets."

"That's amazing! *You're* amazing! Have I thanked you enough already?"

Elizabeth waved his praise away. "It's all for a good cause. Your Lexi is a special girl."

Christopher smiled softly. His face took on a tenderness that warmed Elizabeth's heart.

There's no way he doesn't feel something for this woman… I wonder how long it will be before he realizes it…

She leaned in closer. "Listen, I meant to ask you. Have you heard from Vaughan? Is he here tonight?"

Christopher shook his head. "I'm afraid not. He's still AWOL."

Elizabeth fought off a wave of disappointment and frowned. "But Vaughan's all right, isn't he? Didn't he contact your father and tell him as much?"

"Yes, but that was a while ago."

"Where could he be?" Elizabeth murmured.

"That's exactly what we'd like to know." As if another thought had occurred to him, Christopher frowned. When he looked at her again, his eyes were filled with curiosity.

"Why all the questions about Vaughan? You don't even know him."

Elizabeth cast around frantically for an answer. She knew how perceptive Christopher was and how innately suspicious. The last thing she needed was for him to wonder about her sudden interest in his adopted brother.

She forced a smile. "No reason. Just curious, I guess. Family's important. I'm sure your parents are concerned."

"Not really. Vaughan's got a good head on his shoulders. He's not exactly the flighty type. He told Dad he's okay. I guess we have to trust him and wait for the next email."

The momentary curiosity had disappeared from Christopher's gaze. Elizabeth swallowed a sigh of relief. At the same time, she clenched her fists at Christopher's dismissive attitude.

If only it were that easy for me…

Armed with a fresh beer and a champagne for Lexi, Christopher was perturbed to find her surrounded by half a dozen thirty-something tuxedo-clad men all vying for her attention. She was regaling them with some humorous anecdote and they were hanging off her every word. Her beautiful eyes sparkled with laughter. Her hair glowed under the lights. She looked from one to another, having the knack that few people possessed of being able to speak to a crowd and make every single person feel like she was speaking only to them.

Jealousy surged through him, taking him aback. The feeling made him uncomfortable. He'd been in short-term relationships in the past, but never had he felt such possessiveness. His hands clenched into fists and he was immediately reminded of the pain in his shoulder. He wanted to tell her crowd of admirers to back off; that this woman was spoken for.

Of course, he did no such thing. He slowly relaxed his fists. He had no claim on her. She wasn't his woman, no matter how much he wished she were. As his gaze traveled over her fine form, he noticed how sexy she looked in her evening dress. The royal blue reflected the cobalt of her eyes. A simple gold chain, gold hoop earrings and a pretty brooch in the shape of a peacock completed the look. Her long hair was swept up into a pile of loosely contained ringlets that spilled over her shoulders and curled enticingly around her breasts.

His cock hardened and he cursed under his breath. Though they'd shared a brief kiss, she hadn't given him any real indication she was interested in him in the romantic sense. He'd offered to help her out of a sticky situation. She was grateful for his intervention. That was it.

He bit down on a surge of disappointment and tried to put the thought out of his mind. The money raised tonight would hopefully go some way toward helping her achieve her goal. While the life insurance money was a decent sum, they both knew she'd need at least a million in order to buy the same kind of property she had. Perhaps he could convince someone else to hold another fundraiser...

In the end, he couldn't stand it a moment longer. He had to intervene. "Excuse me, fellas. I need to speak with Lexi. Excuse me." He pushed his way through the crowd until he stood by her side. He offered her a grin.

"How are you doing? I thought you might like a drink."

He handed her the glass of champagne and she shot him a grateful look. She murmured her farewells to her admirers. Christopher took her by the hand and led her away to a less crowded part of the garden.

"Thank you for rescuing me," she said with a smile.

He shot her a sideways glance. "I wasn't sure if you'd appreciate the intervention. It kind of looked like you were holding court back there."

She pulled a face. "Not likely. I was so nervous it's a wonder you didn't hear my knees knocking. I was only trying to be friendly in order to encourage more donations. Is that terrible of me?"

"Of course not," he reassured her. "And you'll be pleased to know we're already up around one hundred thousand dollars."

Her eyes widened with surprise. "You're kidding?"

He grinned. "No I'm not. And that doesn't include the proceeds from the ticket sales. It's a good result, right?"

"It's a great result! Oh, Christopher! I don't know how to thank you!"

She threw herself against him, her arms going around his neck. He sloshed his beer in the process and then felt the cold trickle of her champagne as it ran down the back of his neck. She immediately realized what had happened and her face flamed with embarrassment. She pulled away and hurriedly swiped at the liquid that glistened on his skin.

"Oh God! I'm so sorry! Your suit! It's ruined!"

"Don't be silly. It's nothing. Don't worry about it."

She stopped swiping at his neck and gave him a chagrined, apologetic grin. "You're going to be awfully sticky."

He grinned back. "I can live with sticky. Especially when you smile at me like that."

His voice was rough with desire. She stared at him. Her eyes flared wide. Her pupils dilated. His heart stuttered and then took off at a gallop. The force of his feelings surprised him.

And then her gaze dropped to his sling. "Oh, I'm so sorry! Your arm! I forgot! Did I hurt you?"

"It's fine Lexi. It's nearly healed. It doesn't hurt a bit," he lied.

The look on her face told him she didn't believe him, but she didn't say anything. Instead, her expression slowly became intense. She reached out and took his good hand and threaded her fingers through his. Their gazes locked. The air around them became charged. Christopher hardly dared to breathe.

"You've been so wonderful to me, Christopher. It was the last thing I expected from a Barrington. That first day you turned up on my doorstep, I was sure you were going to evict us. And even later, I was certain your only goal was to get us out.

"But then I got to know you, and I... I like what I see. I like it a lot. You're not heartless at all. You're good and kind and decent and I'm sorry I judged you so harshly in the beginning. It was wrong of me and you didn't deserve it."

Christopher's face flamed with a combination of pleasure and embarrassment. He was pretty sure he didn't deserve such praise, but he liked it. Better still, she liked him. A lot.

If only you knew the real Christopher Barrington... The man who took delight in causing other people trouble...

A hot wave of shame coursed through him. It totally killed the mood. He didn't deserve Lexi's praise. He couldn't be further from that person.

He'd once mentioned to her that he used to be selfish, but she knew nothing about him or the awful things he'd done. Okay, so he was determined to redeem himself, to turn his life around, but he wouldn't ever be fit to be in her orbit and that was the sad and unavoidable truth. No matter how much he wished things were different.

⁓ ℓℓ ⁓

Lexi reached up and grabbed a mandarin. With a tug, she pulled it free and dropped it into the bucket that was hooked on the side of her ladder. It was Sunday afternoon and she was in the orchard picking fruit. Leroy and Patrice sat on the ground below her in the shade of the tree. They were chattering to each other, but Lexi had tuned out to what they were saying.

It was the day after the night of the fundraiser and her thoughts were consumed with Christopher. Even now, she felt embarrassed about how she'd thrown herself at him. The look on his face... And then she'd spilled champagne all down his neck, for heaven's sake...

Still, she wished she'd had the courage to kiss him. She was shocked that she'd wanted to. There had been no one since her husband. Four years was a long time without the comfort and love of a man. For a long time, she'd pushed her loneliness aside and had focused all her attention on her kids.

But then she'd met Christopher and everything shifted. He made her remember what it felt like to share her life with someone—her hopes, her dreams, even just sharing her day.

Funny things the kids had said or done; issues they were facing. Someone to turn to for advice or just someone to listen.

The more she thought about it, the more she realized how desperately lonely she'd been. But she didn't merely miss companionship. She missed being in love and being loved in return. The giddiness, the butterflies, the anticipation of waiting for that person to come home... It was exciting, exhilarating, heart thumpingly wonderful...

She wondered how Christopher felt about her. Back at the fundraiser, when she'd been surrounded by all those men, she could have sworn she'd caught a look of jealousy on his face. And he'd stepped forward and stolen her away, as if he couldn't bear to watch all those men vying for her attention.

But then as she'd opened up and thanked him and tried to get closer to him, he'd turned distant and she didn't know why. They'd ended the night with him ordering her a taxi and he'd waited out the front with her until it arrived. He'd bidden her goodnight with a wistful smile, but he didn't attempt to kiss her. She didn't know if that was because he didn't want to, or if he was unsure of her response.

Perhaps I need to make my position clearer? Perhaps I should make the first move? Just because he's older than me, doesn't mean he's experienced where women are concerned... After all, he's a mature man and he's still single. Maybe he's just shy...

Yes. That's what she'd do. Invite him over for dinner. A romantic setting would be impossible while they were surrounded by her children, but maybe later, after the kids had gone to bed...

She couldn't hold back a hopeful smile.

~ele~

It was early evening. Christopher tried to concentrate on the paperback in his hands. It was the latest release from his favorite thriller writer and yet the story had failed to capture his attention. He'd read the same paragraph three times and still wouldn't have been able to give an account of what he'd read. The problem was Lexi.

His thoughts kept circling back to her and the evening before. The fundraiser had been a resounding success. He couldn't have asked for it to go better. At last count, Elizabeth had raised over two hundred thousand dollars.

Even better, Lexi had met some of his family and friends. Though that hadn't been his primary motivation for going along with the idea of the fundraiser, it was an added bonus. He'd been able to introduce her without the added pressure of his family assuming she was his girlfriend. It had enabled him to continue the pretense that she was merely a friend he wanted to help out.

He wasn't sure whether his sisters had bought the "just friends" thing. They'd always been more astute than his brothers. He didn't care if they guessed Lexi was more important to him than he'd led them all to believe, but it was important to him that they like her and if the feedback he'd received from Molly and Hannah and Charlotte was anything to go by, Lexi's disposition and intelligence had greatly impressed them. His sisters had given her the thumbs up. That meant a lot to him.

For a long time, he'd denounced anything to do with family —be that Barringtons or Craigdons. He'd never had too much time for any of them. He'd been so consumed with hurt and anger and bitterness over his treatment at the hands of Henry Craigdon to appreciate the family who did love him and had accepted him without question.

But that had now changed and he realized how important his family—*all* of his family—was. He respected them. He loved them. He was glad to be a part of their inner circle. Their opinions mattered to him and he was pleased they'd given Lexi their stamp of approval. And Lexi appeared to have had a good time. She'd mingled with the guests, sharing conversation and laughter. At one stage, he'd even caught her dancing up a storm with Noah Craigdon.

It was only when Christopher had allowed his insecurities to get the better of him that the night had soured for him. Of course, he'd kept his feelings from Lexi, but he could tell she was confused about his abrupt change in attitude. One moment they were holding hands and sharing lingering looks and the next he was suggesting she go home and check on her kids. He'd seen her off in a taxi and hadn't even given her a goodnight kiss. After the looks, the touching they'd shared earlier that evening, she had every right to be confused.

Tossing the paperback aside, he stood and strode to the fridge. He pulled out a beer and popped the lid. He gulped down half of the contents. Then he walked over to the sliding door that led to the balcony and stepped outside.

The cool evening breeze lifted his hair. Leaning over the railing, he contemplated the harbor view. From this perspective, he could see the curve of the Harbour Bridge.

Trains with lit carriages passed intermittently, along with the steady flow of vehicular traffic. People heading home, heading to assignations, meetings, dinner, fun. Everyone had somewhere to be and someone to be with. Everyone except him.

And then he snorted with disgust and shook his head.

Stop feeling sorry for yourself, Christopher. You've no one to blame but yourself for reaching the ripe old age of forty-one with nothing to show for it. Stop moaning and get up and do something about it. You know how you feel about Lexi. Grab hold of your courage and ask her on a date. If she turns you down, well… At least you know where you stand and you won't waste any more time wondering about her… But she might just say yes and how good will that feel…?

The sound of his phone ringing stirred him from his reverie. He reached into his pocket and pulled out his phone. He checked the screen.

Lexi.

His heart skipped a beat and then took off so fast he felt breathless. His chest went tight. And then he pulled himself together. No doubt she was calling to thank him for his efforts last night.

He drew in a steadying breath and was pleased that his voice sounded almost normal when he answered the call.

"Hello?"

"Christopher. It's Lexi. I hope I haven't called at a bad time?"

"No, no. You're fine. What can I do for you?"

"I just wanted to call and thank you for everything you did last night. The fundraiser...the night...your family... I had a wonderful time."

He fought off a wave of disappointment. "You're welcome. What are friends for?"

"You're right." She paused.

"Was there something else?"

"Um..."

He heard the uncertainty in her voice.

"Lexi?"

"I... I was wondering if you'd like to come to dinner. It's probably easier if you come here, to Serenity. That way you could meet everyone. I was telling the kids about you and the event last night. They had a million questions about the fundraiser, especially Kishaya and Denzil. While I haven't given them all the details about what's happening with our property, they know how important the fundraiser was to all of us. They're curious to meet you. And dinner will be a way to thank you for all you've done. So, what do you think?"

Her words had come out in such a rush, it took Christopher a few seconds to process everything. And then he was flooded with elation.

Did she just ask me out? I think she did... Okay, so not exactly a date when we'll be surrounded by eight children, but still...

Excitement surged through him.

"Christopher?"

Her cautious question brought him to his senses.

Dammit! You haven't even told her yes! Answer her, dammit, before she thinks you don't want to come!

"Yes! Yes, of course. I'd love to come. Thank you, that's very kind of you. But you know, it's completely unnecessary.

There's no need to thank me. You don't owe me anything."

"Thank you. That's very nice of you to say so, but it isn't true. You've done so much for me—for us—already. Having you over for dinner is the least I can do."

They made plans for the very next night. Though it was a school night, she was sure the kids would cope. He asked if he could bring anything, but she told him they had everything under control.

With that, he ended the call and after dropping his phone back into his pocket, he finished his beer, crushed the can in his hand and then stared out into the quiet night. He couldn't keep the grin off his face.

Lexi Greenaway just invited me to dinner!

Though a little voice reminded him she was only doing it out of gratitude, nothing was going to dim his excitement. He still had a ways to go to proving himself worthy of her, but he wanted so much to be that man. A man she could be proud of.

The power was within him to bring about change. He was determined to give it everything he had.

Chapter Fourteen

Lexi's belly danced with butterflies. They'd been fluttering all afternoon. Every time she thought about Christopher inside her house for dinner, her stomach somersaulted. It had been a long time since she'd been on a date. More than thirteen years, in fact. The last date she'd been on had been with Ronnie before they'd married.

She remembered it clearly. They'd both been in their early twenties. They'd gone to a pizza place and then to a movie. Some Tom Cruise action thriller. She'd been more interested in making out with Ronnie in the back row than she had been in the movie. The memory brought a smile to her lips.

They'd had some good times. He'd been a good husband. Except when it came to his willingness to take unnecessary risks. He'd always been that way. It's what had attracted her to him in the first place. He was so different from her—a risk taker. Living life to the fullest and to hell with the consequences.

His devil-may-care attitude had been so exciting, so appealing to her younger self, who'd grown up always fearful, always worried about what nasty surprise life might have in store for her next and whether she'd be able to handle it. She guessed that came from her unstable childhood. Being passed from one foster home to another. There had been no stability, no security, no love. It had felt like trying to keep afloat in slowly sucking quicksand, always trying desperately to keep her head above the surface.

Ronnie couldn't have been more carefree, more footloose and fancy free. She'd reveled in his freedom, hoping some of it would rub off on her. But as she'd grown and matured, married and eventually became a foster mother, Ronnie's free spirit lost its appeal. Often it felt like he was just another one of their kids.

After one such afternoon when he'd spent the weekend away with his mates, motorbike riding through steep and uninhabited bushland, she'd pleaded with him to take more care, to think of his responsibilities. He'd fallen off his bike and had broken his arm. There had been no phone service out in the bush. It had taken his mates hours to raise the alarm and bring help. Ronnie had been off work for six weeks. That he had sick leave to cover his lost wages had been beside the point.

"What if you'd really hurt yourself? Cut yourself badly? You'd have bled to death before help arrived. What if you'd died? What then? What would we do without you? How would we survive? You're a husband and father, Ronnie. You have responsibilities. It's not fair that you take such risks with your safety. It's time for you to take care with your behavior and grow up."

Ronnie had remained stubbornly obstinate. His unwillingness to curtail his risky pleasures had been the main source of their arguments. The day he'd come off his bike and been thrown into a tree—breaking his neck and dying instantly—they'd had an awful row about him wanting to go motorbike riding up in the country with his mates instead of staying at home and helping out with their kids. Kishaya had needed help with a school assignment. Denzil had been sick with a fever. Lexi remembered the argument as if it had happened yesterday.

For a long time she'd felt guilty that their final words to each other had been said in anger, but some counseling from a good therapist and from her local priest had helped her to accept that their life together had encompassed so much more than those few heated words said in anger. Angry words hadn't negated everything they'd meant to each other, the love they'd shared, the things they'd achieved, the security they'd given their children.

Ronnie would always have a special place in her heart. Despite the fact his parents had seemingly withdrawn their love and no longer wanted anything to do with her or their grandchildren, she didn't hold that against them. It was their loss. They'd grieved for Ronnie as much as she had. He was their only child. She wouldn't judge them for their uncharitable behavior. Instead, she'd pray for them and hope they found peace.

But right now she was preparing to welcome another man into her home. A man who made her feel things she thought had died along with her husband. To say she was rusty on how to flirt with a man was an understatement. The more she thought about Christopher's imminent arrival, the more nervous she felt.

She'd already recruited Denzil in the kitchen. They weren't cooking anything fancy—spaghetti Bolognese with mozzarella cheese for the younger ones and fresh parmesan for everyone else. It was quick and easy, and best of all, a little went a long way. It was also a favorite among her little ones.

Demi and Stella, ten and twelve respectively, who had both been adopted before Ronnie died, were setting the table, plying her with questions as they did so.

"Who is this man, Momma?" Demi asked.

Stella giggled. "He's her boyfriend."

Lexi blushed. "He's not my boyfriend. His name is Christopher and he's...a friend."

"Are you going to kiss him?" Stella asked.

The heat in Lexi's cheeks burned hotter. "Of course not," she muttered. She turned away, pretending to be busy pulling placemats out of the dresser that stood against the wall.

"I thought we were using the good tablecloth, Momma?" Demi asked.

"You're right," Lexi mumbled and stuffed the placemats back where she'd found them. "Demi, can you get the good cutlery out of the cupboard in the hallway? I'm going to check on the younger ones in the bath," she said quickly and escaped the kitchen.

Patrice, Michael and Leroy were covered from head to toe in bubbles. Lexi couldn't help but smile when she rounded the corner and saw them in the tub. She'd put Patrice in charge of making sure everyone washed themselves, including their hair. It seemed Patrice had taken her duties seriously. Three shampoo bottles floated on top of the water.

"Well, as least you're clean," Lexi muttered. "Careful, Leroy. It's going to get in your eyes. Hang on a minute, honey. It will sting if it gets in your eyes."

Grabbing a face washer, she wiped the three little faces clean. Patrice grinned at her with her toothy grin, her eyes alight with laughter.

"We were having a bubble party, Momma! Michael emptied one bottle and it made so many bubbles, we decided to add more."

"I can see that, Patrice." Lexi tried for a stern voice, but failed hopelessly.

Leroy swished his hands through the water, sending bubbles floating over the side. The three children giggled again and Lexi couldn't help but smile.

"All right. Party's over. It's time to get out."

Amid a chorus of disagreement, Lexi pulled one child out after the other, dried them off and helped them into their pajamas. She brushed their hair and gave each one a kiss before hurrying them out of the room.

"Go and wait in the living room. I'm going to get changed. Christopher will be here soon."

The words sent another rush of nerves dancing through her veins. She hurried into her bedroom and began pulling out clothes. She looked at and discarded several outfits before she settled on a pair of black slacks and a silk blouse in hues of deep emerald green and blue. It was soft to the touch and felt luxurious against her skin. It also emphasized the color of her eyes and it was a blouse she'd always felt good in.

She tucked it into her open slacks, pulled up her zipper and did up the clasp. She then slid a belt through the loops and turned this way and that to survey the results in front of the mirror. She looked nice. Not too over the top. Not too desperate.

God, the last thing she wanted was to look desperate. She might have invited Christopher over with the hope that they might end the night declaring they had feelings for each other, but that didn't mean she wanted him to think any man would do.

Moving over to her dresser, she opened the top drawer and took out a jewelry box. It was made of cheap varnished wood, but it had a pretty faux glass inlay decorated with painted flowers. She'd bought it with money she'd managed to save from the job she'd secured at her local supermarket when she'd been seventeen.

She kept items of special significance in it, including the only photograph she had of her mother. She didn't even know how she'd come by the picture, but somehow or other it had always been among her things. There were also some beads from a necklace Ronnie had given her not long after they'd first started dating. It wasn't expensive, but the blue glass beads were so pretty and Ronnie had told her they reminded him of the color of her eyes. She'd worn it every day until the cheap chain had broken. She'd gathered the beads as they'd fallen to the ground and had stored them in her jewelry box, always intending to buy another chain but somehow she'd never gotten around to it.

The most expensive item in the jewelry box was the diamond and sapphire encrusted brooch in the shape of a peacock that had once belonged to her maternal grandmother. As with the photograph, she had no memory of how she'd come by it. It had just always been among her few possessions. But she remembered being told it had belonged to her maternal grandmother, a woman Lexi couldn't remember ever having met.

The brooch was beautiful. She'd lost count of the number of times she'd taken it out of her box and had stared at it, fingering the beautiful stones, thinking about the woman who'd once worn it. Lexi tried to imagine what her grandmother had been like. Had she been kind? Pretty? Happy? Or had she been worn down by life? What had happened between her and Lexi's mother that the fifteen-year-old found herself pregnant and alone?

Lexi preferred not to think about that. She'd never know the reasons why her mother ran away from home. What she did know was that most runaways didn't leave without good cause. Still, the brooch was the only connection Lexi had to her real family and she treasured the ornament above everything else.

She'd once shown it to Ronnie and he'd been impressed with the quality. He'd taken it to a jeweler to get valued. They'd both been shocked when the valuation came back at somewhere in the vicinity of twenty thousand dollars. Apparently it was very old and extremely well made. Even older than her grandmother, so more likely than not it had been handed down to her from one of her relatives.

That made it all the more special, but now Lexi wondered if the time had come to part with it. An extra fifteen or twenty thousand dollars would go a long way right now. The money from the fundraiser was fantastic, but it still meant she'd be forced to use the insurance money.

With a soft sigh, she pinned the brooch to her blouse, just above her breast. She only wore it on special occasions. The last time had been to the fundraiser. When she wore it, she always felt close to her mother and the grandmother she'd never known. Besides, if she were forced to sell it, she'd most likely never get to wear it again.

She glanced at her watch and noted the time. She had less than fifteen minutes before Christopher was due to arrive. Hurrying now, she pulled open her makeup bag and began hastily applying foundation, eyeliner, mascara and finally, two coats of red lipstick. Once again, she took a moment to look at the results in the mirror.

"Why are you getting all dressed up? You're even wearing your special brooch."

Lexi jumped with a yelp. "Oh, Kishaya! You startled me."

Kishaya walked further into the room, her gaze narrowed. "You're jumpy as a jack rabbit and you've been rushing around the house cleaning it from top to bottom all day. Now you're all dressed up like you're going somewhere important. All for this guy. Who is he? Why is he so important to you?"

The suspicion in fifteen-year-old Kishaya's brown eyes gave Lexi pause. All of a sudden, she realized in her excitement, she hadn't taken the time to properly explain to the older children what was going on. They hadn't met Christopher before. They didn't know about the sale. All they knew was that their mother was acting oddly and now a strange man was coming around for dinner.

Lexi looked at her foster daughter. With a soft sigh, Lexi perched herself on the end of her bed. She patted the space beside her. With an exaggerated eye roll, Kishaya plopped down on the mattress. Before she could speak, Denzil appeared in the doorway.

Lexi smiled and patted the other space beside her. "Come in, Denzil. You have a right to hear this, too."

Denzil loped into the room and sat down next to her. Lexi silently marveled how tall and lithe her young fourteen-year-old had grown. It seemed only yesterday that he'd arrived on her doorstep as a scared and sullen nine-year-old, dirty and under-nourished. Now he was as cocky as any teenager. In fact, sometimes she had to rein in his confidence.

"What's going on?" he asked.

Lexi looked from one to the other. She drew in a breath and then eased it out quietly. And then she told them the truth about the sale, the eviction notice, the fact they were low on cash. She also told them about Christopher and his connection to the whole sorry mess.

"So we're going to have to move?" Kishaya asked.

"Yes."

"When?" Denzil demanded.

"I'm not sure, but soon."

"Will I have to change schools?" Kishaya asked, her eyes wide with concern.

Lexi reached out and brushed a strand of long dark hair out of Kishaya's eyes. "I'm not sure, honey. I hope not, but it depends on whether we can find somewhere else suitable to live in this area."

"I don't want to change schools!" Kishaya cried. "What about my friends?"

Lexi kept her voice low and calm. "I'm going to do all I can to make sure you can still go to the same school, Kishaya. That goes for all of you. The last thing I want to do is disrupt that aspect of your lives. In fact, I don't want to disrupt any aspect of your lives, but I'm afraid that's out of my control."

"Why have you invited that man over? Isn't he the reason we're being kicked out of our house?" Denzil cried.

Lexi was appalled Denzil felt that way. She hurried to set him straight. "No, honey. It's not Christopher's fault. He's merely the one who told me it had been sold."

"You said it was his father who'd bought this place. Doesn't that mean he's also one of the bad guys forcing us out?"

Lexi put an arm around each of their shoulders and drew them close. "This isn't Christopher's fault. He's not one of the bad guys. In fact, he's gone out of his way to try and help us. He's the reason I attended that fundraiser on the weekend and we raised a lot of money. Money we're hoping to use to put toward an even bigger facility where we can all live, along with even more kids. Wouldn't that be great? To have the room to bring even more kids home to live with us?"

Both of the teenagers nodded, though Lexi could see they were still far from convinced Christopher wasn't the enemy. She tried again.

"Remember when that police officer came and told us about Dad? That he'd had a serious accident and had died?"

Both nodded somberly.

"Did either of you blame the police officer?"

"No."

"Of course not."

"And yet the officer was the one who'd brought us the bad news. What he told us changed our lives forever and yet, none of us took it out on the officer. He was just doing his job."

"So you mean this Christopher didn't have anything to do with his father's decision to buy our house?" Kishaya asked.

"That's exactly what I mean, honey. He was just the messenger."

"So why's he coming to dinner?" Denzil asked, his eyes narrowed with suspicion.

Lexi tried not to squirm. "I wanted to thank him for all he's done for us. And... I like him. I'd like for us to be friends."

Kishaya eyed her skeptically. "Friends? Is that all?"

As much as she tried to avoid it, Lexi blushed. But true to the vow she'd made to herself a long time ago when it came to her children, she answered honestly.

"No, Kishaya. I like him more than that."

Kishaya whooped. "I *knew* it!"

Denzil's reaction was less enthusiastic. "Don't tell me he's going to be moving in?"

Lexi shook her head. "Oh, heavens! Denzil, honey. We've barely known each other a couple of weeks. I don't even know how he feels about me. If he likes me the way I like him then... Maybe he'll spend more time with us. But no one's moving in. I promise you, before I make any kind of major decision like that, I'll talk to you. I won't do anything without you all being on board. You're more important to me than anyone in the world, including Christopher."

Denzil nodded, appearing satisfied with her response. She hugged them both close. "I love you guys so much," she whispered.

"Momma! Someone's coming!"

The cry from Demi coming from the front of the house snagged Lexi's attention. And then she heard the dogs barking. Her heart skipped a beat and the butterflies went crazy.

It must be Christopher.

With another quick hug for both of her teenagers, Lexi got to her feet. "I think our dinner guest has arrived. Don't forget to mind your manners."

Denzil rolled his eyes. "You want us to be nice to him?"

"I want you to treat him with the courtesy you'd show any guest," Lexi replied. "Now, come on. Let's go and invite him inside."

Chapter Fifteen

Christopher climbed out of his Mercedes amidst the barking of two very excited dogs. He reached down to pat first one, then the other. They greeted him like an old friend. Smoothing out the creases in his pants, he opened the rear door and pulled out the bottle of wine and the bouquet of flowers he'd bought for Lexi. A large box of chocolates for the kids completed his gifts.

Nerves had bounced around in his stomach during the entire drive out there. He'd been excited to see Lexi again and spend more time with her, but he was also nervous about meeting her older children. He knew nothing about kids. He'd never been around them. The fact they were the most important thing in Lexi's life made him more anxious to make a good impression. If they didn't like him, no doubt that would be a deal breaker.

He'd been so nervous he'd changed his outfit three times before he'd settled on the navy-blue slacks and white polo shirt. His first choice had been a suit, but he'd discarded that as too formal. The previous two visits in suits had been about business. Tonight he was here for pleasure, as Lexi's guest.

He'd also contemplated jeans and a T-shirt, but decided that was far too casual. This was a date. Okay, so they'd be chaperoned by eight children, but still... He wanted Lexi to know he'd made an effort. The pants and polo shirt were a compromise. Not too formal, not too casual. Black designer leather loafers completed the ensemble.

Awkwardly tucking his gifts under his good arm, he lay the bouquet of flowers across his other. Though the worst of the pain in his collarbone had subsided, he'd been told by his doctor to continue to wear the sling for another week. The longer he kept the shoulder immobilized, the better.

He walked across the front yard and up the steps to the veranda and knocked on the door. It was opened a few moments later. Lexi stood on the other side looking breathtakingly beautiful. Her chestnut-colored hair fell in loose waves around her shoulders. She was dressed simply, but elegantly. Her blue-green blouse deepened the color of her eyes.

"H-hi," he stammered and then blushed. He'd never been awkward around women, but Lexi seemed to turn him inside out and upside down until he could barely string two words together.

"Hi," she said and gave him a warm smile.

"These are for you," he said and awkwardly thrust the flowers and wine toward her.

"Oh, thank you. They're lovely," she said, burying her nose in the fragrant red roses. "They smell divine."

"Hi, Christopher. Remember me?" a little voice chimed.

Christopher looked down. Patrice looked up at him smiling, her eyes sparkling with mischief.

He winked. "Of course I do. You're the mischievous monkey!"

The little girl giggled. Leroy poked his head out from around Lexi's pants. "Hello, Christopher," he said shyly.

Christopher crouched low and ruffled the toddler's soft blond curls. "Hello, Leroy. Don't you look cute in your pajamas!"

"See? They're the Wiggles!!" Leroy cried.

Christopher wasn't sure who the Wiggles were, but obviously they were popular with children. Michael also made a brief appearance in the doorway before Lexi ushered them all inside and into the combined kitchen and dining area. The smell of tomato and meat cooking reached his nostrils. A tall teenage boy stood by the stove stirring a pot. He looked up as Christopher entered.

Lexi made the introductions. "Denzil, this is Christopher."

"Hello, Denzil."

The boy nodded. He gave Christopher a wary look. Christopher acknowledged the boy's protectiveness of Lexi with a slight inclination of his head.

Denzil continued to regard him somberly. His caramel-colored skin and wide, flat nose, along with a head full of riotous dark curls were evidence of his aboriginal heritage. He also had the typical build of the indigenous: Broad shoulders, narrow hips, long, thin legs. He'd been built to run, like his ancestors who'd lived off the land for so many thousands of years. Western influence meant that he no longer needed to be a hunter or gatherer, but his body shape, inherited through his genetics, provided a strong link to the past.

An older girl stepped forward. She was also unmistakably aboriginal.

"I'm Kishaya," she said and gave him a shy smile.

Her straight white teeth glowed brightly against her dark skin. Like Denzil, she also had dark curly hair and brown eyes. Her expression was a mixture of friendliness and curiosity.

"Hi, Kishaya. It's nice to meet you."

After Kishaya came three more children: Josie, Demi and Stella. Lexi told him they were aged seven, ten and twelve respectively and that all three had been adopted by her and Ronnie when they were toddlers. Josie and Stella were both Caucasian. Demi was another gorgeous-looking aboriginal child.

Lexi announced dinner was ready and asked Christopher to open the wine. The sling made it a bit of a struggle, but he managed it and felt ridiculously proud of himself. He filled the two wine glasses Lexi had set out and handed one to her.

She murmured her thanks. Their fingers touched. Tingles raced along his nerve endings. The contact was so brief he thought he might have imagined his body's response, but then he glanced at Lexi and noticed the adorable blush that stained her cheeks.

A surge of satisfaction went through him.

So, she isn't as immune to me as she might wish me to believe… Interesting.

It gave him the confidence to join in the conversation and barely controlled mayhem that thereafter took place. The table was overcrowded. One long wooden table and two wooden benches that ran along either side. There were kids everywhere, all talking and laughing at once. Leroy sat in a booster seat that lifted him up to the height of the table. Even so, Christopher was sure the little boy spilled more spaghetti on the tablecloth than what actually made it into his mouth. Still, he seemed to be having a good time.

Demi and Stella regaled them with an amusing story from school. One of the second graders had been finger painting and then decided to clean his hands on the teacher's skirt.

"You should have seen Mrs Winters!" Stella squealed. "She was like, 'Oh, Toby! Don't do that! Go and wash your hands! Don't wipe them on my skirt!'"

Stella had used a mock-adult voice that had everyone in stitches. Then Josie got in on the act and relayed another hilarious tale about school.

Christopher hung off every word, fascinated and charmed by their uninhibited joy and affection for each other. Although he was part of a large family, he'd never experienced a meal like this. He'd been an only child for the first twelve or so years of his life. His first sibling was Vaughan, who was adopted at age eleven, well past the age of spilling food all over himself and the telling of funny stories from school. Christopher was sixteen when the next Barrington arrived. By that time, he'd spent more time in his room than at the dinner table and when he did eat, it was often later, after the younger children had been put to bed.

But it seemed the evening meal was a time to bring the whole family altogether, from the three-year-old to the teenagers. The result was loud and exuberant conversation, with plenty of fun and laughter. Enjoying the mayhem, Christopher realized how much he'd missed by being so much older than his siblings. At the time, he'd been glad to escape the noise and mess that often accompanied meal times with his younger brothers and sisters. Now he wished he'd spent less time on his PlayStation and more time interacting with his family.

Ice cream and strawberry-flavored jelly was served among cheers from the younger kids. By the end of the meal, Lexi jokingly commented that Leroy looked like he needed another bath. The toddler merely sent her an angelic grin. She stood and planted a kiss on his chubby cheek.

"I love you Momma," he said.

"I love you too Leroy."

Christopher's heart clenched with emotion. The sweet, pure love between the two of them filled him with a yearning to know that kind of emotion. He was forty-one years old and he'd never been in love. Had never allowed himself to be so vulnerable with another person. Had always felt the need to keep his walls up, to protect himself.

And look what I've missed out on?

Lexi loved openly and unconditionally. Patrice, Denzil and Kishaya were foster children. At a moment's notice, they could be taken from Lexi and returned to their biological parents and there would be nothing she could do about it and yet that didn't stop her from loving them with everything she had. It was a humbling revelation.

While Lexi put the younger children to bed, Christopher helped the five older ones to clean up. It was like watching a production line. Josie and Stella cleaned off the table. Demi scraped the plates into a dish that would be taken out to feed the dogs. Denzil filled the sink with hot, soapy water. Kishaya picked up a tea towel.

"What can I do to help?" Christopher asked.

Kishaya opened a drawer and drew out another tea towel. "You can help wipe up."

She tossed the tea towel in his direction. He caught it in his good hand.

Kishaya grinned. "Not bad for someone who's wounded."

He smiled back. Denzil chuckled. Over the course of the meal, most of his wariness had dissipated. He'd asked Christopher questions about Barrington Developments and what they intended to do with the land. He appeared genuinely interested when Christopher talked about the hotels, the office blocks and apartments they were hoping to build.

"How old are you, Denzil?" Christopher asked.

"Fourteen."

"Another year or so and you can leave school. You could get an apprenticeship. Become a builder or a plumber or an electrician. They're always in demand. Or you could go to university and study architecture, town planning or something completely different."

Denzil merely nodded, but there was a sparkle of excitement in his eyes that hadn't been there before.

"Let me know if you're interested in any of that. I'm sure I could make some calls and get you an interview or two when the time comes."

Denzil smiled shyly. "Thanks. That'd be great. I like being with my friends, but the truth is, I don't care too much for school. I'd much rather be outside."

"Well, then. A builder might just be the thing. They spend a *lot* of time outside." Christopher grinned. It warmed him through when Denzil grinned back.

Then Kishaya spoke. "Mom said something about you raising money to put toward a new place for us."

"Yes. My stepmother held a fundraiser last Saturday night. A lot of important people came. It was a successful night."

"How much did you raise?" Kishaya asked.

"About two hundred thousand dollars."

Denzil's eyes were as round as saucers. "Two hundred thousand dollars! In one night?"

Christopher smiled. "Yes. It sounds like a lot, and it is. But houses cost a lot, too. It's a good start, but we need more."

Kishaya stared back at him. "Why are you helping us?"

Christopher drew in a deep breath and eased it out. "I was adopted, too. I also have an adopted brother. It's important to me that other children in similar circumstances are given a secure and happy home. Your mother's done such a great job, but right now she needs a little help."

"What other ideas do you have to raise money?" Denzil asked.

"What about crowdfunding?" Kishaya suggested before Christopher could answer. "We could set up a Kickstarter or something."

Christopher blinked in surprise. That kind of thing had never occurred to him. Trust a teenager who lived in the world of social media to come up with such an idea.

"What's a Kickstarter?" Lexi asked, returning to the kitchen.

"It's kind of like an online fundraiser," Kishaya explained. "You set it up online and let people know about it through social media and then ask them to donate to your cause."

Lexi glanced at Christopher, her eyes wide. Then she looked at Kishaya. "Wow! I'd love to hear more about that, Kishaya. Maybe you could give me some help to set it up?"

"Sure, Mom. Of course," Kishaya replied.

Denzil chimed in. "It's not hard. I can help too, if you want."

Christopher watched and listened to the ensuing discussion. He could have written Lexi a check there and then to cover any shortfall, but Elizabeth's warning sounded in his ear. No one wanted to be treated like a charity case. Everyone had their pride. No sense in trampling hers when he didn't have to. Besides, he was blown away by their willingness to come together as a family and do what they could to solve their problems. It was what families were supposed to do, to pull together, but many didn't.

Although thinking about it, his family was like that, too. Not only the Barringtons, but the Craigdons, too. Pulling together as one in times of need or crisis. He'd just been too angry and bitter to notice or see the positive in it, but he was determined to do better in the future.

One by one, the kids drifted off to their rooms. They kissed Lexi goodnight and offered Christopher smiles and waves of farewell. Denzil said he'd like to talk to him a bit more about an apprenticeship another time. Kishaya thanked him for the box of chocolates. Finally he and Lexi were alone.

As if suddenly becoming aware of that, their gazes locked and the air between them became charged. Christopher's heart thumped. Blood pounded through his veins. Lexi's gaze lowered. She fiddled with her hair. Her gaze glanced off his again and just as quickly she looked away.

"Would you...like a coffee?"

Christopher blinked and drew in a deep breath in an effort to settle his pulse. "Thank you. That would be nice."

He caught the relief on her face before she turned away. He was also grateful for the distraction. Had the same need for some distance. Never before had a woman made him feel so off-balance.

He wanted to spend every minute getting to know everything about her: Her favorite color, her favorite food, her favorite book, movie, music. But the thought of becoming so enmeshed with her, trusting her with his thoughts, his secrets was daunting. To do that made him vulnerable. If he knew her so well, he couldn't blame mistakes he made on not knowing or caring. Knowing a person, *really* knowing another, created a level of responsibility...

He'd spent the past forty-one years relying on no one, living life on his terms. His mother had always loved him and had done the best she could, but before she'd had the good fortune to come to the attention of Frank Barrington, she'd worked three jobs to keep food on their table. In those days she was too tired most of the time to pay him much attention. That hadn't been her fault. It was just the way it was. Maybe that was one of the reasons he'd become so fixated on Henry Craigdon.

I wasted so many years feeling angry and bitter over his rejection...

He was glad to have finally put that behind him. He'd turned a corner and was determined to live the next forty-one years quite differently. As he'd begun to look at and engage more with his own family, he'd slowly realized how liberating sharing, caring and loving could be. He wanted that for himself. He wanted to take that risk, no matter how daunting.

The kettle boiled and Lexi filled two cups. She added milk and sugar to hers and left his black. Though it had been a week or so since the last time they'd had coffee, the fact she remembered pleased him. She carried the two cups into the living room. It was furnished with two old couches. Toys and puzzles were still scattered on the floor.

She gave him a wry smile. "Sorry about the mess. As quickly as I pick it up and put it away, it appears on the floor again."

Christopher waved her apology away. "Don't worry about it. This is a home full of love and laughter. That's all I see."

To his surprise, her eyes teared up. She waved a hand in front of her face in an effort to get control of her emotions.

"Hey there, Lexi! I'm sorry! I didn't mean to upset you."

"You didn't upset me," she managed. "I got choked up because that's such a lovely thing to say. See, I grew up in a lot of different homes. I can't ever remember having fun, or feeling loved. I work so hard to ensure my kids don't feel that way. Your comment simply made me feel validated...like all the hard work's been worthwhile."

Christopher smiled. "Well, it's true."

Lexi gave him a wobbly smile. She set the cups down on the coffee table and they sat together on the same couch.

Christopher's knee brushed hers. He heard her quick indrawn breath. And just like that, his nerves returned full-force and his heart took off at a gallop. Desire pounded through his veins. His cock hardened.

This is crazy…

Chapter Sixteen

At the intensity that consumed Christopher's expression, Lexi's heart skipped a beat. His pupils had dilated. Desire had darkened the emerald-green of his eyes. They sat so close together, she could see a pulse beat a frantic rhythm in his neck. She felt an answering surge of desire and the force of it was overwhelming. It also scared her to bits.

She wasn't used to feeling so out of control, and especially not around a man. Though she'd felt the butterflies-in-her-stomach, giddy-with-excitement kind of exhilaration in the early days of her marriage to Ronnie, that was so long ago she barely remembered.

Christopher was tense, poised mere inches from her. His breath came fast, like he was waiting for her to make the first move. Her reason for inviting him over to dinner was so that she could tell him how she was feeling. That she liked him, really liked him. In a romantic sense. Had even daydreamed about dating him. But getting past her growing panic was proving difficult.

It's too soon... What about the kids... What if things don't work out...?

In an effort to distract herself, she leaned forward and picked up her cup. She took a sip and then set it back down again. She cast around for something to say and came up with his early life. There was so much she didn't know about him. If she was seriously contemplating a relationship with him, she'd best find out what made him tick, what he was interested in, how compatible they were... And that before she let her sorely deprived libido override whatever common sense she had left.

"Would you tell me about your mother? I didn't get a chance to meet her at the fundraiser."

Christopher raised a single eyebrow, but didn't comment on her attempt to divert the direction of their conversation. He breathed out on a sigh and settled more comfortably on the couch.

"She's a remarkable woman," he said. "Evelyn Barrington. Of course, she wasn't always married to Frank and life wasn't always so easy. She started out as a single mother."

Lexi nodded. "I remember you telling me your biological father refused to recognize you."

Christopher grimaced. "Yes. Henry Craigdon. My mother was his secretary back when Henry worked in his uncle's accounting firm. Mom had a brief fling with him. She was twenty. He was five years older. Of course, she was head over heels in love with him. He was older, good-looking, charming. And then she got pregnant and he didn't want to have anything more to do with her."

"That must have been so hard for her," Lexi murmured on a wave of sympathy.

"Yes. She was left to raise me on her own. It wasn't easy. She didn't have any family to rely on. She worked three jobs just to make ends meet. Eventually she got a job as a secretary for one of the executives at Barrington Mining."

"Is that where she met Frank?"

Christopher nodded. "Yes. Frank met my mother in the staff cafeteria."

Lexi started in surprise. "He ate with his staff?"

"Yes. That's the kind of man he was. Still is. Decent and humble. Not a man with the demanding ego one might expect. So different from Henry Craigdon... The way Frank tells the story, he saw Mom seated at a table in a far corner of the room. She was crying quietly. He was drawn to her beauty, but more than that, he wanted to know why she was so upset.

"So, he took his tray and went and sat across from her."

Lexi grinned, loving the story. "I bet she got a surprise to find the CEO of her company having lunch at her table."

Christopher chuckled. "Yes. More than that, she was embarrassed he'd caught her sobbing her heart out."

"What did he say?"

"He wanted to know why she was so upset."

"And what did she tell him?"

"That she was crying because she was about to get evicted. She didn't have enough money to pay her rent and she didn't know what she and her young son were going to do. I was ten years old at the time. Like most kids do, I was going through a stage, although I was probably worse than most. I knew my biological father didn't want to have anything to do with me. I'd grown up wild and unruly. I was rude and disobedient. I regularly got suspended from school. I had a huge chip on my shoulder and I made sure everyone knew it."

He shook his head and gave her a rueful smile. "I look back now and I'm embarrassed about my behavior. I was a real handful for my mom. I made her life so much more difficult than it had to be, but she never stopped loving me." His voice choked with emotion. "That's the kind of woman she is."

Lexi's heart turned over at the raw emotion on Christopher's face. Whatever troubles he'd caused his mother in his youth, it was obvious how much he cared for her.

"She sounds amazing. I can't wait to meet her," Lexi murmured.

Christopher nodded. "You'll like her."

"So tell me the rest of the story. How did they get together?"

Christopher sat forward and took another sip of coffee before setting the cup back down on the coffee table.

"Well, the way Frank tells it, he spent that lunch hour with the beautiful Evelyn and they talked like they'd known each other for years. Frank went back upstairs to his office and he couldn't get her off his mind. He called her about half an hour later and asked her out to dinner. She turned him down because she didn't have anyone to look after me."

Lexi gave him a wry grin. "I know the feeling."

Christopher chuckled. "Not to be deterred, Frank offered to pay for a sitter. At first, Mom refused. She had her pride, after all. So they continued to meet for lunch in the staff cafeteria. People began to talk. Neither of them cared. For that single hour each day, it was like no one else existed. And once the hour was over, they would return to their respective floors to work."

"How long did this go on for?"

"About a month or so. Frank finally convinced Mom to go out for dinner and he paid for the sitter. They went out to dinner a few more times, but Mom made sure Frank knew they were going to take things slowly. Mom knew I wasn't in a good place emotionally. I hated the world and everyone in it. She knew I wouldn't take kindly to a new man in her life and didn't want to introduce me to him until she knew they were serious."

Lexi compressed her lips against a surge of compassion. She understood all too well how Evelyn had felt. She was lucky her children were so well-adjusted. That they'd spent enough time living with her and feeling safe that they weren't overly threatened by the arrival of someone else who might compete with them for her affection.

"Please tell me you were nice to him when you were finally introduced," Lexi said.

Christopher winced. "I wish I could say I was a perfect angel who welcomed him with polite words and a handshake. The reality was vastly different. I first met Frank after he and my mother got engaged. It was such a shock. I didn't take it well."

He ran his good hand through his hair in a sign of irritation. It left the thick strands standing up on end and made him look younger. He drew in another deep breath and kept talking.

"I knew she was getting serious about him. They went out for dinner more and more often and he was all she could talk about. Frank this, Frank that. It made me sick. The truth was, I was jealous. I didn't want her to have anyone else in her life. I didn't want her to be happy. She wanted me to meet him but I wasn't having it. I guess I hoped he'd just go away."

He raised his tortured gaze to hers. "What kind of spoiled brat was I?"

Lexi reached out and touched his hand. His skin was warm beneath her fingers. "You were scared you'd lose her. Of having to compete for her love. That's perfectly understandable."

He shook his head. "Don't make excuses for me, Lexi. I was a little asshole. During subsequent meetings, I acted out, called him names, told him to leave my mother alone. Of course, he took all the abuse and said nothing. Just told me how much he loved my mother and that he wanted to take care of us both.

"I didn't want him to take care of me. I wanted my real father to do that. Only that asshole wouldn't even accept, let alone acknowledge me as his son." His bark of laughter was filled with pain. "You can see why I was so screwed up."

Lexi's heart filled with compassion. Tears burned behind her eyes. She could picture the young Christopher, so hurt and devastated from his father's refusal to acknowledge his son's existence. She wanted so much to give him a hug and reassure him that everything was going to be all right. Unable to resist the urge not to touch him, she moved closer until their thighs touched. She reached for his hand and threaded her fingers with his. He didn't pull away.

"Tell me the rest of the story," she quietly urged.

Christopher's shoulders slumped on a weary sigh. "Mom was thirty when she met Frank. He was five years older. Frank had spent his life until then, building his empire. He had plenty of money, but no one to share it with. He fell head over heels for my mother and even the prospect of taking on a rude and recalcitrant stepson didn't deter him. They married when I was eleven years old. A year later, Frank legally adopted me and gave me his name. That's how I became a Barrington."

Lexi looked at him. "I bet you didn't feel lucky at the time, but take it from someone who knows, you were one of the lucky ones."

Christopher looked at her and nodded. "Yes. You told me that once before and you know, until that moment, I'd never looked at it that way."

Lexi squeezed his hand. "Every time I was sent to another foster home, I'd pray that this time they'd want to keep me. That I wouldn't be sent away. That they'd love me enough to let me become a permanent part of their family. It never happened."

The emotion on Christopher's face brought tears to Lexi's eyes. "My heart breaks for you when I hear that," he whispered. "And it makes me feel even worse when I remember how ungrateful I was for what Frank did for me. For us."

"What happened after their wedding?"

"I continued to be a little asshole. I was angry at the world and I made sure everyone knew it. I was resentful of my new father and the important role he played in my mother's life.

Frank's willingness to treat me as his son only made me angrier. It highlighted for me how crappy my real father was. Here was a man who had no blood ties to me and yet he was willing to treat me like a son. My biological father wouldn't even acknowledge me. The whole thing messed with my head."

"That must have made it hard for your mother, too."

"Absolutely. She was caught in the middle, although to be fair to Frank, he never fought back. He let me rail against him, say terrible, nasty things and then he'd simply ask me if I felt better and that one day, when I was ready, he'd be there for me."

"Of course, that only infuriated me further. I refused to believe Frank could love me like a son. I was sure the only reason I was there was because it was the only way he could marry my mother. We were a package deal. My mother had always made that clear. And I only wanted to be a Craigdon. I *deserved* to be a Craigdon. Henry Craigdon was my biological father, after all."

Christopher paused and slowly shook his head. "For a long time, Frank and I were caught up in an endless circle of angst. I got furious and raged against him for all my perceived injustices and Frank merely offered compassion, understanding and forgiveness. I didn't know how to deal with his kindness. So I didn't. I shut down."

Once again, Lexi fought the urge to hold him close. She was pretty sure he'd never spoken like this about his past to anyone and she knew how important it was for him to get it off his chest.

"And then Vaughan arrived," Christopher said slowly.

"Your half-brother?"

"No. Mom and Frank had tried for a couple of years to have children. It seemed that they couldn't. So they adopted Vaughan. He was eleven when he came to live with us."

"And how old were you?"

"I was twelve."

"And how did that go?"

Christopher offered a one-shoulder shrug. "Vaughan was like you. He'd been passed around from foster home to foster home for most of his young life. He didn't know his biological parents. I think they both were dead. But there was something about him. Something incredible I couldn't understand. He'd been dealt a far harsher hand than I had and yet he hadn't let it get him down."

"In what way?" Lexi asked softly.

"He had the most incredibly positive attitude. He always looked at life from a glass-half-full perspective. Of all the people to have reason to be bitter and twisted, he took the prize and yet, he chose to take on a positive outlook and forge a different path. He's still that way.

"Whenever I'd get angry at Henry's refusal to acknowledge me, I'd look at Vaughan and remember he didn't have a mother *or* a father. There had been no one in the world who'd wanted him until he came to live with us. At least I had my mom."

Christopher drew in a shaky breath. "I started to let go of some of my anger—not at Henry, but at Frank. I'd spent too long blithely and selfishly taking all Frank had to offer in the way of material things, all the while treating him with utter disrespect. Vaughan made me realize there were plenty of kids who were worse off—including him."

"Don't be too hard on yourself. You were a kid."

Christopher looked at her. His eyes were stormy with emotion. "I was twelve, nearly thirteen. I was old enough to know better. To be really honest, I *did* know better." He drew in a ragged breath. "There's more."

Lexi could tell from his somber expression and the gravity of his tone that what he was about to say was even worse than what he'd already revealed. She put a hand on his arm.

"You don't have to do this, Christopher. I like you. I like you a lot. Nothing you say is going to change that."

"No. I want you to know. You need to know what kind of person I am."

With that, he drew in a deep shuddering breath before he spoke again: "Vaughan's arrival had a positive impact on me, at least insofar as my relationship with Frank, but it didn't stop me from feeling sorry for myself. The hurt and anger I felt toward Henry Craigdon manifested into a hot, bitter ball of hate.

"As an adult, it negatively affected my relationships, the way I interacted with people, the way I viewed the world. I went out of my way to cause trouble and to make people's lives miserable. It gave me an obscene amount of pleasure. I was nasty and malicious. I zeroed in on peoples' weaknesses and then exploited them for my own gain. I did this time and time again, even to my own family. I used to play dirty tricks on them just for laughs. I didn't care who I hurt in the process. What does that say about me?"

Lexi regarded him solemnly. "It tells me you were an angry, disappointed and troubled soul."

Christopher snorted with irritation. "I wasn't troubled. I was rotten to the core. Nasty, malicious, spiteful. I was a prick."

His head hung low as he stared at the floor. "I'm so ashamed of my behavior, of the man I used to be. I don't know how anyone as good and kind and compassionate as you can stand being near me. I'm sorry I unloaded all that shit on you. I'll understand if you think differently toward me, now that you know the unvarnished truth. I won't hold you to your earlier statements. I promise."

"Did you hear what you said?" Lexi asked gently. "*Used* to be?"

Christopher blinked. "So?"

Lexi turned to face him on the couch. She took both of his hands in hers. "Let me tell you about the man I'm getting to know, Christopher. The man I see. From the moment I met you, I sensed your goodness and I wasn't wrong. You've gone out of your way to help me, to help my children.

"We were complete strangers to you and yet you felt the need to do something to ease our plight. You had no obligation to do so. The circumstances were not of your making, but you felt compassion for our situation and took measures to address it."

She paused and looked at him intently, hoping to convince him. "Make amends with those you've wronged if you have to, but learn to forgive yourself. Your family members whom I met were clearly not bearing any resentments for past slights.

Their love and respect for you was evident. Be kind to yourself and let the past go. You deserve to be happy."

Christopher stared into Lexi's beautiful blue eyes absorbing her words. He couldn't quite believe he'd unburdened himself in such a way. He'd never told anyone his deepest darkest secrets. His shameful past had always been that—something to hide. His trust in sharing his past with her further cemented his conviction in his growing feelings for her.

And most surprisingly of all was the fact she still sat there beside him, looking like she wanted to be there. He was a lucky man. He was so grateful she seemed prepared to look past his flaws and see the better man he was trying so hard to be.

He still didn't quite believe he deserved someone as good and kind as Lexi, but he wanted to. The way she looked at him gave him hope. Her eyes were wide, her expression open. Her gaze roved over his face. She lifted his hands and squeezed them and then pressed a kiss on his knuckles.

Her touch was as light as a feather, but he felt it in every fiber of his being. His heart leaped into his throat. His stomach clenched with need. Desire burned like molten lava and centered in his cock.

Something in his expression must have alerted her to the way he felt. Her lips parted on an intake of breath. She looked at him like he was someone she very much wanted. Their gazes locked. Her tongue stole out to lick her lips. She moved slightly forward, bringing her head close. Her mouth came within inches of his.

It was all the encouragement Christopher needed. Angling his head, he captured her lips with his. Unlike their previous kiss, this one immediately ignited. They kissed like their world depended on this connection. It was like a match struck to tinder, set ablaze.

He lifted his arm and put it around her shoulders, drawing her even closer. Their lips devoured each other's and then her palms framed his face, held his head still so that one passionate kiss morphed into another until there was no beginning and no end, just the two of them caught up in a world of heat and friction where nothing and no one else existed.

And all he could think of was how right she felt in his arms.

I'm home.

Chapter Seventeen

Lexi lost herself in Christopher's kiss. She couldn't remember ever being kissed so completely that she felt it down to her toes. Though she'd loved Ronnie with all her heart and had been devastated by his death, he'd never been one for kissing, holding hands, touching unless it was a prelude to sex. Even then, he hadn't demonstrated the kind of uninhibited giving and expertise Christopher did.

The way he slanted his mouth, the way he held her head. At one point she'd even cupped her hands around his cheeks to make sure he didn't move away. Such was her need for him to continue. She'd never felt like this: like he was making love to her with that kiss. It was strange and unfamiliar, but incredibly exciting. She'd never been more turned on.

A part of her felt guilty. She shouldn't be feeling like this with a man who was almost a stranger. She'd been married to Ronnie for nearly a decade and had never felt like this. It wasn't right that Christopher could elicit such a reaction from her without even trying. Somehow it felt like a betrayal.

And then she remembered her earlier misgivings, especially when it came to her children. They needed certainty, stability. They didn't need men being paraded in and out of their lives.

Okay, so that was a bit harsh on herself. Christopher was the first man she'd invited home since Ronnie's death. Her children hadn't been subjected to the kind of thing she was thinking about, but what about now? Were they ready to accept a man into her life? Having to vie for her attention? Of course, in her mind they would always come first, but what if they didn't see it like that?

And what if she and Christopher started something and then it didn't last? Was that fair to her children?

The questions kept circling around in her head and eventually Christopher noticed her response to him had waned. He pulled back with a question in his eyes. She blushed, suddenly embarrassed. After all, he hadn't forced himself on her. Now she was backing away. No wonder he looked confused.

"Lexi? Are you okay?"

She kept her eyes averted, but managed a jerky nod.

The furrows across Christopher's brow deepened. "Are you sure? You don't look okay."

The compassion in his voice was her undoing. Tears welled up in her eyes. She blinked and fought hard to keep them at bay, but they spilled over anyway.

Christopher looked distressed. He pulled her awkwardly into his arms. "Oh, honey! What's the matter? Please don't cry. Why are you crying?"

"I-I-I don't know." She hiccupped.

He drew her head down on his chest and softly stroked her hair. He pressed a kiss against her head and murmured words of comfort. Her tears continued to fall. He let her cry without interruption. Finally, after her sobs had subsided, she pushed away from his chest, swiped at her eyes and looked at him.

"I'm sorry. That was so embarrassing."

He reached out and gently brushed her hair out of her eyes. "Don't be embarrassed. It makes me feel good, knowing you trust me enough to be so honest with your emotions. It's not easy to do that. In fact, I don't think I've ever been as completely open with anyone about my feelings as I just did."

He gave a self-deprecating laugh. "For so many years, all I felt was rage. I didn't want to feel anything else. I fed off it. I used it to feel self-righteous. I used it as an excuse for my poor behavior. I kept telling myself it wasn't my fault I was so nasty. I had my absent asshole of a father to thank for that."

He looked at her again and the tension around his mouth eased. "But this isn't about me, Lexi. Please tell me why you were upset?"

She eased out a shaky sigh. "I was thinking about Ronnie and my kids and how much I like you and how many crazy feelings are bombarding me, but also how things are moving so fast…" She paused and then added, "I'm not sure I'm ready for fast. Would you mind if we took things slowly?"

His face relaxed into a smile. "Oh, Lexi. I'm so glad to hear you say you like me. I like you too. A lot. And I'm so turned on right now it's all I can do not to take you right here on this couch. But I understand your need to take things slowly and I respect that. From all that you've told me, you and Ronnie had something special. I'm never going to compete with that and I don't want to. I want you to want *me,* and I know that's going to take some time."

Lexi smiled. "Wanting you is not going to be a problem. It's the risk inherent in exploring that want and whether it can really develop into something lasting. Thank you for your understanding as well as your honesty. It means a great deal to me. Because this thing between us—whatever it is—isn't just about you and me. I have eight children to consider. Their needs are even more important than mine. I want you to know they'll always be my priority."

Christopher kissed her briefly on the mouth. "I wouldn't expect it to be any other way. That's one of the things I love about you."

He said it lightly, but they both stilled. Lexi stared at him. Her heart thumped. "Love?" she said jokingly.

A blush stained Christopher's cheeks. He looked away from her, but a few moments later, he looked back.

"It was a figure of speech, but... Does the idea that I might fall in love with you scare you?"

Lexi's chest went tight with a mixture of joy and disbelief. The idea of falling in love again was terrifying, but it also filled her with a kernel of hope she hadn't felt since before Ronnie's death. The thought of loving someone again and being loved in return held so much appeal, she almost didn't trust herself to think about it. And yet, if she was truthful with herself, she'd admit she'd flirted with the idea of having Christopher in her life and he appeared to be hinting the same.

She needed time to think about it, to look at it from every angle. She also needed to analyze it from the perspective of her children. She hadn't been exaggerating when she'd said they always came first. Before she made any decision, she'd need to discuss the possibility with them.

Aware that Christopher was waiting for her answer, she bravely met his gaze. "I've always been open to love. It was sorely lacking during so many years of my life but on the occasions I was been blessed enough to find it, I embraced it.

"Losing Ronnie was devastating. I grieved for a long time. Even now, I still miss him. But that doesn't mean I've closed myself off from the possibility of experiencing love again. The fact that you might one day feel that strongly about me is a little scary, but honestly, it fills me with hope."

The smile that spread across Christopher's face was something to behold. The masculine beauty evident in his satisfaction devastated her senses. He covered her face in eager kisses and then finally claimed her lips once again.

This time the kiss was more gentle, slower, more exploratory. They took their time to taste and feel, learning the shape of each other's lips. Christopher's were full and supple and soft. Lexi could go on kissing him for hours. Then he broke off the kiss and nibbled his way down her neck. He nuzzled one of her earlobes. His good hand came up to cup her breast. She shivered with delight, her nipples pebbling with desire.

His thumb stroked her sensitive flesh and she instinctively leaned into his palm. His lips found hers again and he kissed her thoroughly once more. Her hand splayed over his chest. She felt the force of his heartbeat thumping against her palm.

When they finally came up for air, both of them were breathing hard.

"We'd better stop," Lexi rasped.

"Yes. We'd better. Before we can't." Christopher leaned his forehead against hers and drew in some deep breaths. "Just give me a moment."

Lexi marveled at the power she had in causing him to lose himself so completely. His breath came fast. His skin was hot to touch. His erection strained against his pants. She felt a pang at leaving him in such a state, but it was too soon for more.

After a few long minutes, he moved away from her and she immediately missed his presence. But then he reached out and put his good arm around her and drew her close against his side. She leaned her head on his chest. He felt so warm, so solid, so dependable. All good qualities in a mate. Still, she had to determine whether their fledgling feelings were worth taking the chance.

On his drive back home to the lower north shore, Christopher's head was full of Lexi. His cock still ached at the memory of kissing her. He'd had his fair share of women, but none of them had made him feel like this. Admittedly, he'd never been emotionally involved with any of his former lovers. Maybe that made all the difference.

He was still a little embarrassed at having offloaded his past on Lexi, but she'd been so incredible in her acceptance and support. For that alone, he could love her.

He suspected he was falling for the whole package and he was glad she appeared to feel the same way. He completely understood her request to take things slowly and how her children had to be her priority. The last thing he wanted to do was come between her and her children or disrupt in any way the amazing work she'd done with them.

The only thing to do was to plan their next date. It had to be something incredible. He wanted to blow her mind. Do something she'd never experienced. It also had to be something that included the children. He was nearly back at his apartment when the idea came to him: Raging Waters.

Yes, that's exactly where he'd take them. It wasn't so far from where they lived and it was the biggest water park in the state. It catered to all ages, with jaw-dropping water slides, along with a range of family friendly rides. With this late burst of warm April weather, it was the perfect location for a day of fun.

Of course, he'd make sure to hire some nannies to help out. Or at least discuss the idea with Lexi. It had been challenging enough when it had been just the three younger kids for lunch that time in the city. Taking on all eight of them without some professional support was a daunting prospect. He'd consult with Lexi first. After all, she knew her children best. He just wanted to ensure that all of them had a good time, including Lexi.

—— *ele* ——

Lexi woke the next morning with a smile on her face. The early morning sunshine leaked golden rays of light under her faded curtains. The house was quiet and still. It was too early yet for the children to be up and about. She took a moment to enjoy the serenity and a few more moments just to lie in bed. She stretched her arms above her head. Then she rolled over on her side, dragging the bedclothes with her.

Though her situation was as precarious as ever, after spending the evening with Christopher, the future didn't look quite so bleak. Oh, she was still short a lot of money if she wanted to replace her property with something equally large or larger and not too far out, but there were more important things than money. Happiness, for one. And right now she felt happier than she had for a long time and it had everything to do with Christopher Barrington.

She'd been surprised by his candid self-reflection and willingness to share some of his past. His courage in laying out the person he had been, had enabled her to open up about her painful childhood. It had been an emotional outpouring for them both. And the kisses! Oh my, the kisses. They'd been both wonderful and scary.

The kisses were definitely a bonus, but if she were truthful he'd begun to capture her heart when he'd stepped up to offer support to her and her children. Despite the involvement of his stepfather's company and her immediate challenges, he'd set out to exhaust all possibilities to lessen the impact. The fundraiser, his exploration of legal avenues... had all been about finding a solution to her predicament.

His efforts were a priceless gift from someone who barely knew her and who had nothing to gain by helping her. His actions spoke loudly of his good character and had created a strong bond. If their relationship didn't deepen, she was sure that at the least, she'd always have a friend she could rely on.

The amount of money raised by Christopher's stepmother was phenomenal, but they were still a fair way short. Lexi didn't want to downsize. They were squashed in already and she wanted to expand if possible, to provide a safe haven for other children. She also didn't want to move so far away that the children would be forced to change schools. Such a move would be disruptive and traumatic, particularly when security and stability were two of their greatest needs.

She had to come up with a way to raise more money. Kishaya's suggestion of crowdfunding might be a possibility, though she still wasn't exactly sure how it worked. Her gaze strayed to her dresser. Climbing out of bed, she padded across the bare wooden floor, opened the dresser drawer and pulled out her jewelry box.

She opened the lid. Her grandmother's brooch lay against the cheap velvet lining. The sapphires and diamonds winked at her as they caught the morning light. Her fingers hovered over the beautiful ornament.

Twenty thousand dollars… A lot of money… Not enough to get them over the line, but right now, every dollar counted.

But could she bear to part with it? Other than the single photograph she had of her mother, this was the only thing she had left of her forebears of whom she had no memory. But right now the living members of her family needed her. They needed the money the brooch could bring to help secure their future.

Carefully picking up the brooch, she stared at it a long time and then, with a resolute sigh, she closed her fingers around it and dropped it into her handbag. As soon as the older kids had left for school and she had the younger ones dressed for the day, she'd head into town to find the nearest pawn shop. No doubt she wouldn't be offered anywhere near what it was worth, but right now, anything that went toward their million-dollar goal would help.

Decision made, she opened her door and calling out to her children to get out of bed and get to breakfast, she headed for the shower.

— ele —

Saturday morning dawned bright and sunny with the temperature predicted to climb hot enough that a day at a water park sounded like bliss. Christopher had run his plan by Lexi a few days earlier and had been pleased when she'd responded with excitement and delight.

"You want to take everyone to Raging Waters?" she'd asked, her tone filled with incredulity.

"Yes. Why not?"

"Well, apart from the fact it'll be crowded with people, what about the cost? Admission to that place doesn't come cheap, especially for a group as large as ours. We're trying to save every dollar we can."

"Don't worry about the cost. This is on me. I want to do something special for you and the kids. To give them a distraction from the uncertainty of the pending move. Let them have some fun. What better way to do that than at the water park?"

Lexi's answering laughter had thoroughly warmed him. "I see you, Christopher Barrington. You make out you're this ogre, but underneath you're a softy. I can't wait to tell the kids. They're going to love it! Thank you."

Christopher had also discussed his plan to hire a couple of nannies to be on hand if they were needed. At first, Lexi had protested, but Christopher had managed to convince her that they'd all have a better time with the extra help.

He'd carefully made his argument so it didn't come across as a criticism, not wanting her to think he was judging her ability to look after her kids in a crowded public space.

"This day is all about having fun and that includes you. With a couple more adults on hand, you won't need to be so vigilant all the time. Who knows, you and I might even enjoy a ride by ourselves."

When she continued to prevaricate, he sealed the deal by saying, "When was the last time you got to do something like this without having to constantly worry about everyone, particularly the younger ones?"

"Not since Ronnie was alive," she grudgingly admitted. "And even then, I was the primary caregiver. Ronnie was just as unpredictable and worrisome as the kids most times when we went out."

But as they pulled up to the park in the minibus Christopher had hired for the day, complete with car seats for the younger children, he took a look at the thousands of cars lined up in neat rows across the acres of car park and his gut filled with dread.

Oh, my God! Look at all the cars! This is madness! What the hell was I thinking? Eight kids among thousands of strangers. What if I lose one of them? Or worse? What if one of them is snatched?

He'd heard about that kind of thing happening. Predators trolling places like this for young victims. Kids who disappeared in a crowd, never to be seen alive again. His heart thumped. And for the first time in a long time, he felt uncertain.

Something in his expression must have alerted Lexi to his misgivings. She reached across from the passenger seat and squeezed his arm. "Hey, relax. It's going to be all right. The kids are beyond excited. Let's all go and have some fun."

Christopher looked at her. "Aren't you worried we might lose one of them? What if they go off with someone?"

She gave him a gentle smile. "The older ones are very aware of stranger danger. I'm sure they won't go off with someone voluntarily, no matter the enticement."

"But what about the younger ones?"

"We'll keep a close eye on them," she assured him. "They know how to stay together and thanks to you, we have a couple more sets of eyes, remember?" She looked meaningfully behind her toward the two nannies Christopher had hired. "Besides," she added, "Leroy will spend most of the time in the stroller. The other little ones can hold our hands."

She gave him a sideways glance. A single dark eyebrow quirked upwards. "You might find this hard to believe, but this isn't the first time we've all been on an outing together, Christopher. We have a routine the children are familiar with. We all look out for each other and no one wanders off. At least, not without permission and never on their own. It's always worked in the past."

"Have you ever taken them to a place like this? With so many people around?" Christopher asked, still feeling anxious.

"No, but only because we could never afford to go to a place like this, not because I deemed it less safe."

Christopher nodded and took a deep breath. He'd forgotten the nannies. Silly really, but this was his first foray with a group of children who were important to the woman important to him. The brief bout of anxiety was unfamiliar and, he thought deprecatingly, probably not the last time he'd feel such concern. Still, the whole point of the visit was for the family to have fun. Lexi was right. He needed to get with the program and relax. Starting now.

He forced a wide grin and looked over his shoulder at the wall-to-wall children who sat behind him.

"Who's ready for some fun?"

His question was met with a chorus of cheers.

Lexi was right. They could do this. After all, how hard could it be?

Chapter Eighteen

Lexi had never been to a water park, or any other kind of theme park. Money had been tight in the foster families she'd been homed with and things like holidays and days out for nothing more than fun had been out of the question. She wouldn't admit to anyone, but she was just as excited as her children to be at Raging Waters for the day. Christopher's thoughtful generosity in hiring help would enable her to relax and enjoy herself even more.

The last four years of single parenting, as the sole responsible adult for eight children, had demanded all her energy. That had also meant knowing where each and every one of her children were at all times and ensuring they were safe. While she'd always been willing to take on the role of parent, she'd never envisaged she'd be doing it on her own.

But she hadn't shied away from taking in needy children, including adopting Leroy after Ronnie's death. She'd continue to do whatever she could to help them feel loved, secure and safe. The unexpected luxury of having three other adults to share the burden, even for a day, was a tremendous and much appreciated gift.

And again, I have Christopher to thank for it…

His thoughtfulness didn't mesh with the picture he'd painted of himself. No matter how awful, how selfish, how nasty he thought he might have been in the past, she could only judge him on the way he'd treated her and her children. As far as she was concerned, he'd been nothing but kind and generous. If he hadn't expressly confided in her about his previous shortcomings, she'd have been none the wiser.

He'd taken a great risk in doing so. The risk that she might reject him; feel disgusted and not want anything more to do with him. But instead, his honesty and his actions had showed her his integrity. He was someone she could trust with herself and her children. She actually liked him very much. In fact, if she allowed herself, she knew she could fall in love with him…

The thought made her giddy with a mixture of hope and apprehension. Her contemplation was suddenly interrupted by the kids shouting to be let out of the minibus so they could queue at the entrance gates.

"Come on, Momma! Let's go!" Josie cried, flinging off her seatbelt.

"Let's go! Let's go! Let's go!" Patrice chanted, her eyes wide with excitement.

Even the teenagers looked keen to get moving so the fun could begin.

Lexi looked at Christopher and grinned. "I guess we'd better get this adventure started."

He winked. "Sounds good to me."

Christopher left them gathering their towels and gear and headed for the entrance. He approached the ticket booth, handing over the tickets he'd purchased online. In short order, they'd all received wrist bands that allowed them to move freely inside the park.

Lexi pushed Leroy in his stroller. One of the nannies had another stroller ready for when Michael decided he was too tired to walk. Right now he was bouncing around like a kangaroo, eager to get inside, but there would come a time later in the day when he'd be grateful for the stroller.

To save time having to change, the children had worn their swimsuits underneath their clothes. The second nanny hefted their two beach bags filled with towels, and slung one bag over each shoulder. As Christopher rejoined their party, he offered to take one of the bags. Lexi noticed the nanny blush and avert her gaze, but she gratefully handed over one of the bags.

"Let's pile them in the spare stroller for now," Lexi suggested. "That way no one has to carry them."

Christopher grinned. "Good idea."

Lexi's heart flip-flopped. She almost pinched herself to remind herself this was real. *He* was real.

He was so sexy with his three-day stubble on his face, his shiny dark hair, his designer sunglasses. He wore a white T-shirt that stretched taut across his well-defined pectorals and drew attention to his flat stomach. A pair of colorful board shorts completed his outfit. He no longer wore the sling and had assured her his injuries had healed enough he could carry things and do without it. He'd teased her by saying that he was even up for going on one of the slides, providing she joined him.

As they walked through the gates and before the kids got so excited they stopped listening, Lexi gathered everyone around and set out the rules. No one was to go off on their own. If someone wanted to go on a particular ride, they were to tell one of the adults. The teenagers were to keep their phones close at all times in case Lexi or one of the other adults needed to get in contact with them. The younger children, including Josie, Stella and Demi were to stay with the adults.

When Josie opened her mouth to protest, Lexi held up her hand. "No, Josie. That's not negotiable. There are a lot of people here. You can see for yourself. Only Kishaya and Denzil have permission to walk around together without the rest of us. Do you understand?"

The seven-year-old nodded reluctantly and remained silent.

Lexi continued: "We're all going to meet at a pre-arranged place at half-past twelve for lunch and to check in and make sure everyone's all right." She looked at her teenagers. "Once we get further inside and find somewhere suitable, I'll text you the details, okay?"

Both Kishaya and Denzil murmured their assent. Denzil moved his weight from one foot to the other, obviously keen to get started.

"Can we go now?" Kishaya asked.

Lexi grinned. "Yes. Go and have fun! We'll see you for lunch."

The teenagers turned and disappeared into the crowd before Lexi had even finished speaking. The younger children started jumping up and down and pleading to be allowed to go on a ride. Lexi looked at Christopher who grinned and gave her a wink.

"Let's go!" he shouted.

"Yay!" the kids chorused.

Michael and Patrice reached for Christopher's hands, clinging on enthusiastically. Josie, Stella and Demi skipped along beside Lexi. The two nannies brought up the rear with Leroy and the second stroller.

Lexi consulted the map they'd been given and suggested a couple of slides that looked both age appropriate and fun. They headed in that direction. The morning passed in a blur. Lexi had never seen her kids have so much fun. They laughed and giggled and screamed with delight. They went flying from the highest slide, landed in the pool and climbed out with grins a mile wide. And then they did it all over again.

In deference to his recent injuries, Christopher chose more kid-friendly slides, and took Michael and Leroy with him. No sooner had the three of them reached the bottom and the boys were begging him to take them up again. Lexi noticed he never looked bored or irritated or impatient. In fact, he always acquiesced to their demands with a smile that looked genuine.

When Patrice tugged on her hand and asked her to go on the Breakers, Lexi's heart skipped a beat. The ride was ridiculously high and looked way too scary. She tried to persuade Patrice to try something a little less frightening, but the five-year-old was having none of it.

"Please, Momma! I want to go on that one!"

Christopher and the younger boys were standing nearby, all of them dripping wet. Christopher looked at her and laughed. "Go on, Momma! What are you waiting for?" he teased.

Lexi's heart somersaulted at the casual use of "Momma." Somehow, it sounded so sexy coming from him. Coupled with the heat in his gaze as he waited for her reaction, it was all she could do not to throw herself against him and kiss him senseless.

As if sensing the direction of her thoughts, Christopher's eyes darkened. He took a step toward her just as Patrice tugged on her hand again.

"Come on, Momma! Let's go!"

With a helpless shrug and a smile in Christopher's direction, she let the little girl drag her away in the direction of the Breakers. They shucked their clothes down to their swimsuits. It was even higher at the top than Lexi had imagined. She put on a brave face for Patrice's sake, but she needn't have bothered. The child grinned from ear to ear, loving every minute of it.

When it was their turn, Patrice took off with a shout of triumph. Lexi followed her down. At the bottom, they stood in the pool laughing and pushing back their wet hair. Christopher, standing nearby with the younger boys, watched her intently, his gaze moving slowly over her scantily clad form. Lexi flushed hotly.

"That was so much fun!" Patrice shouted. "Let's do it again!"

Pulled from her distraction, Lexi didn't know if her nerves would hold up for another turn, particularly with Christopher looking on, but unwilling to disappoint her little girl, she held on to her courage, climbed out of the pool doing her best to ignore the hot eyes that followed her, and headed back to the top of the slide to do it all again. When Patrice begged for a third turn, Lexi laughed and shook her head.

"That's enough for now, honey. It's time for lunch. Let's retrieve our clothes."

"Okay. Can I have some ice cream? With chocolate sprinkles on top?"

Lexi scrunched up her nose. "That doesn't sound like much of a lunch to me. I was thinking maybe a sandwich..."

Patrice looked horrified. "A sandwich! Momma! We're supposed to be having fun!"

Lexi laughed and hugged the little girl to her. "Okay, okay. Ice cream it is!"

"Yay! Wait until I tell the boys! They're going to be so happy!"

Lexi had texted the older kids earlier with directions on where to meet for lunch. Together, she and Patrice walked back to where Christopher and the boys were waiting for them. A short time later, the nannies appeared with Demi, Stella and Josie. All five were dripping wet.

"It looks like you've been having fun," Lexi commented.

The younger girls shouted in unison. "Yes!"

Lexi laughed. "I'm glad. It's time for lunch. Let's go and meet the others."

While they gathered their possessions, Lexi studiously avoided Christopher's burning gaze and busied herself by strapping Leroy back into his stroller. They made their way over to the food stalls where they'd agreed to meet Denzil and Kishaya. Lexi was both pleased and relieved when she spied the teenagers already waiting for them.

Denzil and Kishaya stood there with towels wrapped around their bodies, hair wet and grinning from ear to ear.

"Hey, guys! How's your day been so far?" Lexi asked.

"It's been the best fun ever!" Kishaya enthused.

"We've been on 360Rush four times!" Denzil crowed. "Talk about a rush, all right. It's wicked."

Lexi grinned. "Well, I'm glad to see you've been having a good time."

"Who's ready for some lunch?" Christopher asked.

He was met with a chorus of cheers. An enthusiastic discussion followed, with everyone keen to make their own suggestions. Ice cream, hot dogs, pizza and burgers were all part of the mix. In the end, it was decided each child could make their own choice.

They walked together. Kishaya and Denzil took the lead. Josie, Stella and Demi skipped along beside them. Michael asked if he could ride in the spare stroller and one of the nannies kindly strapped him in. Lexi pushed Leroy, and Christopher walked beside her. He reached for Patrice's hand. She shot him a cheeky grin.

"This is the best day ever Christopher," she announced. "I never want it to end."

He laughed and affectionately ruffled her hair. "I'm glad you're having fun, squirt."

Patrice looked momentarily outraged until she caught Christopher's teasing grin.

Lexi watched their interaction. It had been a long time since she'd seen her children so outwardly joyful and trusting of another adult. It had been a long time since *she'd* felt such joy. Her heart turned over. She was falling head over heels for this man and there was nothing she could do to stop it. His patience with her children added to the growing list of things she liked about him.

Careful… I need to take things slowly… Make sure I'm certain about him… I won't be the only one affected by any decision I make regarding a possible relationship…

Her cautionary thoughts had the desired effect. She forced her heart rate to slow and the smile eased from her lips.

Catching sight of the ice cream stand, Patrice dropped Christopher's hand and took off. Lexi called out to her, but she didn't hear. A few seconds later, the little girl tripped.

Over she went amid a cry of alarm. Her hands went out to break her fall. She skidded her bare knees against the concrete. Lexi's heart leaped in her throat and she hurried as quickly as she could. Christopher got there ahead of her and was already kneeling beside Patrice, comforting her and gently wiping away her tears when Lexi arrived.

"There, there. It's all right, squirt. You've just taken a bit of skin off your knees. You're going to be fine. Nothing a double scoop of chocolate chip ice cream won't fix, right?"

Patrice looked up at him, tears leaking from her eyes. She gave him a shaky grin. "Right, but… Can I have caramel?"

Christopher gave her a spontaneous hug and Lexi's heart turned over. "Of course you can!"

They high-fived and Patrice smiled. Slowly, Christopher helped her to her feet. Lexi came over and put her arm around Patrice's shoulders and pulled her close.

"Are you all right, honey?"

Patrice nodded. "Yes, Momma. I'm fine. Just a little scratch, right Christopher?" She looked at him, seeking reassurance.

"Absolutely," he replied without hesitation, "and I know for sure a little scratch isn't going to stop a strong, brave girl like you. As soon as we've had something to eat, how about you and I go over to Nickelodean Beach and make some sandcastles?"

"Yay!" Patrice cheered, her skinned knee all but forgotten.

"Can I come?" Michael asked from the stroller.

"Of course you can." Christopher winked at Leroy. "How about you, buddy? You want to come build sandcastles on the beach?"

Leroy beamed. "Sandcastles!"

Lexi's heart filled with warm emotion. She looked at Christopher and mouthed *thank you.*

He gave her a smile so soft and tender, her stomach somersaulted with nerves. On top of all of his other amazing qualities, he was wonderful with her children. He'd make a perfect dad. She wondered if he was willing to take on all of them. It was an important consideration and something she needed to find out about before she fell all the way with no chance of a return.

Christopher saw the rush of emotions that passed across Lexi's face and his gut clenched with something that felt akin to panic. The way she looked at him, like he was beyond reproach; she'd put him on a pedestal and he sure as hell didn't deserve to be there.

Okay, so he'd been trying hard to be a better person, the kind of man she deserved, but he was still finding his way and right now, it felt like he could slip off just was easily. He was falling for her fast. Hell, he might already be in love with her. But she and the kids were a package deal and he had to be sure none of them would be hurt. He'd known that from the start.

Am I up for that? Am I up for that kind of responsibility? What if I let them down? Then again, Frank managed it. He took on someone else's son and he raised me to be the man I am today. If anyone let someone down, it was me...

He'd always wanted a family, but eight kids, with a promise of more to come was beyond anything he'd ever imagined. He wasn't at all certain he had what it took to be a good husband and father. What if he couldn't do it? What if he tried the best he could, but it still didn't work out? Did he even want to try?

Am I crazy?

Yes, he was crazy all right. Crazy for Lexi. And there wasn't a damn thing he could do about it.

Chapter Nineteen

Lexi sighed quietly as the lights of the farmhouse came into view. Christopher pulled the minibus into the driveway and switched off the ignition. Though it was only going on for six in the evening, all but Kishaya and Denzil had fallen asleep on the drive home.

The kids had wanted to stay at the water park right up until closing time to take advantage of every second of their time there. They'd been tired but happy when the security guards hunted them down.

After loading everyone back into the bus, Christopher had headed toward home. The trip had taken a little longer than it should have because Christopher had thoughtfully offered to drop the two nannies to their homes. Lexi didn't expect anything less of the Christopher she was fast falling for.

In the darkness of the interior, she turned to him and smiled. "Home sweet home."

His teeth glowed white in the dimness. "How do you want to do this?"

"Are you up to carrying Leroy inside? He's not all that heavy."

"Of course."

"I'll take Michael and come back for Patrice. We'll wake the others and they can walk."

Christopher grinned again. "Sounds like a plan." He paused and then added, "Do you want me to put Leroy straight to bed?"

"Yes, please. If he wakes later, I'll give him something to eat. Quite frankly, I think he ate enough junk food today to tide him over for a week."

Christopher smiled. "They had fun, didn't they?"

Lexi's heart melted. "Yes, they did. Thank you. What you did for us today... It was wonderful. You helped create special memories they'll have with them for life."

Christopher tried to dismiss her words with an embarrassed wave of his hand, but Lexi was having none of it.

"Trust me, Christopher. I know about this stuff. I've been there. I wish someone had done for me what you did for these kids today. For them it was like having a fairy godfather granting them their every wish. It was as incredible, as magical and as momentous as that."

She saw him swallow and then he compressed his lips and merely nodded, as if words were beyond him at that moment. She understood. She was feeling fairly emotional too.

Between the two of them, and with the help of Kishaya and Denzil, they got everyone inside and ready for bed. Christopher returned to the bus for the beach bags of wet towels and after asking Lexi for directions to her washing machine, he proceeded to put on a load. Lexi dressed the last child in her pajamas and tucked her into bed with a kiss before returning to the kitchen to put the kettle on.

She had just set it on the stove and lit the gas burner when Christopher walked back in. She looked at him and smiled.

"Thanks for that. If I don't stay on top of it, the washing we accumulate in this house would just about take over the place. I usually put on at least one load every day. And wet towels especially. They just start—"

"Smelling if you leave them lying round," Christopher finished.

Lexi's smile widened. "Exactly."

Christopher winked. "That's why I thought I'd throw them in the machine right away."

"Thank you. That was very thoughtful."

The kettle began to whistle. She looked back at him. "Would you like a cup of tea?"

"Thanks. Sounds good. Are the kids all in bed?"

"Yes. I think they were all asleep before I even left the room."

"It was a big day."

"Absolutely. The best day ever. They'll remember this day for a long time. So will I."

Their gazes caught and held. For a long moment, neither moved. Lexi flushed and broke the silence. "How do you take your tea?"

"Black, no sugar."

"The same as you take your coffee."

His answering smile made her belly flutter. "Yes."

Lexi busied herself pouring the tea. She added milk and sugar to hers. "Shall we sit on the couch?"

"Yes, let's. After you," he said, stepping aside for her to lead the way.

They settled on the sofa, close enough that if Lexi moved even a little, their legs would touch. She wondered if he'd done that deliberately when he settled down beside her. She hazarded a glance in his direction and found his gaze on hers. Her heart skipped a beat at the intensity in his green eyes. Heat crept up her neck and spread across her cheeks. She nervously averted her gaze.

She'd been so aware of his physicality all day. His nearness...his expensive cologne. His size and strength and dependability. He'd been so hands-on at the theme park. He'd helped out at every instance with the smaller children, taking turns watching over them, taking them on rides. Several times over the course of the afternoon he'd gone for a food run and come back with his arms laden with hotdogs, popcorn, fairy floss and soft drinks. The kids thought they were in heaven.

And then, of course, there had been the tantalizing sight of him near-naked. At several times during the day, he'd pulled off his T-shirt. His board shorts had hung low on his slim hips. His broad, tanned chest, with only the sprinkling of dark hair, was muscular and oh so enticing.

Now, with him seated a few inches away, her awareness of him skyrocketed. Her heart rate galloped, her palms were suddenly damp. She risked another glance at him and found his gaze still locked on her.

"Lexi..."

The desire that glittered in the green depths of his eyes made her breathless. Her chest went tight with an answering need. And then he leaned over and kissed her.

"I've been wanting to do that all day."

His voice was husky, with the same desire reflected in his eyes. Once again, her body flooded with the need to touch him, to kiss him, to have him touch and kiss her. There were so many questions that remained unanswered, but right then she couldn't think of a single one. On a sudden sigh of surrender, she took his head between her palms and kissed him back.

Just like the first time, passion ignited the moment their lips touched. She kissed him with everything she felt inside and was gratified at his equally passionate response. Though a part of her was nervous her lack of experience might be a turn-off, she figured making love was like riding a bike. She might not have done it for a while, but she was pretty sure she'd remember how when the time came.

And she wanted to find out. But she also didn't want any of the children stumbling across them if they happened to leave their beds for a drink or something to eat. Pulling slowly away from him, she stared at him.

Her breath came fast. So did his. He looked at her with a question in his eyes. It felt good knowing he wasn't pressuring her into anything she didn't want to do. She nodded slightly and the tension around his mouth relaxed.

"I want to make love to you, Christopher."

"I want to make love to you, too."

"But not here. The kids..."

He nodded. Some of the passion in his eyes dimmed. "I understand."

Lexi took his hand and squeezed it. "I don't mean not now. I mean, not *here*." She looked around them.

His eyes widened with comprehension. "Oh. So… You want to go to your bedroom?"

She blushed, but nodded shyly. "Is that all right?"

"Of course it's all right!" came his swift reply. And then he frowned. "But I want you to know, if you want to wait, that's fine with me, too. Today wasn't about scoring brownie points with you. Today was about you and the children. I wanted to do something special for them. For you. I don't expect anything in return."

Lexi stared at him and her heart filled with love.

Where did you come from? How can you be so perfect? I don't deserve someone as giving as you…

In response, she threw herself against him and kissed him thoroughly again. His lips, his eyes, his cheeks. She smothered his face in kisses. She'd never felt happier or more in love. There were still so many things they needed to talk about, to work through, to sort out… But practicalities could wait. Right now she wanted nothing more than to feel his bare skin moving against hers and love him all night long.

Christopher stood and lifted her in his arms like she weighed nothing. She protested, arguing that his shoulder wasn't ready for that kind effort, but he silenced her with a slow and sultry kiss. Full and sensuous, his lips felt like magic. She'd never been kissed like this. Like he was making love to every inch of her lips. Like that kiss was just as important as anything else they were going to do.

With her arms draped around his neck, she kissed him back. Murmuring quietly in his ear, she directed him down the hallway to her bedroom, grateful she'd had the foresight to close the doors of the children's bedrooms. He reached her partially open door and pushed it wider with his shoulder. Stepping inside, he slowly slid her down his long body until her feet finally touched the floor. She reveled in the feel of every hard, muscular inch of him.

They kissed again, over and over until finally it wasn't enough. She reached for his T-shirt and he helped her ease it over his head, revealing the same broad, tanned chest that she'd ogled at the water park. Now she ran her hands over the muscular peaks of his pectorals and the planes of his chest, relishing the feel of heat, strength and suppleness.

"I've been wanting to touch you like this ever since you first took off your shirt this morning."

He nuzzled her neck. "Why didn't you?"

She giggled. "In front of the children?"

He kept nuzzling. "Why not? Do you think they would have been shocked?"

"Of course! Well, maybe. You know, they probably would have just laughed, especially the little ones."

He gave her a wicked grin. "See? All that touching you could have done. You denied yourself for nothing."

She laughed. "Good thing I don't have to deny myself any longer."

With that, she ventured further to flick the pads of her thumbs across his nipples. They immediately pebbled in response. His eyes darkened. A groan escaped his lips. She marveled at her power.

"You like that?" she asked shyly.

"God, yes. I like it a lot. Do it again," came the husky response.

She smoothed her palms over his chest again, this time in a circular motion. As she drew closer to his nipples, she saw him tense. Instead of using her thumbs, she bent her head and flicked the hard nubs with her tongue.

"Lexi…"

Her name came out part cry, part groan. She swiped her tongue over his nipples again and this time took one of them into her mouth and suckled. His hands buried themselves in her hair, holding her head in place. She responded by kissing and licking and sucking his nipples, doing her best to drive him wild.

"You're driving me wild," he muttered, as if he could read her mind.

She looked up and grinned. His reaction gave her confidence. "Do you want me to stop?"

"Hell, no. But I think we need to remove some of your clothes. Fair's fair, right?"

She suddenly felt unaccountably shy about getting naked in front of him. The only other man to see her without her clothes on had been her husband. She was glad for the drawn curtains that largely shrouded the room in darkness, but still…

As if sensing her nervousness, Christopher kissed her gently on the lips. "Please, Lexi. I want to see every beautiful, desirable inch of you. After seeing you today in your bikini… I was in torture all day. I want—no, I need—to love you with my hands, my fingers, my lips. I promise we'll go as slow as you wish. Please…"

His final plea was low and husky. She felt it deep inside. Heat centered in her core and blossomed into almost overwhelming desire. While it had been four years since she'd slept with anyone, she was sure she'd never experienced such intensity of feeling.

Dragging in a fortifying breath, she stepped slightly away and began working on the buttons of her cotton blouse. Shrugging it off her shoulders, she let it drop to the floor. She still wore her bikini top beneath. Christopher reached behind her and loosened the tie. In short order, it was also on the floor.

She stood before him, topless. He looked his fill. When she went to automatically cover herself, he reached out and stilled her hands.

"Please, let me look at you. You're so beautiful."

To her relief, he took her in his arms and kissed her hungrily. His erection strained against her belly, full and hard. Suddenly impatient to feel his skin against hers, she reached down between them and began working on the drawstring of his board shorts. Her fingers got tangled. She cursed under her breath. Christopher brushed her hands away.

"Let me," he rasped.

In no time at all, he'd loosened the drawstring and shucked the board shorts down his lean hips. His underwear quickly followed. He stood before her naked, tall and proud and fully aroused. He looked down at her with eyes that glittered with possession. She now understood how he'd felt when he'd looked at her. She was mesmerized.

Slowly, he reached out to her and unsnapped the button on her denim cut-offs. He slid down the zip and then eased her shorts off her hips. She wiggled in an attempt to assist him and then stepped out of them. The only thing that remained was her bikini bottom.

The tiny black scrap of Lycra could hardly be called clothing. It barely covered anything and yet, when she stood fully naked before him, it was all she could do not to turn and hide herself under the bedclothes.

Once again, Christopher appeared sensitive to her needs. He took her by the hand and led her to the bed. They sat down together and tenderly cupping her face in his hands, he kissed her long and thoroughly. As the passion and heat began to build once again between them, they slid sideways and rolled onto the bed. Christopher lay on top of her. Her arms went around his shoulders and then clung to his neck.

Like she'd done to him, he made his way down her body, licking and suckling her nipples, flicking the hard nubs with his tongue. She arched up against him, moaning with desire. He caught her moans in his mouth.

They kissed like they couldn't get enough and for Lexi, that was true. She arched her back, pressing her breasts against him. He responded by rubbing his chest against hers. His erection felt hot and heavy against her stomach. Reaching down between their bodies, she encircled the thick length with her fingers and squeezed.

"Lexi... Oh, God..."

His tongue invaded her mouth, thrusting in and out of her warmth. Her hand mimicked the rhythm of his tongue, opening and closing around his cock. Sticky fluid leaked from the tip. She smeared it over the head of his cock.

Once again, he groaned her name. He moved his hand down lower, finding her slick with need. He slid one finger inside her, rubbing back and forth. She gasped at the movement. He added a second finger, stretching her. She burned with need. She had to have him before she combusted. She let her legs fall further open and moaned for more. He shifted and came up on his elbows, gazing down at her.

"Are you sure you want this?" he asked.

She couldn't believe he was prepared to stop if she only said the word.

"I'm sure."

Excitement leaped in his eyes. He moved away from her and fished around on the floor for his wallet. A few moments later, he sheathed himself and came back to her, settling himself between her thighs. He leaned over her and kissed her deeply. At the same time, he nudged at her opening. She braced herself for his entry.

Instead of a hard thrust, Christopher eased himself into her wetness. She clung to his shoulders, feeling her inner muscles stretch to accommodate him. When he was fully seated, he rested his forehead against hers to catch his breath.

"Oh, God. Lexi... You feel so incredible... So warm... So wet... So tight..."

His erotic words sent her desire skyrocketing. She lifted her hips and urged him on. Taking the hint, he began to move. His thrusts were strong and sure and filled with confidence. He made love the same way he kissed—with a thoroughness and a level of expertise she'd never experience. He was a considerate lover, holding back from reaching his own fulfillment until she'd found hers.

As desire built deep inside her, she concentrated on the powerful feelings he generated inside her. She held onto his shoulders and met his thrusts, her legs tightened around his hips. Together they moved and soared. She reached the precipice and with a gasp of ecstasy and relief, toppled over the other side, finding her release.

She'd hardly had a chance to catch her breath before Christopher picked up the pace and began thrusting hard. His face grew taut as he drew closer to his goal. She tightened her hold on him and as he reached his climax, she pulled him close against her.

His breath was harsh in her ear. Gradually, his breathing slowed, as did the sound of his racing heart. He came up on one elbow and gazed down at her, a look of wonder on his face.

"I love you," he whispered.

She fell asleep with a smile on her face.

Chapter Twenty

The sun peeked through the faded curtains in Lexi's bedroom. Christopher slowly came awake. He looked at the woman who was still asleep beside him. He couldn't believe they'd made love. It was everything he could have dreamed of and more. He'd been with countless women, but he'd never before been with a woman he was in love with.

At least, he was fairly sure love was what he felt. He wanted to be with Lexi every minute of the night and day. He wanted to make her happy. Make her laugh. He wanted to take care of her, protect her, keep her safe. He wanted to share his dreams, his fears, his joys with her, and her children.

He never dreamed he'd be happy at the thought of becoming an instant father to eight children, but he wasn't only happy at the idea, he was excited. He just hoped Lexi felt the same way. After all, he'd said the "L" word and she hadn't said it back. Of course, she'd fallen asleep right afterwards.

He couldn't help feeling slightly smug at having worn her out so thoroughly with his lovemaking. It had been an indescribable feeling seeing her head thrown back in ecstasy and the soft pleasure in her eyes as she came down.

Would she say it back? Did she feel the same?

Feeling suddenly nervous, he cleared his throat. She stirred beside him and slowly opened her eyes and smiled.

"Good morning," she said.

He smiled back. "Good morning. I was beginning to think you might not ever wake. How does a mom of eight get to sleep in so late?"

She stretched and grinned. "What time is it?"

"Seven."

"It's Sunday. The kids always sleep in on Sunday. It's an unspoken rule."

He kissed her on the nose. "I like that rule."

Her grin widened. "I thought you might."

Christopher put his good arm around her and drew her close. She rested her head on his chest. It felt so good, so natural.

"I had such a great time yesterday," he said.

Lexi looked up at him tenderly. "So did I. We all did. Thank you again for making it happen. You're the kindest, most generous, sweetest man I know."

Christopher frowned. Though he'd confessed to her about his past, about the kind of man he used to be, it still concerned him that she had him up on some kind of pedestal, imagining him to be much more than he was. Better than he was. He might be doing all he could to improve himself, but he was a long way from sweet.

"Have you forgotten what I told you? How much of an asshole I was?"

Lexi reached up and cupped his cheek, her gaze fixed on his. "*Was*. Not *now*. I don't know what happened to make you change your ways, but the fact is, you have. You're not that person when you're with me and the children. All I see is someone good and kind and decent. Honest, generous and real. I'm an excellent judge of character. Trust me, I know you. I *see* you, Christopher Barrington. I see a man I've fallen in love with."

Christopher's jaw dropped. He stared at her. His heart pounded. "Did you... Did you just say you've fallen in love with me?"

Lexi grinned. "Yes. How does that make you feel?"

"Terrified. Elated. Overjoyed." He gathered her close and kissed her over and over on her eyes, her lips, her cheeks.

"I love you, Lexi Greenaway. I don't know when it crept up on me, but you've stolen my heart. I'm so happy you feel the same way."

They shared a tender, loving kiss that left them both breathless. When Lexi finally pulled away, she looked up at him and then a slight frown appeared. Christopher's heart tightened on a frisson of concern.

"What is it, Lexi?"

She averted her eyes and chewed on her lower lip. His consternation increased. "Please, Lexi. What's wrong?"

"I'm thrilled that you love me, Christopher. I truly am. After Ronnie died, I didn't think I'd ever feel this way again. But... It's not just me you have to love. I come with eight children. Probably more in the future. I can't see a time when I won't want to foster needy children. So it's not just me. We're a package."

Her gaze was still fixed on the bedspread. He could almost feel the waves of uncertainty that washed over her. With infinite gentleness, he tilted her chin up with his finger and almost teared up at the vulnerability in her eyes. He pressed a soft, lingering kiss against her lips, her eyelids.

"You silly duffer," he teased. "Don't you think I know that? Of course you're a package deal. I'll admit the thought of becoming an instant father to eight children is a little daunting, but I've never backed away from a challenge and I look forward to taking this one on. With help from you, of course."

The love in her eyes took his breath away. "I couldn't think of anyone I'd rather have by my side."

He dragged her back into his arms and kissed her thoroughly. Feeling more at peace than he ever had in his life, he threaded their fingers together and pressed a kiss against the back of her hand.

"There's something else I'd like to run by you," he said and then felt a fresh wave of nervousness.

She quirked an eyebrow at him. "Oh?"

"I've been thinking about our problem."

"Which problem is that?"

"The fact you have to vacate this farmhouse and don't have enough money to buy another place at this point. Or at least one close to the city."

She smiled slightly. "Oh, so it's *our* problem now? That's so sweet."

He chuckled, feeling a little more confident. "Of course it's our problem. I want to help you find a solution and... I think I have."

She came up on one elbow and looked down at him, her eyes now filled with curiosity and a little wariness. "I'm all ears."

"It's actually something Kishaya came up with. Do you remember the crowdfunding idea?"

Lexi nodded.

Christopher continued. "I've done a little research. It's a good idea. I think we could raise some serious money that way. Whatever you still need. I've always figured you'd need around a million dollars. It's possible we could crowdfund the shortfall."

Her eyes widened in shock. "But I'm short fifty thousand dollars!"

He kept his gaze on hers. "Yes."

"Fifty thousand dollars! Are you insane? Would ordinary people actually donate that much?"

Christopher nodded. "People love to get behind good causes. What you're doing for so many vulnerable children is more than worthy. Being a foster mom is something a lot of people can't take on, but they'll gladly support you in other ways—like, with their money.

"I give regularly to my favorite charities. I'm not one to go and volunteer on a stand somewhere or hand out flyers to raise awareness, but I'm more than happy to lend my support in a financial way. I know a lot of other people, even big corporates, who'd gladly assuage their social conscience by donating to a worthy cause. You might not even have to dip into the kids' college fund."

Lexi's eyes were wide. "Really? You think that would work?"

"Yes. I'd be happy for the kids to help set it up and then to make a few calls, call in some favors…" He paused and gave her a crooked grin. "I have friends in high places. With a bit of luck, you'd have enough money to buy somewhere else that suits your needs. I'm thinking some more acreage—but maybe with a house that is in slightly better repair than this."

She shook her head, as if dazed. "I can't believe you'd be willing to do that for us. For me."

Christopher sat up. Lexi wriggled up to sit beside him. He turned to her and framed her face with his hands.

"I love you, Lexi. I want to take care of you. But even before that, before I knew how I felt about you, I wanted to help you. You're the most amazing woman I've met! You're good and kind and wonderful. What you've done for these children and all the other children who've come into your care… The whole twenty-seven of them… It blows my mind! I've never met anyone like you. You're… You're a saint!"

Lexi burst out laughing. "Oh, my goodness Christopher! A saint? Hardly! But I thank you for your kind words. Truly. I'm no one special. Just an ordinary woman trying to live the best life I can. I want to help needy children. So I do. There's nothing more to it."

Christopher pulled her close and hugged her tightly. "There's so much more to it and you know it," he muttered against the softness of her hair, "but we're not going to argue about it. As long as you agree to let me help you raise the money, we'll be fine."

She pulled back and looked up at him. "Of course I'll let you help! I'd be mad not to! You know, I would never have said this a month ago, but if what you say is true, this might be a blessing in disguise. Just imagine if your father's company had never purchased this place from my in-laws? I'd still be here, living in this old place, patching up leaks and thinking nothing of it.

"Now I'm dreaming about how we could expand things, buy a bigger place, with more bedrooms, more space for the kids to play. There'd be no limit to the number of kids we could help."

Christopher's chest exploded with warmth. Unfamiliar emotion burned behind his eyes. Lexi noticed the change in his expression and frowned.

"Christopher? What is it? What did I say?"

He bit his lip to stop it from trembling and shook his head. "It's nothing."

Lexi's frown deepened. She laid her hand against his cheek, forcing him to look at her. "It doesn't seem like nothing."

Christopher drew in a deep, cleansing breath. "Okay. I'll tell you. You mentioned the word 'we.'"

Lexi looked confused. "I don't understand."

"You said *we* could expand and *we* could help more kids. I'm not sure if you're aware of it, but... You included me in your plans."

Her expression softened. She leaned forward and kissed him softly on the lips. "So I did. Are you okay with that?"

He grinned. "More than okay."

⸎

Christopher ran to the shops and stocked up on bacon, eggs and pancake mix and made it back to Lexi's just as the children began stirring. They'd decided that getting the children used to having him around should begin with finding him in the kitchen, not Lexi's bedroom. Patrice was the first one to appear, quickly followed by Michael and Stella. The children saw him standing by the stove wearing Lexi's apron and laughed.

"You look funny," Michael said.

"Are you cooking breakfast?" Patrice asked.

"Yes. Bacon and eggs and pancakes. Who's hungry?"

"Me!" all three of them chorused.

Twelve-year-old Stella moved closer. "Why are you still here? Did you stay the night?"

Christopher blushed under her curious regard. "Um, yes. I did. Is that okay?"

Stella merely shrugged. "I guess."

Leroy toddled into the room, still dressed in his pajamas and wiping sleep out of his eyes. He saw Christopher and a smile broke out on his face. He walked over and tugged on Christopher's leg. "Up."

Christopher frowned. Fortunately, Stella came to his rescue.

"He wants you to pick him up."

"Oh," Christopher responded, feeling a little flustered. Though he'd spent all day with the children yesterday that had mostly been in the company of Lexi and the two nannies. The thought of interacting with them by himself was daunting.

Leroy lifted his arms up above his head. Taking the hint, Christopher set down the spatula he'd been using to turn the pancakes and picked up Leroy. The little boy straddled Christopher's hip and snuggled against him.

"Pancakes. Yum," the boy said, pointing to the pan.

"Yes. You like pancakes?"

"Yes!" Leroy replied.

The next two people to appear in the kitchen were Josie and Demi. Though both girls were dressed in T-shirts and shorts, their hair was in a mess. They both looked surprised to see him.

"Christopher! What are you doing here?" Josie asked.

Demi gave him a sly smile. "Did you spend the night with my mom?"

Once again, Christopher felt a guilty blush steal across his cheeks. Instead of replying, he prayed silently for Lexi to hurry up and finish in the shower and busied himself at the stove.

"Who wants pancakes?" he asked.

Once again, he was met with a chorus of cheers. He directed the children to get plates out of the cupboard, including plastic ones for Leroy, Patrice and Michael, and began serving pancakes.

"There's also bacon and eggs in the oven, if anyone wants them. I cooked them earlier."

He didn't get any takers and made a mental note not to bother with the bacon and eggs next time. And then Kishaya and Denzil walked in.

"I smell bacon," Kishaya said. "Is there any left?"

"Yes," Christopher said, turning to her with a grin. "It's in the oven."

Denzil was a little less talkative. He shot Christopher a wary look. "You stayed the night."

Christopher regarded him solemnly. He was sensitive enough to the teenager's feelings that he understood the need to tread carefully. The last thing he wanted was for the boy to feel Christopher was usurping his place as the man of the family.

"Would you like something to eat?" Christopher asked.

"Yes thanks," Denzil said quietly. "Bacon and eggs, please."

"Grab a plate and I'll serve you," Christopher replied.

Denzil did as he was asked and Christopher filled his plate. The boy murmured his thanks and turned and headed toward the table where the younger children were already busily eating their pancakes and chattering loudly, non-stop. Then Lexi walked in and Christopher breathed a silent sigh of relief.

"Good morning everyone!" Lexi cried. Moving from one child to the next, she greeted them all with a kiss.

Christopher filled two more plates and came to join them at the table. Like they had the last time he'd eaten with them, the children shuffled along the long wooden bench and made room for him beside Lexi.

"Are you and my momma in love?" Demi asked.

Christopher stole a glance at Lexi. Her cheeks were just as hot as his felt. He turned back to Demi and answered her.

"Yes, Demi. We are. Is that okay?"

Demi and Stella looked at each other and giggled. Then Demi looked back at him again. "I guess so."

"Are you going to get married?" Patrice asked in an earnest voice.

Once again, Christopher fought against a blush and once again, he sought help from Lexi. She merely looked at him and grinned.

"Well, we haven't talked about marriage, but...maybe...one day. If your mom wants to..."

Eight pairs of eyes turned toward Lexi. Christopher felt sorry for her coming under so much intense scrutiny.

Maybe we should have thought this over a bit more when I suggested I'd cook breakfast for everyone? Maybe I should have simply left before any of them woke up?

Now it was too late. Now everyone at the table knew he'd spent the night and those old enough to know exactly what that meant were looking at him with questions in their eyes. No doubt this was only the beginning of the inquisition, and to be fair to the children, they had the right to know. Any change in their mother's relationship status would have a direct impact on the kids and they knew it.

Lexi still hadn't responded. Christopher came to her rescue. He looked around the table. "Would you be okay with it if we did get married?"

"Yes!" Patrice and Michael chorused.

Christopher's gaze moved from one child to another. Most of them nodded their approval. Only Denzil remained quiet, neither affirming nor denying. It was more than Christopher expected and he felt himself relax. He smiled toward Lexi.

"It looks like I've won at least some of them over. Good thing we have plenty of time."

He looked directly at Denzil. "Feel free to speak your mind, Denzil. Ask me anything you want. I understand your reservations. After all, your mother and I haven't known each other very long. But sometimes when you're with the right person, time's immaterial. You just know they're the one." His gaze went back to Lexi and his heart swelled. "That's how I feel about your mother."

Once again, his gaze traveled slowly around the table. "I meant what I said to Denzil about asking me questions. The same goes for all of you. Ask me anything, anytime. One thing I promise is that I'll always be upfront and honest with you. That's the least you deserve."

From the corner of his eye, he saw Lexi swipe at her eyes. She cleared her throat. "I just want to say how proud I am of you all. Having Christopher here, in our lives, has come as a surprise. To me, too. But what he says is true. I love him with all my heart. He's a good and caring man and I feel blessed that he's in my life. You all know how important you are to me. You are my first priority and that won't change. I've explained that to Christopher and he understands. I hope as you get to know him, you'll embrace him into *your* lives. And maybe one day you might even love him as I do."

Unable to help himself, Christopher stood and tugged Lexi to her feet. In front of all the children, he took her in his arms and kissed her thoroughly. The children cheered. Even the older ones smiled. When it was over and Christopher had released Lexi—who looked a little dazed—he took a theatrical bow. The children cheered again.

Breakfast continued to be a noisy, rowdy affair with Christopher fielding several questions and asking a few of his own. They relived their experience at the water park and then argued good-naturedly about which were the best slides. There were also plenty of comments about Christopher's pancakes. The general consensus was that they were good and the key question was when he could cook them again.

The conversation switched to the imminent move and where the family might relocate. Lexi had told Christopher she'd talked to all of the children about the sale and what it would mean for them. The little ones were excited about moving to somewhere that might have a pool. The older kids were concerned they might have to change schools.

Though Christopher hadn't yet started searching for real estate nearby that might suit their needs, he was confident that with the money they'd raised at Elizabeth's event and the potential success of crowdfunding, they'd find something suitable. He needed to move forward sooner rather than later as his father was keen to make a start on phase one of his development project. Christopher was getting the same kind of pressure from Nicholas Craigdon. Everyone involved was keen to get started. Christopher was pleased he'd be able to report back to his father that everything was on track.

With that thought in mind, he excused himself from the table and found a quiet spot outside. He composed a text to his father.

Good news! Your little problem with that recalcitrant tenant has been solved. She's moving out. Start those excavators!

He added a few wink emojis so that his father could tell he was speaking tongue in cheek and then walked back inside.

The table had been cleared and Lexi and the older children were now in the kitchen attending to the washing up.

Kishaya wore rubber gloves and had her arms in a sinkful of suds. Denzil was clearing the table. Lexi held a tea towel. Christopher offered to help. Lexi told him they had everything under control.

"In that case, I might use the bathroom." Leaving his phone on the counter, he headed down the corridor to the only bathroom.

Chapter Twenty One

After Denzil left the room, Lexi shot a sideways glance at Kishaya. The girl appeared to have taken their declaration of love pretty well. She'd even smiled when Christopher had so spontaneously and passionately kissed her. But it was important to Lexi that she be certain that her oldest child was on board with her burgeoning relationship.

"So, what do you think about Christopher?" Lexi asked. She deliberately kept her tone casual and continued to dry the plate in her hand.

Kishaya glanced at her and then focused her attention on the sink. "He's all right, I guess."

"What do you think about me dating him?"

A one-shouldered shrug. "I think it's good."

Lexi blinked in surprise. "You do?"

"Yes. You and Ronnie were a great couple, but he's been gone a long time and I hate to tell you this, Mom, but he's not coming back."

Kishaya lifted her gaze to Lexi's. They sparkled with tears. "Ronnie was cool. I really liked him. I know you did, too. Those of us kids who knew him, we miss him, but we have to go on. That includes you. You're not so old. You deserve to have someone to share your life with. You've got us, but I'm not so stupid to think you mustn't be lonely for some adult companionship every now and then." She paused and then added, "Christopher seems nice enough and he said he loves you and you love him. Maybe that makes it worth a shot."

Tears burned behind Lexi's eyes at the sensitivity and maturity in her oldest young daughter. It took her completely by surprise.

"When did you get so wise?" she choked and then hugged her close.

"Okay, Mom. You need to let go now."

Reluctantly, Lexi released her hold and swiped at the tears on her cheeks.

Kishaya gave an exaggerated eye roll. "You're not going to cry on me, are you?"

"No, of course not. You know I'm not a cry baby."

Kishaya smiled wryly. "Yeah, right."

Lexi picked up another wet plate and started wiping it. Kishaya returned her attention to the sink.

"So, just to be clear, Christopher has your stamp of approval?" Lexi asked.

Kishaya looked at her steadily, a grin tugged at her lips. "Yes, Mom. He has my stamp of approval. If you want to jump his bones, I say go for it!"

"Kishaya!" Lexi gasped in mock outrage.

Kishaya grinned unrepentantly. "Just saying."

They continued to work in silence. Kishaya was the first one to break it.

"What happened to your grandmother's brooch?"

Lexi frowned. "What do you mean?"

"I was in your room yesterday looking for a hairband and I noticed it was gone. I know how important it is to you. I wanted to make sure no one's taken it. I caught Patrice and Michael playing in your room the other day."

Lexi shook her head. "I appreciate your concern, but it's fine. No one's taken it. I... I sold it."

Kishaya's mouth gaped. "You *sold* it?"

"Yes. We needed the money. You know we have to find somewhere else to live. I have some money set aside and we raised a good deal from that posh event I went to last weekend, but every bit counts."

Kishaya looked upset. "But it belonged to your grandmother! Don't you care about that?"

Kishaya had been with Lexi the longest of all her children. She knew the most about Lexi's past.

"Of course I care, honey, but... Like I said... We need the money. I can't expect Christopher to raise all of it."

"I could help! I could get a part-time job. Maybe at the local supermarket. I could work there after school."

Lexi's heart melted. Once again, she pulled Kishaya in for a hug. "You're so sweet. I love that you'd do that for me, for us. But it isn't necessary. We'll find the money. In fact, Christopher thinks your crowdfunding idea might just work. He said we might even raise as much as fifty thousand dollars. Can you believe that?"

Kishaya grinned. "Really? He liked my idea?"

"Yes, he sure did. He's going to get you to help set up a page and he's even willing to contact some big corporates and see if they'll donate to our cause."

"That's great news! I like him even more now." Kishaya winked. "He's a keeper, Mom. Don't let him get away."

Lexi laughed, so relieved Kishaya was on board. Stacking the dry plates in the plate rack, Lexi spied the small pile of letters she'd received from Barrington Developments tucked away down the side. It seemed so long ago since she'd received the first one, when she'd thought her world had been turned on its end. Now she'd met Christopher and her life couldn't get any better.

It's funny how things work out. What I thought was a curse has turned into a blessing...

She recalled all that Christopher had told her about Frank Barrington. He sounded like a truly remarkable man. She hadn't been given the opportunity to meet him at the fundraiser and now she wished she had. On impulse, she pulled out one of the letters and scanned it for a phone number. She'd call their office and let them know she was no longer a thorn in their side.

She could hear Christopher talking to some of the children in one of the other rooms. They were laughing about something. They sounded like they were having fun. Her heart turned over with love.

Pulling out her phone, she tapped in the numbers. She didn't expect anyone to answer at Barrington Mining because it was Sunday, but just on the off chance someone was there... Just in case Frank was there... She really wanted to speak with him. She wanted to thank him for all he'd done for Christopher and to congratulate him on his wonderful son.

The call rang out. She braced herself for a message service to cut in and was surprised when the call was answered.

"Barrington Mining."

"Oh, this is Lexi Greenaway. I was wondering if I could speak with Frank Barrington."

"Mrs Greenaway. This is Frank Barrington. It's nice to hear from you again."

"Oh, Mr Barrington. I—"

"Please, call me Frank."

"Okay, Frank. I… I just wanted to call to let you know I'm no longer fighting your eviction orders. We… We're going to be moving out. Just as soon as I find somewhere else to live."

"I'm pleased to hear that. Might I ask what changed your mind?"

"Your son. Christopher. He's…a very special man."

Her voice had gone husky with emotion. She cleared her throat and spoke again. "You've done a wonderful job in raising him. He… He told me a bit about his past. You're a truly lovely man. I look forward to meeting you."

Frank didn't bother to hide his surprise. "Wow. That's very nice of you to say. I can't take all the credit. His mom had a fair bit to do with it, too. And Christopher has worked hard to become the man he is today. He should rightly feel proud of himself."

"That's what I keep telling him," Lexi said.

"I hope he's listening to you. Anyway, thanks for the call. I appreciate it," Frank said.

"No problem."

With that, Lexi ended the call. Setting the phone down on the counter, she breathed out a gentle sigh. Frank Barrington sounded every bit as nice as Christopher had painted him. She couldn't wait to meet him face to face.

***

Frank stared down at the phone he still held in his hand. He'd already read the text sent by Christopher confirming the deal had been done: Lexi Greenaway had agreed to vacate. The contents of her call hadn't come as a surprise. What was surprising was the way she'd talked about his son. She'd told Frank how special Christopher was. It was because of Christopher that she'd agreed to move out. But it was the tone in her voice whenever she mentioned Christopher's name that had Frank curious.

He recalled the lavish way Christopher had described the woman the last time they'd discussed her situation. Christopher had called her amazing. Frank had even joked that Christopher sounded like he'd fallen in love with her.

I wonder what's really going on… Has my son finally found love?

The thought pleased him. For too long, Christopher had lived his life through a prism of bitterness, hurt and disappointment. It had turned him into a man he wasn't proud of. But lately, he'd been working hard to turn his life around, along with his attitude. It seemed from what Lexi Greenaway had said that he was succeeding.

Christopher had agreed to take on the challenge of finding a workable solution for all concerned as far as the eviction went and it appeared he'd gone out of his way to help her. Of course, if what Christopher said was true, she was an extraordinary woman doing extraordinary things, but Frank's gut told him this was something more. This woman was important to Christopher. He really hoped his son had found true love.

He thought of Evelyn and smiled. Three decades married and she still made his heart beat faster. He wanted that for Christopher. In fact, he prayed for that for all of his children. So far, he was still waiting for his prayers to be answered.

Not that he was deterred by the fact not a single one of his nine children were married. Not a single one of them were even in love. It would happen. All in good time. And from what he could tell, it might have just happened for Christopher first. Frank couldn't help but smile.

Tapping on his phone, he replied to Christopher's text.

Congratulations! Job well done! Looks like you scored yourself $500k.

Lexi grabbed the broom and started sweeping the kitchen floor, like she did after every meal. With eight kids in the house, two of them under five, there were always messes and spills to clean up. It was all part of the job. After their chat, Kishaya had headed off to somewhere else in the house, most likely to her bedroom to text with her friends. Christopher was still playing with the younger ones. He'd come in a while ago looking for a hairbrush.

"Josie wants me to plait her hair," he'd explained.

Lexi had shot him a dubious look. "Have you ever plaited hair before?"

"No, but it can't be that hard. Besides, we'll have fun trying."

Lexi had grinned and shook her head and told him where he could find the hairbrush. He'd taken the time to give her a quick kiss and then disappeared again. The sound of Christopher's phone beeping snagged her attention. He'd left it on the counter. It pleased her that he didn't feel the need to stay tied to it every second of the day, like some people did. In fact, he hadn't looked at it since he'd used it earlier that morning.

She walked over and picked it up. Curious, she looked at the screen. It was a text from Frank. She wondered if he'd said anything about her call. Feeling a little guilty, she quickly scanned the message and froze.

"Looks like you scored yourself $500k?" *What the hell does that mean?*

An icy trickle of dread crept through her veins. Shock and a burgeoning anger, along with a growing sense of betrayal flooded through her. Rooted to the floor, unable to move, she wasn't even aware of Christopher entering the room until he spoke.

Christopher bounced into the kitchen bursting to tell Lexi about how well he'd done plaiting Josie's hair, but one look at her pale and stricken face pulled him up short.

"Lexi? Honey? What's the matter? What's happened?"

She turned her dazed gaze toward him. Without a word, she handed him his phone. He glanced down at the screen and dread filled his gut. He looked up at her.

"Lexi. Please, let me explain. This isn't what you think."

"Oh, so your father isn't paying you half a million dollars for successfully convincing me to leave without a fight?"

Her eyes narrowed, filled with accusation. Her voice was harsh with anger and hurt.

This isn't good… This isn't good at all… I need to make her understand…

He thought fast, canvassing several ideas and discarding them just as quickly. The old Christopher would have reached for the easiest lie he could find and put it across so convincingly, everything would be smoothed over in no time. But he wasn't that man anymore. He'd vowed to live his life with more honor and he'd meant that. So he settled for the truth.

In a calm, soft tone, he explained himself. "My father told me about the difficulties he was having with a tenant who was refusing to vacate. I was in between jobs. I offered to help him. He told me how important it was for his development project and the time when the first sod could be turned was fast approaching. He offered me an incentive if I could persuade the tenant—you—to leave as soon as possible."

"A half a million dollars. That's some incentive." Lexi's tone was flat, her eyes still hard.

Christopher nodded. "You're right. It's a lot of money, but I would have done it without the financial incentive. You already know how good my father has been to me throughout my life and that there were many years when I didn't appreciate that. You also know how I've been trying hard to turn my life around, become a better man, someone worthy of Frank Barrington's love and respect.

"So I agreed to the deal, but I would have done it anyway because I wanted to help him out. He really needed this place to be vacated so it didn't hold up his plans."

Lexi snorted in disgust. "So all this time, laying on the charm, being so nice to us, to me... It was all a ruse. Part of your stupid game. All aimed at getting me to agree to move out."

"No! Lexi! God, no! Please, you have to believe me."

She glared at him, her expression cold and unforgiving. Feeling a little desperate, he scrubbed a hand through his hair and tried another tack to convince her.

"The first time I arrived, I was here on a mission to convince you to move out. Barrington Developments was the legal owner. We'd given you more than the notice required under the legislation. I came here merely to remind you of your obligation to vacate. I'll admit the thought of using my charm on you had crossed my mind, but more than that, I knew we had the law on our side. I was sure, once you'd taken the time to see that, you'd move out. After all, what choice did you have?"

Her lip curled up in disgust. "You're right. What choice did we have? We never stood a chance against a billion-dollar corporation such as Barrington Developments. You would have squashed us like a bug."

He shook his head, appalled. "No, Lexi. You're wrong. And that's not fair. If my father had wanted to go down that path, he could have instigated legal proceedings against you well before I got involved. That's the thing. Frank didn't want to get heavy-handed. He was hoping you'd see sense. Hence, the reason he asked me to meet with you."

"Oh, yes. You met with me all right," she said caustically. "You charmed yourself right into my life. And into the lives of my children... Into my bed. All on a lie."

Her expression was a mixture of hurt and bitterness. The sight of it broke his heart. It also sent him into a panic.

I have to get through to her... I have to make her see... Before I lose her forever...

"No, Lexi. That's where you're wrong. It wasn't a lie. Never a lie. It didn't take me long to realize how special you were. You'd fostered twenty-seven children! And for the past four years, you'd been doing that on your own! I'd never met someone as good and kind and selfless as you. You were everything I wasn't and like I yearn to be.

"I was drawn to your goodness. I wanted to spend time with you, bask in your joyful positivity, and even though I knew I didn't deserve to be in your orbit, I couldn't stay away."

Some of the tension eased from Lexi's face. Encouraged, Christopher continued.

"My mission had been to meet with you and convince you to leave, but as I got to know you, I realized it wasn't going to be as simple as that. The law might have been on our side, but putting you and your children out of your home and onto the street wasn't just or right.

"Your in-laws had treated you abominably. Selling your house out from underneath you without even having the decency to consult you about it first—or to tell you about it afterwards. The injustice of it infuriated me. You know, I went over to see them. I wanted to impress upon them how despicably they'd acted."

Lexi looked at him in surprise. "You went to see my in-laws?"

"Yes." "How did you know where they lived?"

"I tracked them down through the address they'd provided on the sale contract. It was in Camden."

Lexi nodded, looking a little dazed. "Yes, that's where they live."

"I knocked on their door. Only your mother-in-law was home. Apparently George was out golfing with his buddies."

"He does like to golf..." Lexi said faintly.

"Anyway, I tried to shame your mother-in-law into handing over some of the money, but she refused. We exchanged some pretty harsh words, but she held her ground. So I had a mate of mine look into their finances."

Lexi gasped. "You looked into their finances? Isn't that illegal?"

Christopher waved away her question. "The point is, it doesn't matter. It seems the vast bulk of the money they received from the sale of your house had already been spent."

"That's... That's what they told me," Lexi whispered.

"Yes. That's when I knew pursuing your in-laws through the courts was a waste of time and money. Even if we succeeded in an action against them, it would be a hollow judgement. There's no money left to recover. They have barely enough left to cover the legal costs."

He eyed her steadily, pleased that some of the anger in her eyes had dissipated. "So I started looking at other options. Staying here was out of the question. I had to come up with a solution that helped you find somewhere else to live.

Something that catered to your needs. Somewhere close to your kids' schools."

Lexi looked at him in surprise. "You thought about the kids and their schools?"

"Yes. After you told me about Ronnie's insurance money, I knew it was possible if we could come up with a bit more cash, there was a fair chance we could find another place that ticked all the boxes, or at least most of them. I sought advice from my stepmother. She's always been a great source of support and encouragement for me. Elizabeth's suggestion of a fundraiser filled me with hope and excitement. It was an opportunity to set things right."

Lexi nodded. "It was a wonderful night."

"Yes. And though we raised a good chunk of change, it wasn't enough. I kept thinking about other ways I could make up the difference." He shot her a sideways glance. "I thought about simply writing you a check, but I didn't think you'd accept it and I'd have understood your reaction. Everyone has their pride. I didn't want you to feel like a charity case, because you're not.

"I remembered Kishaya talking about crowdfunding. The idea had real appeal. We talked about it this morning, remember?" He scrubbed a hand over the bristles on his cheeks. "Hell, was it really only this morning?"

"I told Kishaya how much you liked her idea," Lexi said slowly. "She was stoked."

"I still think it's a good idea and I think she can help. I hope you do, too."

Lexi slowly nodded. "Yes."

Christopher moved slowly toward her and closed the distance between them. When he was a few feet away, he stopped.

"I'm sorry, Lexi. The deal with my father was nothing. A bit of fun. Yes, it's a lot of money, but it has nothing to do with you or the way I feel about you. As soon as I met you, everything changed. My world was turned on its end. This wasn't a game for me. The way I feel about you... The fact I love you... I've never been more serious about anything in my life. I hope you believe that."

Her expression softened. Her mouth tilted upwards in an uncertain smile. "I believe you."

Relief poured through Christopher. He took a big step forward and enveloped her in a hug. He held her tightly against him. He kissed her and then buried his face in her hair. He couldn't believe how close he'd come to messing everything up. Messing up the only good thing in his life, the best thing to ever happen to him.

After a long moment, Lexi lifted her head. "Thank you for being honest with me. I appreciate that."

Christopher smiled. "I promised the kids I'd always be upfront with them. I mean that for you, too. I hope that's okay with you?"

Lexi's face lit up. Christopher's heart turned over at her glowing smile.

"That's more than okay," she whispered.

They shared another tender kiss. When they finally pulled away, Lexi spoke again.

"There's just one request."

"Name it."

"Could you do me a favor and hold off on the bulldozers until we've found another place and the kids get settled? Would that be okay?"

He grinned. "They'll be using excavators. Bulldozers aren't suitable for this kind of demolition work, but absolutely. Nothing will happen until you and the kids are well clear of this place. You have my word."

Chapter Twenty Two

The next few days for Lexi passed by in a blur, made up of school commitments for the older children, poring over property listings on the Internet and spending her nights wrapped in Christopher's arms. She knew there would come a time when he'd be too busy or too tired to make the long trip from his apartment in Waverton to her place well south of the city, but she decided she wouldn't think about that and instead, would enjoy whatever time they had together.

Though they'd both declared their love and Christopher had mentioned the "M" word, there had been no further discussion about the future. Lexi was fine with that. There was a lot going on, not the least being the pressure to find a new house. Christopher had told her Frank was keen to move on the project. No doubt he wouldn't wait forever.

But right now she had dental appointments for the three youngest in the city. She'd driven them all to the train station and they'd caught the train into town. It was a ninety-minute train journey, but one they'd done plenty of times before.

Leroy was in his stroller. Michael and Patrice walked on either side of her. When she needed them to stay close in the crowds, she made sure they held onto the stroller. It worked well and was easier than trying to battle the traffic into the city, and dealing with the hassle of finding somewhere to park near the dental clinic.

On the way in, she'd called Christopher, hoping they might be able to catch up for lunch, but he'd apologized and told her he was stuck on a job site about an hour out of the city and would be tied up there all day.

Lexi had swallowed her disappointment. "I guess I'll see you later then."

Christopher had promised to call her again when he had more time to talk. "Oh, by the way," he added. "I've got good news."

"Oh?"

"Yes. Remember the crowdfunding page we talked about? Well, I took directions from Kishaya and with some other help, set it up a couple of days ago. Good news is we're already at the twenty thousand-dollar mark."

Lexi gasped in surprise. "People have donated twenty thousand dollars in just two days?"

"Yes. See? I told you. People want to help. They want to give to good causes. What cause is more worthy than offering a better life to vulnerable children?"

Lexi silently agreed, but the generosity from strangers still filled her with surprise. It also helped restore her faith in people.

The dentist was busy. The receptionist had thrown Lexi an apologetic look and explained they were running about thirty minutes behind. Lexi settled her children in the play area and occupied herself by using her phone to continue her search for a suitable property in her neighborhood. She was surprised to discover there were quite a few possibilities, but a lot of them needed considerable work. She chuckled to herself.

Work? What would I care about that? All of these places are in better condition than the farmhouse... They all have more than one bathroom, for one...

Eventually, the dentist called her children in. They all went in together. One by one, they received their check-up. Lexi was pleased when they were all given a bill of good health.

"Not a single cavity between you!" the dental nurse beamed. "Well done!" She rewarded them each with a balloon and a new toothbrush.

"Don't forget your manners," Lexi cautioned.

There was a chorus of "thank yous."

Lexi strapped Leroy back into his stroller and they all headed outside. The sun was high overhead. The sky was a clear blue, with hardly a cloud in sight.

"Who's hungry?" Lexi asked.

"Me!" the children shouted simultaneously.

Lexi grinned. "Well, let's go and find something to eat."

She pushed the stroller along the footpath. She cautioned Patrice and Michael to stay close as she wended her way through the lunchtime crowds. She found a vacant table in the food court underneath the MLC building. Though there were a lot of eateries, there were none of the popular fast food chains in sight. In the end, they settled on pizza and finished with ice cream as a special treat.

By the time she made it back to the train station, Leroy had fallen asleep. The other two were also showing signs of fatigue. Thankfully, they found seats together on the train. She took Leroy out of his stroller and settled him on her lap. Michael and Patrice snuggled in on either side of her. She put her arms around them and they rested their heads against her chest. Within minutes, the gentle sway of the train had put all of her children to sleep.

Ninety minutes later, they arrived at Liverpool Station where Lexi roused them all and together they left the train. She helped them walk the short distance to where she'd left the car. After strapping everyone into their respective car seats, Lexi headed for home.

She rubbed at her eyes. It had been a long day. She looked forward to a bit of quiet before the rest of the children arrived home from school. In fact, she could almost do with a nap herself...

As she rounded the corner that led to her driveway, a cloud of dust in the distance caught her attention. She frowned. It looked like it was coming from the vicinity of her property.

No, that can't be right. There's no reason for there to be dust hovering over Serenity...

The closer she got, the more bewildered she became. By the time she turned into her driveway, the reality of what was happening right before her eyes hit her like a sledgehammer. Despite Christopher's promise, the demolition team had moved in.

Lexi brought the car to a sudden halt and gaped at the sight in the front of her. Two large excavators and a couple of dump trucks filled her front yard. One of the machines had already taken a chunk out of the side of her house. With fury igniting her veins, she floored the accelerator and came to stop beside the machinery. She leaped from the car and started running toward the excavator, waving her arms.

"Hey! Hey, you! Stop! Stop!"

Finally the operator spied her waving like a crazy woman. He switched off the engine and climbed out of the cab. His gray hair and grizzled cheeks were covered in dust. He swiped a hand across his face and then came to a halt beside her.

"What the hell are you doing, lady? I could have run right over the top of you!"

"What the hell are *you* doing? This is my home! You don't have permission to be here!"

The man shook his head. "I'm sorry, but you're wrong. I was given the go-ahead by my boss. I have orders to level this place."

Lexi stared at him, aghast. "No. There's been some mistake. They told me we could stay here until we'd found somewhere else. Christopher gave me his word..."

The man looked at her. "I don't know anything about that, but my orders came from the top. As far as I'm concerned, you're the one who's confused."

Panic held Lexi in a death grip. She grabbed the man's arm. "No! Please! You don't understand! All our things are still in there. Our clothes and furniture and books and toys and food and...everything."

When the man opened his mouth and looked like he wanted to argue further, Lexi squeezed his arm.

"Please," she implored him. "Just give me a few minutes to make a phone call. You can't destroy our house. It contains everything we own."

The man eventually gave her a reluctant nod. "All right. Make your phone call. But be quick about it. These machines are hired out by the hour. Time's money, if you know what I mean. We've been contracted to demolish this place today. That's all I know."

With her heart pounding and her hands shaking with a combination of shock and anger, Lexi pulled out her phone and dialed Christopher's number, praying he'd pick up.

"Lexi! Hi! I was just thinking about you."

The cheerfulness in his voice grated on her like fingernails across a chalkboard. How could he be so cheerful when her life had just been torn apart?

"The bulldozers are here. Or the excavators. Or whatever the hell you call them."

"*What?*"

She ignored the shock in Christopher's voice. "Don't even pretend you didn't know! You promised me! You gave me your word!" Her voice cracked under the force of the emotion that coursed through her.

"Lexi! I swear to you, I knew nothing about this! Hell! Are you sure? They're already there?"

"Am I *sure?* Are you *kidding?*" she cried. "They've already demolished part of my house!"

"Shit. Oh, God. I'm sorry, Lexi. I'm so sorry. I don't know what happened. Somehow, someone's been given the wrong information. I can promise you, it didn't come from me. Please, I need you to believe me."

"Why should I believe you? You told me so many times how awful you used to be, lying, deceiving, playing tricks on people you loved. I didn't want to believe it. I told myself you'd changed. That I'd seen no evidence of that person. But now it appears that I've been a gullible fool. My home and all of my possessions are in the process of being reduced to rubble! What am I going to tell my children? How am I going to explain?"

Once again, her voice cracked with emotion. Her breath came fast. Her chest was so tight it felt like she might be having a heart attack. The thought that Christopher had betrayed her trust was like a knife to her chest.

"Please, Lexi! Let me make a call. Let me try and fix this!"

I can't do this anymore...

Stabbing at her phone, she ended the call.

Christopher jumped into his Mercedes and floored the accelerator. Weaving in and out of the traffic, he cursed every time he caught a red light.

I need to get to Lexi... I need to make her understand... I need to get to Lexi... I need to make her understand...

The mantra kept cycling through his head on an endless loop. While pulled up at his third set of lights, he punched in Frank's number and drummed his fingers impatiently against the steering wheel while he waited for his father to pick up. When he did, Christopher didn't hold back.

"What the fuck, Dad? There are excavators out at the Greenaway place. They've already started on the demolition. What the fuck is going on?"

"Whoa! Steady on there, son. What the hell are you talking about?"

"Lexi's house. The Greenaway place. There's machinery on site. She just rang to tell me they've already knocked down part of her house. I thought we had a deal? You agreed to wait until she'd found somewhere else. For fuck's sake, she hasn't even moved out!"

"Oh, dear. I'm sorry Christopher. There must have been a mix up in communication. I told the head foreman that we had the final approvals from the council and all was a go for demolition. I didn't mean right that minute. The contractor must have gotten confused. Oh, dear. Leave it with me. I'll call him right away and explain."

"Confused? A mix up in communication? Dad! This is a disaster! I gave Lexi my word we wouldn't move on the place until she'd found somewhere else to live. She thinks this is my fault. That I broke my promise."

"Then I'll call her too. Explain this had nothing to do with you."

Christopher made a sound of frustration deep in his throat. "It's too late, Dad. The damage has been done! She's never going to trust me again."

"You don't know that son. She's a good woman. She'll understand."

"Dad! You're not listening! Her house has already been partly demolished! She's furious and she has every right to feel that way. There's nothing you can say that will make a difference."

"Where are you?"

He sighed heavily. The lights changed. He hit the accelerator. "I'm on my way over there. It's the least I can do."

"I'm sorry son. I'm really sorry. I know how much this woman means to you..."

There was nothing more to be said. Feeling sick to his stomach, Christopher ended the call.

Lexi got the kids out of the car and inched them around the heavy equipment. The site had fallen silent. She could see the excavator driver standing off to the side on the phone. Anger still boiled through her veins. Her face felt hot. But worse was the feeling of betrayal. Christopher had broken her trust.

He'd told her he hadn't known about the order to go ahead. Who knew if that were true? Not so long ago, she would have immediately come to his defense if someone had suggested he was being dishonest, but how well did she really know him? All she knew was that it seemed awfully convenient for him to deny any knowledge about the demolition order when he'd been put in charge of this part of the project. Even more so when she knew there was half a million dollars on the line.

She picked her way over the debris that already lay in piles on the ground. With Leroy perched on her hip and the other two walking carefully behind her, she made her way over to the side veranda that had sustained the most damage. Thank God she'd arrived back when she did. It appeared they'd only just begun the demolition. Though both windows along that side were broken and part of the wall was no longer there, it appeared the rest of the house was intact.

"What's happening, Momma?" Patrice asked. "Why are they knocking down our house?"

"My toys are still inside!" Michael wailed.

With her free hand, Lexi drew them close against her side. "Hey. It's going to be all right. It looks like we got here in time. Your toys should be fine."

By the time the older children had climbed off the school bus and walked down the drive, Lexi had managed to sweep up the mess that had fallen inside. The excavator operator had left, but the heavy machinery remained parked in their front yard. Kishaya was the first through the door.

"What's going on? What are those machines doing out there?" she cried.

Lexi grimaced. "There's been a bit of a misunderstanding. The digger operator thought he'd been given the go-ahead to start demolishing the place."

"How could that happen? We're still living here!" Kishaya shouted, her eyes bright with anger and tears.

I know exactly how you feel…

Lexi had to stay strong for her children. She drew in a deep breath and squared her shoulders.

"Look, it's not as bad as it seems. I've managed to salvage most of our things."

"Christopher said—"

"I know what Christopher said," Lexi interrupted. "I've spoken to him. He claims he didn't know anything about the demolition team moving in."

"Then what's he going to do about it?" Kishaya demanded. "These people can't just come in and bulldoze down our house!"

Lexi's phone rang. She pulled it out of her pocket and checked the screen.

Frank Barrington.

With a sigh, she answered the call. "Frank. I don't really have time to—"

"Lexi. I'm so sorry. This is all my fault. I told my supervisor we were good to go. I meant that we'd received the final approvals and... You'd told me you'd agreed to move out. Unfortunately, there was a misunderstanding... The supervisor gave the go-ahead to the demolition team... They didn't even go inside the house to check that it was clear... A serious breach of protocol... There will be consequences, never you mind... I'm so sorry, Lexi."

His words faded in and out as she tried to concentrate over the angry buzz in her head. There was only one thing she wanted to clarify.

"Did Christopher know about what was going to happen today?"

"No Lexi. He didn't. We talked about your willingness to leave. Naturally, I was pleased. I've been eager to make a start on this project. But Christopher told me he'd promised you that you and the children could stay there until you'd found somewhere else to live. I assured him I was on board with that." He paused and then added, "I've just had a very terse conversation with him. He's very upset about what's happened. This wasn't his fault. Though he hasn't said anything to me, I can tell he cares for you a lot, Lexi. Don't forget that."

Before Lexi could formulate an answer, the sound of Michael and Patrice yelling interrupted her. She walked closer toward the noise and saw that they were shouting and waving at Christopher who had just pulled up in her drive. Stabbing at her phone, she ended the call and glared at the man she'd professed to love and who had just trampled all over her heart.

Chapter Twenty Three

Christopher saw the way Lexi stood on the front veranda glaring at him and his heart sunk. He'd been hoping she might have had a chance to cool down, to think about what he'd said, but it appeared he was mistaken. Michael and Patrice bounded toward him and threw themselves against him. He bent down and hugged them both, pleased that at least someone in the Greenaway family was happy to see him.

"Hey guys! How are you?"

"Someone knocked down our house!" Patrice announced.

"Lucky they didn't hurt my toys," Michael added.

Christopher gave them another quick hug and then set them aside and stood. Lexi remained on the veranda, her expression still cold and unforgiving. Swallowing a sigh, he made his way toward her.

"Hi," he said.

"Look. Look what they did!"

He glanced toward the side of the house that had sustained damage. Inwardly, he was relieved there hadn't been more damage done. Still, it shouldn't have happened at all.

"I'm sorry, Lexi. It shouldn't have happened."

"Yes, well that's cold comfort now, isn't it? My house has been destroyed."

He shrugged, feeling helpless. "How can I fix this?"

She looked at him with such cold finality, his heart sunk. "I don't think you can." With that, she turned her back on him and headed inside the house. He went to follow. He only made it halfway down the hallway when he saw her go into her bedroom. She closed the door behind her. The click of the lock turning sounded so final it tore pieces off Christopher's heart.

Christopher veered into the kitchen. Kishaya was there making herself a snack. She looked up as he entered and swiped at her eyes. He could tell she'd been crying. His heart sank. He'd never felt so low. The worst of it was, for the first time the damage hadn't been his doing. There was a sad irony in that.

"Would you like something to drink?" Kishaya asked.

"No, thank you." He lowered himself onto one of the stools that lined the breakfast bar. "I'm sorry, Kishaya. This had nothing to do with me."

She looked at him solemnly with her big dark eyes. "Is that true?"

He held her gaze. "Yes." He blew out his breath on a heavy sigh. "The decision was made by my father. There was a misunderstanding with some of his crew. He didn't mean for the demolition to start right away."

"How does something like that happen? If Mom hadn't come home when she did, they might have leveled our whole house and everything in it!"

"You're right and I'm sorry. It shouldn't have happened. The thing is, your mom blames me. She thinks I had something to do with it. That I lied to her when I told her we wouldn't move on the house until after she'd found you all somewhere else to live."

"Why doesn't she believe you? Have you lied to her before?"

"No, of course not. But the thing is, I have lied in the past. Not to your mom," he added hurriedly, "but to others. I'm not proud of my behavior and I've tried so much to change my ways, but I'm afraid your mother thinks I've reverted back to form. I'm not sure what I can do to make her believe me."

Christopher's voice cracked. He was devastated to think he'd finally found someone to love and who'd loved him in return, and he'd messed it all up. Okay, so he wasn't directly responsible, but the outcome was the same. She hated him.

Kishaya moved closer and leaned over the counter toward him. "Do you still love her?"

"Of course I do!" he said without hesitation. "I never imagined I could love anyone the way I love Lexi. She's my moon and stars and sunshine. She makes me want to be a better person. And now I've gone and ruined everything. How am I going to make amends?"

Kishaya looked up at him, her eyes welling with fresh tears. "My mom has been sad for so long, about a lot of things.

Losing Ronnie, then the house. She's been so worried about the money. She even sold her grandmother's brooch! Apart from a single photograph, it was the last remaining link she had to her family. It was so important to her. It cuts me up inside thinking about how she pawned it—for us. For our family." Kishaya's breath hitched on a sob. "I wish I knew how to help her. I love her so much!"

Christopher stood and pulled Kishaya against him for a hug. Her breath came out on a shudder, but after a while, she pulled back. He dropped his arms.

"It's going to be okay, Kishaya. You don't have to worry about the money or anything else. We're going to find a solution everyone will be happy with."

Kishaya nodded gratefully. "I hope so." She paused and then added, "And you know what, I think I have an idea about how you can make this up to my mom."

Christopher stood straighter. "You do?"

"Yes."

Kishaya went on to tell him more about the brooch that had once belonged to Lexi's grandmother.

"It was so beautiful," Kishaya continued. "It was in the shape of a peacock and had all these sparkling blue and green sapphires. Mom said there were even real diamonds in it."

Christopher recalled seeing Lexi wearing the brooch the night of the fundraiser and again the night she'd invited him over for dinner. "And you said she pawned it?"

"Yes. Like I said, she was worried we didn't have enough money. She knew we had to leave this place and buy another. She said every dollar counted."

Christopher frowned. It pained him to think of Lexi parting with something so special to her when he could have just as easily given her the extra money.

"Do you know where she took the brooch?" he asked.

Kishaya shook her head. "No, but she probably took it somewhere local. She does most of her shopping locally."

Christopher absorbed the information. Though it was already after four, he could still make a start on canvassing the pawn shops in the area. Hopefully there wouldn't be too many.

He gave Kishaya a grateful smile. "Thank you, Kishaya. I really appreciate you telling me this."

"Are you going to buy it back for her?"

"I'm going to give it my best shot."

Kishaya grinned. "Way to go, Christopher!"

Christopher smiled again, feeling better than he had since he'd taken Lexi's phone call.

"You take care, okay? And look after your mother and your brothers and sisters. I'll be back soon."

"Okay. See you round like a rissole."

Christopher raised an eyebrow. Kishaya merely laughed.

After a quick search on the Internet revealed there were sixteen pawn shops in a three-mile radius of where Lexi lived, Christopher spent the next forty-five minutes going from one pawn shop to another and making enquires about Lexi's brooch. So far, no luck. But he wouldn't be deterred. He was on a mission and nothing was going to dissuade him.

He glanced at his watch. It was five minutes before closing time. Enough time to try his luck one more time before calling it quits for the day. He walked into the dusty old shop that was jammed packed from floor to ceiling with what looked to Christopher to be nothing more than junk. He strode up to the counter and asked to see the owner.

"That'd be me," the gray-haired man with the sizeable paunch hanging over his tight belt replied.

For the eighth time that afternoon, Christopher explained what he was looking for.

"Yeah, I know the piece you're talking about," the man replied.

Christopher started in surprise. "You do?"

"Sure. A really pretty piece. I paid a fair price for it too."

Christopher collapsed against the counter with relief. "So you have it?"

"No."

"What do you mean, no? You just said you'd bought it."

"I did buy it. And then I sold it again. You must be a bit slow. This is a pawn shop. That's how I make my money."

"How long ago did you sell it?"

"Yesterday."

Christopher stared at him in disbelief. "Yesterday?"

"Yep. Bloke came in who owns an antique shop. He drops in now and again on the off chance I might have something of interest he can sell in his shop. He liked the look of the brooch. Gave me good money for it, too."

"How much?"

"Ten thousand dollars."

Christopher blinked. "Ten thousand dollars?"

The man chuckled. "Yeah, nearly double what I paid for it. Not a bad day's work, eh?"

Christopher tried hard to get his mind round the fact Lexi had owned a brooch worth ten thousand dollars—and no doubt even more, if that's what the antique dealer had paid for it. He obviously thought he'd make money, even at that price.

"Who is this antique dealer? Do you have a name?"

"Course I do."

Christopher waited, his patience almost at an end. He gave the man a look. "So? Can I have it?"

"How much is it worth to you?"

Christopher gritted his teeth. He reached into his back pocket for his wallet, but before he could pull it out, the man waved him away.

"Just kidding. Put your money away. I'm not that much of a jerk."

The man tore a piece of paper out of a notepad he drew out from under the counter. Reaching for a pen behind his ear, he scribbled down a name and phone number and then handed the paper to Christopher.

"That's all the details I have for him."

Christopher glanced down at the paper. "Is he a local?"

"Not sure. Never asked."

Knowing he wasn't going to get anything else of use from the man, Christopher tucked the paper into his pocket, thanked the man for his help and left. Once outside, he glanced at his watch. It was already past five. Most businesses closed their doors by then. But not all of them. On the off chance this antique dealer might be one of those still open, Christopher pulled out the paper and reached for his phone. He tapped in the numbers and listened as the call rang out.

To his relief, the call was answered.

"Roberto Silviani."

"Mr Silviani. It's Christopher Barrington. I was wondering if I could stop by your shop this afternoon."

"Sorry. I'm closed."

"I understand, but it's kind of an emergency. See, it's my wedding anniversary and I've completely forgotten to buy my wife a gift," Christopher improvised. "She'll be so disappointed if I arrive home empty-handed. Apart from that, if I turn up with nothing, I'll be hearing about it for the next six months."

Christopher held his breath. He'd taken the punt the man might be married and would empathize with his plight. He was right.

The man chuckled knowingly. "Ah, the anniversary gift. How many years?"

"Years?"

"How many years have you been married?"

"Uh...five."

"Five. So, you'll be looking for something carved from wood then."

Christopher frowned. "Uh... Carved from wood?"

"Yes, that's what you traditionally give for the fifth wedding anniversary."

"Oh. Right. Actually, I had something else in mind." He described the brooch.

"Oh, a lovely piece. And it is the right combination of colors. Blue and turquoise. Those colors are also traditionally used for the fifth wedding anniversary."

"So you still have it?" Once again, Christopher held his breath.

"Sure I do. I only acquired it yesterday. A piece like that's for a very special buyer."

"So I heard. Do you mind if I stop by your shop now?"

The man sighed. "Sure. Come on over. I'll keep an eye out for you and unlock the door when I see you coming."

The man gave Christopher an address not too far away. With a sigh of relief, he returned to his car and sped toward the antique shop. He was pleasantly surprised to discover the place had a smart and well-maintained shop front. Large glass windows artfully displayed a range of wares. The name "Silviani Antiques" was stenciled in elaborate, faux gold lettering in a semi-circle on the glass front door.

Christopher tapped on the glass. The door opened before he'd finished knocking. An elderly man who barely came up to Christopher's chest stood on the other side.

"Mr Barrington, I presume?"

"Yes. And you must be Mr Silviani."

"Call me Roberto," the man said magnanimously and stood back to allow Christopher to enter.

"I really want to thank you for letting me stop by," Christopher said as he walked further into the shop. "You might have just saved my marriage."

"Ah, marriage. Yes, it's not for the fainthearted."

"I take it you're speaking from experience?"

Roberto smiled. "Does forty-two years count?"

Christopher stopped in surprise. "Forty-two years? That's... a lifetime!"

Roberto merely shrugged. The smile continued to hover around his lips. "I was twenty-one. She was nineteen. Her family said we'd never last, but look at us? Forty-two years and still in love. A match made in heaven."

Christopher smiled back. With the divorce rate climbing higher each year, it was nice to see some marriages went the distance. He'd always had a good role model in Frank and his mother, but it was reassuring to meet someone else who'd managed to stick it out.

"What's your secret?" Christopher asked, curious.

"Love, of course. There must be that. But there must also be respect for each other and forgiveness. You don't always have to agree, but you have respect each other's opinion. We all mess up sometimes. That's when forgiveness really matters. If you can apply those qualities to your marriage, you'll be fine."

Christopher merely nodded. He felt bad about lying to the old man about being married, but he wasn't about to correct things now. Not when he still hadn't set eyes on the brooch. He reminded Roberto what he was there for.

"Ah, yes. The brooch. A beautiful piece. Your wife's a very lucky lady."

"Yes, she is."

The old man disappeared for a few moments and then returned carrying something in his hand. He set it down on the counter for Christopher to see. The overhead lights picked up the blue and green sapphires and diamonds that decorated the piece. Christopher picked it up to examine it more closely. It truly was a remarkable piece. He wondered at the woman who'd owned it and had handed it down to her daughter. And then he wondered how that very daughter had become a runaway at the tender age of fifteen and had given birth to a baby that nobody seemed to want.

There was a story there and one day he hoped Lexi would share it with him, but right now, he needed to secure the brooch and get back in her good books.

"How much do you want for it?" he asked, pulling out his wallet.

"It's a beautiful piece," Roberto said. "It's been created by an artisan. Beautifully designed, unique. Your wife will be the envy of all her friends. It will be an anniversary gift she'll never forget!"

Christopher swallowed his impatience. "Cut the sales pitch. I want the brooch. How much?"

"Twenty thousand dollars."

It was more than double what the old man had paid the pawn broker, but Christopher wasn't in the mood to negotiate. After all, he'd already made it clear the deal was as good as done. He pulled out his credit card and slapped it on the counter.

The man rang up the transaction and Christopher tapped his card onto the machine and then entered his PIN when prompted. The transaction was processed and finally the brooch was in his possession. He closed his fingers around it and then dropped it into his pocket.

He looked at Roberto and smiled. "Thank you."

The old man grinned widely. "The pleasure was all mine. Happy anniversary."

Chapter Twenty Four

Lexi spent more than an hour in her bedroom getting control of her anger and disappointment and clearing her head. She'd come to the conclusion that she either had to believe Christopher's protestations of innocence, which had been backed up by his father, or bring their fledgling relationship to an end.

Do I really think he's the kind of man who could have gone back on his word? Do I really think he was behind the premature arrival of the demolition team?

Now that she'd had a chance to calm down and look at the situation through a lens that wasn't so clouded with hurt and anger, she had to admit she didn't think Christopher was that man. He'd told her he'd been like that in the past and she had every reason to believe him. After all, she didn't know of anyone who would confess to such shortcomings to someone they were apparently trying to impress. And in all the time they'd spent together, she'd seen no evidence of the man he used to be.

Trust in a relationship was vital. Without it, the relationship was doomed. For all Ronnie's lack of maturity, she'd never doubted his word. She felt the same way about Christopher now. Despite her earlier misgivings, she conceded that she'd reacted out of fear more than anything else. Their relationship was still so new; they had so much to learn about each other. It wasn't surprising she might react in a way she wasn't proud of when their fledgling relationship hit its first road bump.

She owed Christopher an apology. She should have given him the benefit of the doubt. With that thought in mind, she climbed off her bed and opened the door and padded down the hallway to the kitchen. She found the younger kids on the couch, watching TV. She could see Denzil out in the front yard, playing a game with the dogs. Kishaya sat on a stool at the kitchen counter, texting on her phone.

"Where's Christopher?" Lexi asked in the most casual tone she could manage.

"He went out," Kishaya said, barely looking up.

Lexi quelled her disappointment. "Oh."

"He said he'd be back."

"Oh? Tonight?"

"I think so. He said he'd be back soon."

"Oh. Okay."

Lexi was still trying to work out whether that was a figure of speech or whether she could take it as a literal interpretation when the dogs started barking and Christopher's car appeared in the driveway. Her heart skipped a beat.

He's back…

She watched him climb out and say a few words to Denzil. The boy broke into a smile. Christopher said something again and then ruffled Denzil's hair. Once again, Denzil responded with a grin. Then Christopher turned toward the house and Lexi's pulse took off. She tried desperately to slow her breathing, but to no avail. The closer he got, the faster the nerves churned her stomach. And then he was climbing the stairs and had crossed the veranda to knock briefly on the front door.

Lexi stood on the other side and opened it, her heart in her throat. She prayed silently that Christopher would forgive her outburst.

"H-hi," she stammered. "I didn't know if I'd see you again tonight."

Christopher bent his head and pecked her on the cheek. "I told Kishaya I'd be back."

Lexi's skin tingled where he'd kissed her. It was a good sign that he wasn't too mad at her. "So you did," she managed.

"May I come in?" he asked.

She blushed. "Of course." She stood back to allow him to enter and then turned and headed toward the kitchen. Christopher followed her.

"Do you mind if we go somewhere and talk?" he asked.

She tensed momentarily and her stomach filled with dread, but she forced herself to continue walking on through the kitchen and dining area and out to the screened-in veranda at the rear of the house. She closed the door behind them, providing a modicum of privacy.

He looked so somber. Her heart beat double time. She decided the best course of action was to rip the Band-Aid off.

"I'm really sorry, Christopher. I said some awful things. I—"

He held up his hand to silence her. "Lexi, it's fine. I appreciate your apology, but it's okay. I understand. Arriving here and finding your house being torn apart... It would have come as a shock to anyone, let alone someone who'd been promised that her house was safe until she was ready to move out."

He moved closer and gripped her gently by the arms. "*I'm* the one who's sorry. I wasn't directly responsible for what happened, but I should have made sure everyone involved in the project was completely clear about the rules of engagement. I'm sorry I let you down."

"Oh, Christopher! You didn't let me down! I should have believed you when you said you had no idea about what had happened. I'm the one who's let *you* down!"

He smiled tenderly and reached out and brushed a long strand of hair off her face and tucked it gently behind her ear.

"How about we just agree to forgive each other and put this behind us?"

Her chest went tight with emotion. Tears welled up in her eyes. Her voice came out strangled. "Th-that sounds like a good idea."

Christopher bent and pressed a soft kiss against her lips. "Don't cry, honey. I don't like to see you cry."

"I'm not crying," Lexi choked out.

Christopher kissed her again. This time he lingered and together they relearned the shape and feel of each other's lips. When they finally pulled apart, Lexi sighed and rested her head against his chest.

"I'm so glad you came back."

"Me too."

They stood holding each other in silence. After a while, Christopher dropped his arms and stood back.

"I have something for you," he said.

Lexi looked at him in surprise. "You do?"

"Yes." He reached into his pocket and pulled out her grandmother's brooch.

Lexi gasped. Her eyes went wide. Her heart leaped in her chest. "You have my brooch?"

"Kishaya told me what you'd done. She also told me how much it meant to you. It didn't seem right that you had to part with such a special piece of your past. So I bought it back for you."

"Oh, Christopher! I don't deserve this kindness..."

She threw herself against him. The tears fell in earnest now. She buried her face against his shirt and sobbed.

Christopher put his arms around her once again and held her close. He whispered words of comfort against her hair.

"Hey! I thought this would make you happy."

"I *am* happy!" she sobbed through her tears. "So happy." She looked up at him through her tears. "I love you, Christopher Barrington. I've never known a sweeter, kinder, more wonderful man."

His gaze darkened with emotion. "I love you too, Lexi Greenaway. More than I could ever have imagined. I'll love you all the days of my life."

Their lips met in another tender kiss. When they finally pulled apart, they shared a tender smile, threaded their fingers together, then turned and walked back inside to rejoin the rest of the family.

Though they'd all spent the night at Serenity, Christopher's concern about potential structural damage to the house had them urgently assessing options the following morning.

They were seated around the breakfast table. Once again, Christopher had done the cooking.

"I've been thinking about what to do," he said and then popped a piece of bacon in his mouth.

Lexi waited impatiently for him to stop chewing. "And?"

"And what?"

"Have you come up with any suggestions? There are nine of us, you know. It's not like we can all go to a hotel."

Christopher grinned. "Yes, Lexi. I think I'm aware of that."

She made a sound of frustration. "Christopher! Would you just tell us! Please!"

"Well, my parents have this huge house outside of Broken. It's about ninety-minutes' drive south of Sydney, in the southern highlands. In fact, it's not too far from here. There's just the two of them living there now and they have like nine bedrooms or something, most of them empty."

Lexi looked at him, her eyes wide with surprise. "Your parents' place? I'm not sure they'd want eight children running around their house."

"Why not? They raised nine of their own. I don't think a few more would frighten them off. In fact, I've already passed it by my mother. She's thrilled at the idea."

"You passed it by your mother? Already? Why would she want to help us? She doesn't even know us!"

Christopher shrugged. "She's just that kind of woman. Besides, she knows me and she knows how much I love you."

Lexi looked even more surprised. "You told your mother about us?"

Christopher grinned and nodded. "Yes. I also told my dad. They're both ecstatic and beyond excited to meet you." He looked around the table crowded with children. "*All* of you. Better still, it's close enough to here that no one would have to change schools."

Lexi shook her head, as if still trying to come to terms with the idea. "Wow. I mean, wow. How long can we stay?"

"As long as you like. But I checked the crowdfunding page this morning and we've reached the one hundred thousand-dollar mark."

Lexi gasped in disbelief. "One hundred thousand dollars? Are you kidding?"

Christopher laughed. "No. I'm one hundred per cent serious."

"Oh, my goodness! I never imagined we could raise so much."

"So I'm thinking we ought to kick the house hunting into gear. We have more than enough to buy something that will suit everyone's needs."

Lexi continued to look dazed, as if she couldn't quite believe how much her life had changed for the better. The kids started talking all at once. Christopher sat back in his chair and absorbed it all. He'd never been happier.

After breakfast, when the plates had been cleared away and the older kids had left for school and the younger ones had dispersed to other corners of the house, Lexi made them coffee. They went out to the front veranda and seated themselves on the old wicker chairs that stood there. Though Lexi was excited about the prospect of moving into the Barrington mansion, she was uncertain about what that meant for her and Christopher.

He'd been spending most of his nights with her at Serenity. Would he continue to stay overnight with her at his parents' place? Would they mind? She had no idea how Frank and his wife viewed such things. They might be totally traditional… Perhaps they frowned on couples sleeping together before they were married.

The uncertainty of it was the only blight on Lexi's horizon. Christopher seemed to sense something was wrong.

"What is it, Lexi?" he asked gently.

She took a sip of her coffee and tried to think of a way to broach the subject.

"I can tell you're worried about something. Just tell me," Christopher urged.

She drew in a deep breath and took hold of her courage. "Okay. I was just thinking about what it would mean for us if the kids and I move in with your parents. I mean, would you visit us there?"

"Do you want me to?"

"Of course I do! I want to live with you! I want to spend every morning and every night with you. Does that scare you?"

Christopher's grin was breathtaking. "It doesn't scare me one bit. I'd love to move in with you! I didn't want to presume... You and the kids... You're a real family. I didn't want to intrude..."

"You couldn't ever intrude on our family. You're as much a part of this family as any of us!"

Tears glinted in Christopher's eyes. When he spoke, his voice came out choked. "Really? You really mean that?"

Lexi leaned over and planted a kiss on his mouth. "I really mean that."

He leaped up off the chair and started across the veranda.

Lexi frowned. "Where are you going?"

"Back to my apartment. I'm going to pack my bags. And then I'll be back to help pack up the house for the move. I don't want to spend another night away from you."

"What about your parents?"

"They'll be thrilled. They're going to love you and your kids as much as I do."

As Christopher backed out of her driveway, Lexi couldn't keep the smile off her face.

THE END

Get a free book when you sign up for Chris Taylor's newsletter at: http://www.christaylorauthor.com.au

If you enjoyed Christopher and Lexi's story don't forget to leave a review at your favorite digital retailer. Every review is really appreciated and helps with visibility so that other readers can find my books.

Broken Promises is the next book in the Barrington Family Series. Keep reading below for a sneak peek at *Broken Promises*:

CHAPTER ONE

It was as if the heavens had opened up and decided to drop a year's worth of rain in one afternoon. The deluge battered Charlotte Barrington's BMW 4 series convertible as she fought to see through the mountain of water that bounced off her windscreen. Despite the fact she had her wipers going flat out, it was as if they remained motionless.

Thank goodness I had the foresight to close the roof before leaving the supermarket. I'd be soaked through…

Though the sky had been dull and gray and filled with heavy clouds before she'd left home a couple of hours earlier, there had been no hint of the tsunami waiting right around the corner. Now she was stuck in the middle of it, fighting to get home.

She'd gone out for cat food. The thought of her chocolate point Siamese baby going hungry had forced her out to the shops when she would have much rather spent the afternoon binge-watching the current TV serial she was hooked on. There was something so addictive about all those sexy doctors facing life and death situations on a daily basis – sometimes several times a day. Of course, she knew it was only TV. Real life wasn't quite as dramatic, thank goodness. She ought to know.

As a cop employed by the New South Wales police force, she'd faced her fair share of drama and dangerous situations. Thankfully not so dangerous that she'd ever feared for her life. To date, she'd been posted in a rural town so far from Sydney it should have been described as the outback. The biggest excitement in Watervale had been a purse-snatching a couple of months into her twelve-month stint. Poor old Rosie Robinson, eighty-five if she were a day, had been sent flying when fourteen-year-old Jaxon Pitt had stolen her handbag. It was lucky the great-grandmother hadn't broken a hip when she'd landed awkwardly on the concrete footpath right outside the local supermarket.

Charlotte had conducted a thorough investigation and the perpetrator had been arrested and charged within the hour. That was one thing about small towns: Everyone knew everyone. Rosie had taught Jaxon's mother in high school. Everyone said he was the spitting image of his mother.

Still, Charlotte had learned a lot from the cops in Watervale. Detective Chase Barrington was her cousin and he'd taken it upon himself to show the probationary constable the ropes and a few tricks of the trade besides. Her brother, Wade, was also a resident of Watervale. As the local park ranger, he'd been only too willing to take her hiking on some of the trails. They'd even camped out in the bush once or twice, toasting marshmallows before a campfire and recalling adventures from their childhood. She'd enjoyed her time in the country, but it was the city where she really yearned to be.

Nothing beat the glitz and glamor, the noise, the excitement, the sheer *vibrancy* of the city. Directly after the year she'd spent in Watervale, she'd been lucky enough to be posted to the affluent beachside suburb of Cronulla. It was sixteen miles south of the city of Sydney, but it was still a decent enough place to live. The combination of relaxed beachside living and the cosmopolitan vibe of trendy cafés, theaters and restaurants made the place popular with locals and tourists alike. Better still, it was only a ninety minute drive to her parents' house outside Broken in the southern highlands. She'd been spending a lot more of her days' off at the house she'd grown up in now she was single again.

But not today. Today had been all about sleeping late, eating junk and watching TV on her way-too-comfy couch. What better way to spend her last day off before starting back to work first thing in the morning? The ink had barely dried on her promotion to the homicide department of the Sutherland Shire Police Area Command and she still felt the need to impress.

She was most definitely the new kid on the block. So new she was yet to be part of a homicide investigation. She was itching to get started. Not only was she more than ready to cut her teeth on her first homicide, she was also more than ready to have a decent distraction from her ex-boyfriend.

It had been three months since Keith had broken things off. Her self-esteem was still smarting from the fact. Her sisters had accused her of hiding out in her apartment every night, moping about the future she'd thought was hers for the taking that had now been blown to pieces. And they were right. She hadn't been out since Keith had leveled the death blow to their relationship.

It's over… We both want different things… I don't love you… You're more devoted to your job than you are to me…

The accusations had come thick and fast. He'd even insulted her prowess in the bedroom. It had been unnecessarily hurtful and even though she'd wanted to dismiss his cruel words, a part of her had wondered if there wasn't some truth to them...

At least her career was on track. After five years of policing, she'd finally made detective. The only blight on the landscape was that she'd been partnered with Tony Sabattini, a veteran cop who should have retired a long time ago. Though his decades of homicide experience would benefit a rookie like her, his rude and taciturn attitude toward almost everyone and everything were proving difficult to take. Still, even that couldn't put a damper on the fact she'd finally made it on the homicide team.

The thought triggered a slow smile of satisfaction. Then a jagged shard of lightning cracked against the sky. Charlotte yelped in alarm and jumped. Her thoughts went immediately to Raoul. She hoped he was okay. She wasn't sure what had caused the sheer terror he felt at the slightest hint of thunder, but there was no denying he hated storms.

Her four-legged feline companion was currently the most important male in her life. She'd bought him from an animal shelter when he was a few months old. She didn't know anything about his early days. No doubt there was some past trauma that had made him the way he was. At least she had his favorite food in the back of the car. That would help him get through the rest of the day.

With a sigh of relief, she arrived at her apartment complex and parked in her allotted parking space. Unfortunately it wasn't undercover and by the time she'd carried her purchases in, she was sopping wet. Not that she could complain about her apartment: Two-bedroom, two bath, modern and stylish and all within walking distance to the beach.

She'd never have afforded such a place on her cop's salary, but a year earlier she'd been given a generous sum of money from her parents as a twenty-fifth birthday gift, along with the BMW. She'd used the money as a deposit on the apartment. Of course, the responsibility of the ongoing mortgage payments fell to her. Though Frank and Evelyn Barrington were more than prepared to help out their nine children financially, they also expected that each one would take responsibility for their lives and make something of themselves. There was no pressure for any of them to enter into the family mining business, but they'd all grown up knowing there was most definitely an expectation that they work hard and succeed in their chosen field. For Charlotte, it was the police force. Two of her brothers, Trace and Zac, were also cops.

The extra pay from her recent promotion would certainly help with the mortgage. Even with a hefty deposit, the monthly mortgage payments were steep. After her weekly expenses, there was never a whole lot left over. She'd learned the hard way about sticking to a budget.

Dropping her grocery bags on the kitchen counter, she pushed her long wet hair back off her forehead. Kicking off her shoes, she padded barefoot down the hallway.

"Raoul? Puss, puss? Where are you, baby?"

She passed the bathroom and stripped off her wet clothes. Grabbing a towel, she dried off and then wrapped the towel around her and continued her search.

"Raoul?"

She found him hiding under her bed, curled up in a ball and shivering.

"Oh, my poor baby!" She bent down and picked him up. Drawing him close, she pressed a kiss against his soft fur. He burrowed in against the towel. She sat on the bed and petted him until he'd stopped trembling, reassuring him all the time that the storm was almost over and he was fine.

Satisfied at last that he was over the worst of it, she set him down on the carpet and headed back to the kitchen. Diving into the grocery bags, she found a tin of cat food and pulled open the lid. Spooning the contents into his dish, she tapped the edge of the bowl.

"Raoul? Baby? Dinner's ready."

"Miaow."

He rubbed himself against her bare legs and then began to eat. Leaving him to it, she padded back to the bathroom and dropped the towel on the floor. She opened the door of the shower and started the water. The hot spray felt good on her shoulders. After shampooing, shaving and moisturizing, she pulled on her old bathrobe and went back out to the kitchen. Raoul had finished his dinner and was seated by the sliding door that led out onto the balcony, cleaning himself.

"How was that, my gorgeous boy?" she crooned. "Are you feeling better?"

Pouring herself a glass of wine, Charlotte took it out onto the balcony. The storm had passed as quickly as it had started and the air smelled fresh and clean. She filled her lungs. Just then, the sun burst out from behind a cloud and the sky was filled with a brilliant rainbow.

Charlotte's spirits lifted. She might have been down in the dumps since Keith's abrupt departure, but life was looking up. The rainbow was a sign, she was sure of it.

The swish of passing cars below reminded her there were people with places to go, things to do, dreams to fulfil. She was overcome with a sudden wave of discontentment. She was twenty-six. In the prime of her life. She ought to be out dancing, drinking, having fun with friends. Flirting.

Wow. I can't remember the last time I did that...

She and Keith had been together for three years. They'd met by chance at the train station and had bonded over books. She'd been reading an autobiography of a famous Australian cricketer. Keith had once played cricket for his state. He'd been cute in a slightly feminine way, with longish brown hair and glasses that kept
sliding off his nose. He'd been sweet and funny and attentive. Their relationship had been more of a slow burn than an instantaneous combustion, but it had been nice. Comfortable.

Though they'd dated for three years, they'd never moved in together. They'd spent time at each other's places, including sleepovers, but Keith was an accountant and liked to think things over long and hard before he made a decision about anything – including whether they should share an address.

She just wished he'd called it quits before he'd broken her heart.

No, that wasn't right. She wouldn't lie to herself. He hadn't broken her heart. In fact, though she liked him a great deal and enjoyed his company, she was pretty sure she'd never been in love with him. Not the kind of heart-stopping, butterflies-in-stomach, sweaty hands kind of love she read about in romance novels. Then again, they were fiction books. Make believe.

Does that kind of love really exist?

She didn't know and she sure as hell wasn't going to find out by hiding out every night in her apartment.

She took a sip from her glass and sighed. Another long, empty night stretched out before her. Raoul found the courage to venture out onto the wet tiles and wrapped himself around her legs. Setting her glass aside, she bent and picked him up, pressing her face against his soft fur.

"You're the only man I need in my life," she murmured.

A sudden image of her as a crazy old cat woman filled her mind. Living alone in her apartment, surrounded by cats. The neighbors' children whispering about her as she walked by...

Charlotte cursed. She set Raoul down on the tiles. A surge of determination went through her. She'd be damned if she'd spend another night moping about and bemoaning the sad and sorry state of her love life. It was time she went out and did something about it. Starting now.

Returning to the kitchen, she finished her wine and left the empty glass on the counter. She glanced at the clock above the fridge. Half-past four. Though it was a little early to be hitting the bars, she was determined to get out and socialize.

After all, it was five o'clock somewhere. She strode down the hallway to her bedroom. Dropping the bathrobe to the carpet, she flung open the doors to her wardrobe. She moved clothes aside, searching for the perfect something. At last she settled on a skin tight, black leather dress.

She pulled it off the hanger and slipped it over her head. The sleeveless bodice cupped and lifted her generous breasts, leaving a fair amount of cleavage on display. The hem kissed the top of her thighs. A zipper ran up the middle from top to bottom, the zipper tab lying innocently near the cleft of her breasts. It was a dress she'd only worn once. Keith had taken one look at her in it and had nearly had a fit. He'd been overwhelmed and embarrassed by its blatant sexuality and had asked her to take it off.

She remembered the night as if it had happened yesterday. They'd been going out on a date to celebrate their third anniversary. She'd bought the dress with that in mind, hoping it might re-ignite the spark. She should have known then something was up.

She looked in the mirror at her reflection and ran her palms down the curves of her body. Though she was a diminutive five foot three, she was naturally slender and worked hard to stay fit, with regular visits to the gym.

What hot-blooded male wouldn't want a piece of this?

Determined to find out, she went into the adjoining bathroom and quickly and efficiently applied her makeup. Dark eyeshadow, mascara, bright red lipstick. She set about blow-drying her hair and then brushed it into loose, shiny waves. What she lacked in height, she made up for by being perfectly proportioned and she knew just how to gain a few extra inches. She padded back into her bedroom and pulled out a pair of four-inch stilettos. She slipped them on and then stood back to survey the results.

The woman who stared back at her was sophisticated, sexy and with enough mystery in her gaze to create interest. For a moment, she was paralyzed with indecision.

I'm not the kind of woman to indulge in a one night stand... Is that what I'm contemplating? Taking a stranger home for the night?

Charlotte would never have described herself as spontaneous. Her siblings often teased her about the length of time it took her to make a decision, especially about something important. That was something she and Keith had had in common. Like him, she preferred to examine an issue from all angles, make lists of the pros and cons and yet here she was, contemplating something that could have significant repercussions and she'd barely thought it through.

She stared at her reflection in the mirror. She looked good. She felt good. It was time to reclaim her life. Time to remember she was an attractive, single,

twenty-something woman with her whole life ahead of her. With that thought in mind, she picked up an evening bag and after tossing in her house keys, lip

gloss and a credit card, she snapped the clasp shut and slid the strap over her shoulder. Bidding Raoul a good evening, she left her apartment.

Grayson Thorpe tilted the glass toward his lips and gulped at the yeasty, cold beer. The Brass Monkey was a popular bar in Cronulla and one that just happened to be his favorite hangout. Fortunately, it wasn't far from where he lived.

He'd been there since he'd left work more than two hours earlier. Truth be told, he'd probably already had more than his fair share of drinks, but he couldn't bring himself to go home. Earlier that day, he'd found out his wife was cheating on him. He didn't know how long it had been going on for, but he suspected it had been several months.

It was at least that long since she'd lost interest in their relationship, including having sex. He'd tried to be understanding, but when she'd continued to reject his advances, he'd finally suggested they see a marriage counselor.

Lydia had merely smirked. "A marriage counselor? Really, Grayson? How quaint. Have you forgotten I'm a psychologist? I counsel people for a living. You don't think I can't work through my own shit?"

He'd winced and tried to explain he hadn't meant it like that, but she'd refused to listen. He'd ended up spending yet another night alone in the spare room. A few days ago, he'd taken off his wedding ring. It was a big step, but he'd gotten to the point that he refused to wear it until he felt like her husband again. She probably hadn't even noticed.

With a sigh, he picked up his glass and drained his beer. The bartender moved closer.

"Can I get you another?"

Grayson looked down at the empty glass. "I probably shouldn't. I need to get home."

A knowing look passed over the bartender's face. "You got someone waiting for you?"

Grayson grimaced. "Nope."

The truth was, Lydia would mostly likely still be at work. And after that, she took a Pilates class. If for some reason she'd left work early or passed on her class, she wouldn't think anything of the fact he wasn't home. On a normal day, he'd still be at the office. On a normal day, he wouldn't be home for hours.

Lydia knew how much he wanted to make junior partner. It was one of the things they fought about. The fact he worked too hard, spent too many hours at the office. He'd tried to explain that it was important to work hard if he wanted to get promoted, but Lydia didn't seem inclined to accept that or to understand. In the end, he'd stopped offering explanations and she'd stopped asking where he'd been.

The sound of raucous laughter behind him caught his attention. He swiveled on the bar stool and surveyed the crowd. The place had filled up since he'd arrived. The clock above the bar showed it was a little past five. The bar was brimming with young professionals, both men and women, wearing power suits, tasteful ties, shiny shoes. Everyone seemed in high spirits, laughing and joking and sharing conversation. He'd never felt so alone.

His gaze slid further along the bar and snagged on a woman. She sat alone at the bar and sipped from a glass of red wine. Her bare legs were crossed, drawing his attention to their shapeliness. His gaze moved higher. She was a little overdressed for so early in the evening, but what the hell. Maybe her day had been as shitty as his.

His gaze skimmed over her tight, black leather dress and then paused on her breasts. They swelled generously above the zipper that divided the bodice, almost spilling over. Reflexively, his cock hardened. As if sensing his scrutiny, she turned and saw him. A slight smile turned up her ruby-red lips.

His heart kicked against his chest. Another rush of blood filled his cock. It strained against his boxers. It had been a long time since he'd felt such immediate attraction.

Christ, she's a stunner…

She sent him another look of encouragement from beneath her thick dark lashes. Once again, her lips taunted him with a teasing smile. Knowing he shouldn't, but unable to resist the temptation, he moved closer to her, seating himself on the empty stool beside her.

"Hi. I'm Grayson."

She inclined her head. "Charlotte."

She was even more beautiful up close. Her olive-toned skin was flawless. Her eyes were a deep blue, their almond shape accentuated by her makeup. Her dark brown wavy hair was rich and glossy and hung down past her shoulders. She moved to re-cross her legs and he caught a whiff of her perfume. Dark, heavy, exotic…

"Do you come here often, Grayson?"

Her voice had a husky tone to it that ignited a fire in his groin. Desire coursed through him. He struggled to remember what she'd asked.

"Um. No. Yes. Sometimes. After work. To blow off steam, you know?"

He covered his discomfort with a laugh, silently cursing his awkwardness. He couldn't remember the last time he'd flirted with a woman and never one as beautiful as this.

She took another sip of her wine, seemingly unfazed. "What do you do?" she asked.

"I'm a lawyer."

She pulled a face and this time, his laugh was genuine. "I know, right?" He winked.

She chuckled. "Well, now I know why you need to blow off steam."

He caught the eye of the bartender and signaled for another drink before returning his attention to Charlotte.

"So, how about you? I take it you're not a lawyer?" he teased.

She chuckled again and the husky sound of it shivered across his skin. "God no! I'm a cop."

This time it was his turn to pull a face. "A cop? You don't look like a cop."

She stared down at her wineglass, but a secret smile turned up her lips, sending another rush of heated blood to his cock. And then she turned to him with one perfect, shapely dark brow arched upwards.

"What do I look like then?"

Their gazes caught and held. His heart thumped. The air around them grew charged. He leaned closer. "You look like someone who wants a fuck."

Her eyes flared wide. He heard the sharp intake of her breath. A pulse fluttered under the smooth skin of her neck. He waited for her words of rebuke, or maybe even a slap across the face, but neither were forthcoming. Instead, she drew in a deep breath and smiled.

"You sound very confident of that."

He continued to hold her gaze. "I am."

She turned away abruptly and took refuge in her wine. His beer arrived and he thanked the bartender and handed the man some money. Grayson returned his attention to the woman.

"So... Shall we?"

She frowned and moved slightly away. "Shall we what?"

"Shall we dance?"

The lines on her forehead cleared. She smiled. "Oh. I thought you were going to suggest..."

Her voice faded away. Twin spots of color appeared on her cheeks. Her embarrassment touched something inside him. She looked younger than he'd first guessed and even more beautiful.

He gave her a wicked smile. "Suggest what? That we get the hell out of here and do what we've both been wanting to do the moment we set eyes on each other?" He ran the tip of his finger down her bare arm. Her eyes flared wide with awareness. He smiled with satisfaction and added, "Don't worry, we're going to do that too. But first, let's dance."

With that, he took her by the hand and led her confidently toward the dance floor.

CHAPTER TWO

With one hand on Grayson's shoulder and the other grasped firmly in his big hand, Charlotte couldn't help but admire the confident way he led her around the dance floor. The music had changed to something slow and Grayson pulled her in close. His body was hard and muscular. Her breasts brushed his chest and she gasped. Her nipples immediately pebbled. He shot her a knowing look.

She averted her gaze and stared at his jacket. He wore a charcoal-gray suit that fit him like it had been made for him. And perhaps it had. Lawyers who worked in the city were usually paid well, especially if they were good. He moved and the firm muscles in his shoulder bunched beneath her hand. Her heart skipped a beat. Her nostrils filled with the smell of his expensive cologne. Her chest went tight on a wave of desire. She looked up at him and caught the glint of amusement in his eyes.

"Don't look at me like that," he drawled.

"Like what?" She cursed silently at the breathless sound of her voice.

"Like you want to eat me all up."

The heat of embarrassment washed over her cheeks. She ducked her head and then brought it back up again to stare him boldly in the face. She'd come out tonight to have some fun, to throw caution to the wind. And yes, to take somebody home for the night. She'd never had a one night stand before, but somewhere between when she'd left her apartment and walked through the door of the Brass Monkey, she'd made up her mind to do something completely out of character.

After having her boyfriend wound her with a parting shot about her lack of flair in the bedroom, she needed something to boost her self-esteem and to restore her faith in her attractiveness as a woman. What better way to do that than to pick up a willing man? Some no-strings-attached sex. An orgasm free from emotional entanglements. That sounded exactly what she needed.

She'd noticed Grayson the minute she'd stepped inside the room. He'd been seated alone at the bar, drinking steadily. She'd taken a seat a few yards away from him and waited for him to notice her. It hadn't taken long.

His short blond hair, the color of ripened wheat, was mussed, like he'd run his hands through it more than once. His cheeks and jaw were rough with a five o'clock shadow. He was tall and his shoulders were broad. He looked like he worked out. Best of all, he wore no wedding ring.

She might have been prepared to set aside her morals for the night, but she drew the line at sleeping with married men. Of course, she was well aware a lack of wedding ring didn't necessarily indicate he wasn't married. There were plenty of men who went without that significant piece of jewelry, not always because they were being deceitful.

Some of them worked with their hands, or in dangerous jobs where wearing any kind of jewelry could have the potential to cause serious injury. This guy had already told her he was a lawyer. Hardly a workplace where the wearing of a wedding ring would give rise to physical injury. The only way to know for sure if he were married was to ask him.

"So, tell me a little more about yourself, Grayson. Are you married?"

He stumbled slightly, but recovered quickly. "Does it matter?"

She merely offered him a shrug. "It does to me."

He compressed his lips. "I'm...recently separated."

She acknowledged his response with a brief nod and a surreptitious sigh of relief. Though she'd been hoping for a different answer, at least she didn't have to feel guilty about potentially breaking up a marriage.

They were dancing so close she could feel the heat from his body. He released her hand and cupped her ass with both of his hands, pulling her even closer. She felt the unmistakable bulge of his erection, pressing insistently against her belly. The obvious evidence of his desire left her feeling weak with need. Her stomach
filled with butterflies.

The music came to an end and the DJ swung into another round of upbeat music. Grayson led her off the dance floor and returned her to her seat. She picked up her wineglass and emptied it. He did the same with his beer. Once again, he reached for her hand.

"Ready?" he asked.

She ignored the instinctive rush of protests on the tip of her tongue and forced herself to remember what this night was all about. With a determined intake of breath, she nodded. "Let's do it."

They walked out hand in hand. Outside on the footpath, Grayson drew her in close and kissed her. His lips were soft and firm and sensuous. He kissed like someone who knew what they were doing. Her arms crept around his neck and she kissed his back. His tongue pressed against her lips. She opened them, granting him access. The kiss deepened. She clung to his shoulders. When she finally lifted her head, she was breathless.

"Wow." She laughed nervously.

He gave a lopsided grin. "That was just for starters."

He grabbed her hand and pulled her along the footpath, keeping an eye out for a taxi. "Do you live close by?" he asked.

She felt a moment of hesitation. What she was about to do was fraught with danger. Any sane woman would never take a man she'd just met home. Anything could happen. He might be a serial killer, a drug dealer, a thief. And even though her gut was confident he was none of those things, he already knew too much about her. She sure as hell didn't want him knowing where she lived.

He regarded her expectantly, waiting for her answer. She smiled. "There's a hotel not far from here. How about we go there?"

He gave her a knowing look. "You don't trust me."

"Don't take it personally. I'm a cop. I don't trust anyone."

He grinned, flashing even, white teeth. "Fair enough."

Grayson pulled the woman in close beside him as she leaned back against the seat of the taxi. Night had settled in and they were cocooned in a seductive blanket of darkness. She gave the driver the address and then snuggled against him. She lay her head on his chest. He tightened his hold on her.

He thought about Lydia and was filled with guilt, but then he thrust the feelings away. Their marriage was over. He'd known it for months. He just hadn't wanted to acknowledge it, to say it out loud. That made it real. Meant he had to do something about it. Dividing property, refinancing debts. Thank God they didn't

have any kids.

Charlotte's hand stole over his lap and her fingers caressed him through his suit pants. His cock immediately sprang back to life. She pressed and fondled and squeezed and it was all he could do not to take her there and then. But he wanted more from her than a quick toss in the back of a taxi. He wanted her beneath him, clinging to him, her shapely legs around his hips, crying out his name.

His chest tightened on a surge of desire and he was relieved when the taxi pulled up to the curb a few minutes later. He fished in his back pocket for his wallet and handed the driver enough money to cover the fare. Taking Charlotte by the hand, he opened the door and together they slid across the seat and climbed out.

She stumbled slightly in her high heels and he grabbed her around the waist to steady her. He wasn't sure how much she'd had to drink. She didn't appear inebriated, but he didn't want to take advantage of her.

"Are you all right?" he asked.

"Yes. Of course. Why?"

"I just want to make sure you still want to do this."

In response, she draped her arms around his neck and pulled him close. She tilted her head backwards and then came up on her tiptoes and pressed her lips to his. Just the feel of her soft lips against his filled him with another hot rush of desire.

"Does that answer your question?" she asked.

Her voice was husky with need. Her eyes were filled with desire. She smiled slowly and then winked. His gut somersaulted. Blood pounded in his cock.

"I guess so," he murmured.

With his arm around her shoulders, they walked past the doorman and into the plush lobby of the hotel. Grayson murmured for her to stay right there and then went up to the front desk. In short order, he secured a room and came back to her brandishing a room card.

"Tenth floor. Ocean view."

Once again, she wrapped her arms around him and gave him a passionate kiss. "An ocean view hasn't got anything on the view right here."

Grayson clung to his self-control. He walked her over to the bank of lifts and pressed the button. He pulled her close against him while they waited. Finally the lift arrived and he followed her in. He was relieved to discover it was empty. As the doors closed silently behind them, he couldn't wait a moment longer to kiss her
again.

Pushing her up against the wall of the lift, he held her immobile with his body. His head came down and he claimed her lips, kissing her urgently, filled with pent-up passion. They stayed that way, lips locked together, until the slide of the lift doors opening at their floor registered in his mind. He pulled back with
reluctance, pleased that she looked as dazed as he felt.

He took her hand and led her halfway down a long corridor, coming to a halt outside a door that had the number "18" stenciled on it in fancy silver lettering. He pushed the keycard into the slot. The light flashed green and he opened the door. With her hand still in his, he pulled her inside and immediately took her in his arms again.

Their lips met in another heated kiss, this one more frantic than the last. It was as if they'd both come to the decision that now they were in the privacy of a hotel room, they were free to explore the powerful desire they'd both felt the moment they'd laid eyes on each other. Grayson cupped her face in his hands and kissed her over and over again. His body was on fire. He burned to feel every inch of her, skin to skin, on a mattress, buried deep inside her.

With that objective in mind, he backed her up toward the bed, his lips fused with hers. Desire pulsed through him, driving him wild. He felt like he might explode. It had been months since he'd had sex with Lydia. His balls were heavy and tight. But this wasn't just about that. He'd never felt so turned on by a woman. Not even during his university days when he'd slept with more women than he cared to remember.

This is madness… I don't even know this woman… How can she drive me so wild?

Slowly, he pulled away so that he could snatch a breath of air. He was pleased to see Charlotte's chest heaved, too. He moved to switch on one of the bedside lamps and flooded the room with soft, golden light. Glancing around him, he took note of the spacious hotel room. Like the girl behind the counter had told him, it boasted sensational ocean views.

Decorative street lights illuminated the wide, sandy-white beach. Night had stolen all but the slightest glimmer of moonlight on the water. They could be looking at a desert for all they could see. Not that the view mattered. He couldn't care less what was outside the window. His entire focus was on the woman in the room.

She reached for his tie and began loosening it, smiling softly to herself as she did so. Holding his gaze, she slid the tie from around his neck, flung it over her shoulder and then started in on the buttons on his shirt. Emboldened by her eagerness to get him naked, he reached out and took hold of the tab on her zipper.

Their gazes meshed. The heat of desire that burned in her eyes nearly did him in. He inched the zipper halfway down, slowly exposing her large round breasts. They were encased in a scrap of sexy black lace. His breath caught. It was all he could do not to fling her on the bed and fuck her.

With an effort, he held onto his self-control, his breath hissing through clenched teeth. Seemingly oblivious to his inner struggle, she made a sound of impatience and pulled the tail of his shirt out of his suit pants. She pushed the soft cotton off his shoulders and tossed it to the floor. She stared at his naked chest as if

mesmerized. He knew exactly how she felt. He was having a hard time dragging his gaze away from her breasts.

Reaching out, he eased the zipper of her dress lower. The leather parted, exposing more and more of her skin. Grayson's breath caught. She was even more beautiful in the gentle glow of the lamplight. With her dress half undone and her black lace encased breasts overflowing the opening, he was filled with the need to touch her. He stepped forward at the same time she did and they came together with a passion that left him breathless.

Frantic now, he reached for the zipper tab and pulled it all the way down. Her dress separated in two pieces of shiny leather. She shrugged out of it and dropped it to the floor. He stared at her in amazement. She was the most perfectly formed woman he'd ever seen.

She barely came up to his shoulder, even in her extra high heels. Petite in stature, yet curvy in all the right places. Her generous breasts, the flare of her hips, the slim, shapely thighs and calves. He was overawed by her beauty. And then her hands went to his waist and she started in on his belt. Her fingers brushed his cock and he sucked in his breath.

The smile she gave him was filled with satisfaction. Her eyes teased him, along with her fingers. And then she had his button popped and the zipper of his pants down. He shucked them off his hips and kicked them aside. She put her hand inside his boxers and encircled his cock. He barely suppressed a moan.

"You like that?" she asked, her voice husky with need.

"I like it a lot," he managed.

She looked at him, her eyes intense. "I want to see you naked."

Charlotte heard the words fall out of her mouth and could hardly believe she'd said them. She was hardly experienced when it came to sexual partners. Especially when it came to taking the lead. Before Keith, she'd only had one other lover. But somehow, with Grayson it seemed natural. She felt so feminine, so powerful, like she was the one calling the shots. She saw the way he looked at her, the heat, the desire in his eyes: Like he'd die if he didn't have her. It was a heady feeling.

The soft light from the bedside lamp illuminated his pectorals. They were tanned and toned and well-defined. His washboard stomach drew her gaze. She reached out and raked her fingernails across it. She heard him suck in his breath and smiled to herself, loving the fact she could elicit from him such an involuntary response. His muscles were as hard and firm as they looked. Unable to help herself, she then traced the line of dark hair that went from his belly button and disappeared into the top of his boxers.

He stopped her hand before she had a chance to caress his erection once again and placed her hand palm-down on his chest. She could feel the pounding of his heart and it matched the rhythm of her own.

"Can you feel that? Can you feel what you do to me? I want to fuck you, Charlotte."

His coarse language excited her. Her nipples tightened in response. Grayson noticed. His lips parted on a silent intake of breath. His eyes darkened with desire.

His reaction sent another wave of need coursing through her and all of a sudden she was impatient to feel his skin against hers. She reached around and unclasped her bra and let the scrap of lace fall to the floor. Grayson's eyes flared wide. She held his gaze as she slowly stepped out of her panties.

"God, you're so beautiful."

She basked in his obvious admiration and then reached out for his boxers. He helped her remove them and then stood while she looked her fill. He was fully aroused and every bit as beautiful as she'd imagined. Broad shoulders. Narrow hips. Long, muscular legs. Everything about him turned her on.

"Fuck me," she breathed and was gratified by his husky growl.

He took her in his arms and kissed her roughly, almost savagely, as if his control had finally snapped. Bending low, he picked her up in his arms and carried her to the bed. He lowered her to the mattress and followed her down, covering her body with his. Hardness melded against softness until they were as one. He kissed her mouth, her cheeks and eyes and then made his way down to her breasts. He suckled one nipple and then the other and she writhed against him in an ecstasy
of delight.

Desire burned in her core. She stirred restlessly against him, urging him on with small moans of encouragement. And then reality reared its head. She flushed with
embarrassment, unable to believe she'd left her apartment with the single purpose of finding a man for the night and she'd forgotten all about protection. Averting her gaze, she pushed gently against him.

He frowned down at her. "Charlotte? Is something wrong?"

She uttered the solitary word. "Condom."

Relief passed over his face. He moved off her and reached into his suit pants. He pulled out a small packet and quickly sheathed himself. He rejoined her on the bed and once again kissed her deeply, thoroughly, flooding her with desire. Then he settled himself between her thighs. His cock nudged at her entrance. Her legs fell open in silent encouragement. In one swift thrust, he was inside her. She gasped from the sudden intrusion.

He felt huge and hard and hot, filling her like no other had. She clung to his shoulders as his hips moved in a familiar rhythm. The desire inside her built to a crescendo. His breath was harsh in her ear. And then she was there, at the precipice. Her fingernails dug into his shoulders. Her inner muscles clenched and contracted. With a gasp, she cried out her relief and crashed over the other side. Grayson thrust harder, faster, deeper and a few minutes later, he also found his release. He collapsed on top of her for a moment or two, panting.

And then he rolled off her and she was left thinking about how wonderful it had been. If this was how one-night stands felt, she was all for them. In fact, she looked forward to doing it all over again.

❦

CHAPTER THREE

The sound of Charlotte's phone ringing dragged her from a deep sleep. She opened her eyes and blinked, feeling disorientated. She squinted through the dimness at the unfamiliar room. The light was all wrong. It was too dark. A faint headache made itself known. She closed her eyes against it, wanting nothing more than to escape back into sleep.

And then memories from last night came back to her in a rush. Her eyes flew open and her gaze went to the other side of the bed. It was empty.

He's gone.

The mess of the bedsheets, her scattered clothes and the pleasant soreness in her thigh muscles were the only reminders of what had happened. Struggling to sit up, she reached for the lamp switch. The illuminated numbers on the clock radio told her it was a little past four in the morning.

"Ugh!" she groaned.

The phone kept ringing from somewhere far away. Her thoughts immediately went to her family. While her parents were only in their sixties, it was always possible that something might have happened to them. A heart attack. A stroke. A car accident. Or maybe it was one of her brothers or sisters who was the subject of the early morning call?

Get a grip, Charlotte. For goodness sake! Answer the damn phone!

Climbing out of bed, she found her evening bag on the floor. Studiously avoiding looking at her crumpled pile of underwear, she picked up the bag and pulled out her phone. She checked the screen.

Wendell Boney.

Shit. Her boss. Pushing back a hank of hair, Charlotte sat down on the bed. She drew in a deep breath and plastering a smile on her face, she answered the phone.

"Good morning, sir. What's going on?"

"Sorry to call you so early, Charlotte, but there's been a murder. I thought you might want to ride along. Tony's lead investigator, of course, but you could—"

"Yes! Yes!" Charlotte shouted, coming fully awake. "Of course I want to ride along."

"Well, okay. I'll text you the details. You can catch up with Tony at the scene."

Tossing the phone on the bed, Charlotte threw on her underwear and the leather dress. She wasted another few moments searching for her stilettos and then grabbed her evening bag, tossed her phone back inside, and headed for the door. She thought fleetingly of the sexy lawyer who'd shown her such a good time, but there was no time left to think about that now.

Pulling the door closed behind her, she headed for the lift. Excitement and apprehension coursed through her. Her first homicide. Better not mess it up.

By the time Charlotte arrived at the crime scene, the sun had peeked its head over the horizon. The rush of catching a taxi home, showering and changing before heading out again had her adrenaline pumping, along with the knowledge she was about to front up to her very first murder scene. She found herself in an upmarket Cronulla neighborhood, a couple of miles from the beach. In fact, it wasn't all that far from her apartment. The realization was slightly disconcerting.

Climbing out of her car, she observed a large freestanding home, *circa* mid-2000s, rendered pale gray brick structure, white trim and a black tile roof. It was of a similar style and age to all the other houses in the street. The wooden front door was painted charcoal and currently stood wide open.

Uniformed officers traipsed in and out of the house. Charlotte hoped someone had secured the scene.

Blue-and-white checked police tape cordoned off the front yard. Charlotte ducked under the tape and flashed her newly-minted homicide credentials to the general duties cops who were gathered on the lawn.

"Is Sabattini here yet?" she asked.

"Tony? Haven't seen him," one of the cops said.

The other cop snickered. "No doubt he's sleeping off another hangover. Surely you know what he's like."

Charlotte bit down on a surge of irritation. Her partner might very well be the joke of her department, but it annoyed her to see two junior officers blatantly disrespecting him. She pulled out her phone and dialed Tony's number, praying the officers were wrong. To her relief, he answered on the third ring.

"Barrington, what the hell? It's half-past five in the morning. This better be good."

She swallowed a sigh. "I'm sorry, Tony. Didn't Wendell call you?"

There was a pause and then Tony spoke again. "Looks like I might have missed his call," he mumbled.
"What's going on?"

Charlotte swallowed another sigh. "We have a situation. I've been called out to a homicide. I thought you might want to tag along."

He grunted in response. "Mind what you're saying, Barrington. I'm the senior detective here. You're nothing but a—"

"Okay, okay. That was a joke. But you know what, I'm here and you're not. If you want to hold my hand and guide me through the murder scene, I suggest you get over here fast."

With that she ended the call and then texted him the address. She was relieved when he sent her a thumbs up in response. Though she didn't doubt her investigative abilities, the pressure to do things right was enormous. She'd be pleased for some support, even if it was in the form of Tony Sabattini, a cop with an enviable success record in his day, but who'd seen too much in his time as a homicide detective and who should have been put out to pasture a long time ago.

Knowing he was on his way over, Charlotte gave instructions for the uniformed officers to canvass the neighborhood for witnesses and then waited for Sabattini before entering the house. Drunk or not, she'd feel much more confident with Tony by her side. He was a veteran homicide cop. She was a newbie. She wasn't arrogant enough to assume she knew all she needed to. Someone's wife-daughter-mother-sister was lying dead inside. They deserved answers. They deserved to have the perpetrator caught.

Sabattini arrived in his beat-up old Ford about fifteen minutes later. It ground to a halt among a choke of smoke. He climbed out and slowly made his way up the garden path. It took him a couple of attempts to duck under the police tape. He drew closer and Charlotte's heart sank. She could smell alcohol on his breath.

"Thanks for coming," she murmured, deliberately ignoring the other. Even with a few drinks under his belt, she had no doubt Sabattini was still much better at this than she was.

He grunted a response and then cleared his throat and turned his head. He hawked up a lump of phlegm and spat it out. Charlotte ignored him. Together, they walked over to the uniforms.

"What do we have?" Sabattini rasped.

The oldest officer cleared his throat. "Lydia Thorpe. Caucasian, mid-to late twenties. Has suffered multiple stab wounds. We're still waiting for the guys from the morgue to arrive, but it appears our vic's been dead several hours. She's cool to the touch and rigor mortis has set in."

"Who found her?" Sabattini asked.

"The husband. Says he arrived home around four this morning and found her dead on the living room floor."

"Where is he?" Charlotte asked.

"Over there." The cop indicated a tall, broad-shouldered man who stood with his back to her in the front yard. Short blond hair. Tall, athletic. He certainly looked strong enough to overpower a woman. In the dawn light, something about him looked familiar, but she couldn't place him.

Charlotte returned her attention to the uniforms. "Has anyone spoken to him yet?"

"No. We were waiting for you guys to arrive."

Charlotte and Tony walked over to the husband. "Mr Thorpe, I'm Detective Sabattini and this is Detective Barrington. Would you mind answering a few questions?"

The husband turned slowly to face them. Charlotte gasped in shock.

Oh, God... It's him... Grayson... The man from the bar... The man I spent the night with...

He looked just as shocked as she felt. She'd told him she was a cop. She hadn't told him she worked in homicide. Green eyes that were clouded with pain and confusion stared back at her, filled with questions neither of them could ask. Even so, she felt a familiar kick of attraction. She could feel herself being drawn in. Her mind was filled with flashbacks of her running her hands over his chiseled jaw, his biceps, the toned planes of his stomach...

He still wore the same charcoal-gray suit, though the tie was missing. She cataloged each of his features, her mind in turmoil. Her heart thumped. Her chest went tight. All of a sudden, she couldn't breathe.

I need to tell Sabattini...

Oblivious to Charlotte's turmoil, Tony pulled out his notebook and a pen. "Can you think of anyone who'd want to do this to your wife?" Sabattini asked, his gaze fixed on Thorpe's face.

Grayson looked pained. "I don't know. No. I... I can't think of anyone."

"What do you do for a crust, Mr Thorpe?" Sabattini asked.

"I'm a lawyer. I specialize in probate law and litigation. I mainly represent disgruntled beneficiaries who want to challenge a will."

Sabattini snorted. "Sounds like that could get ugly."

Thorpe shrugged. "I guess. From time to time. No one likes to lose, especially when there's money involved."

"Could this have something to do with you?" Sabattini asked. "Did you piss anyone off lately?"

Thorpe paled and looked visibly shaken. "Oh, God. I hope not."

Charlotte finally found her voice. "So there could be someone with that kind of anger against you?"

Thorpe frowned and then slowly shook his head from side to side. "No, surely not. No, I've put some people off side from time to time, but I don't believe any of them would be capable of murder."

"Are you thinking of anyone in particular?" Charlotte asked.

"Maybe. My latest case. The judgement was handed down last week. We... we won. There was a lot of money at stake. Ten million. I represented two of three siblings who were unhappy with their share. It got pretty nasty."

"How did the others fare?" Sabattini asked.

"Not so good. The judgement was in the sum of six million dollars, plus costs. That's going to come out of the losing party's share."

"That's enough to make most people angry," Sabattini observed. "Why are you so sure the disgruntled relative couldn't be responsible for your wife's murder?"

Grayson scrubbed at his hair. "Well, he knows nothing about me, for one! I'm just another lawyer. And he sure as hell knows nothing about Lydia! I work for Sydney Legal. It's a large law firm in the city. Lydia rarely comes into the city. I think she's been to my office all of three times over the five years I've worked there."

He told me he was separated...

Once again, she was bombarded with images of them naked. With an effort, she forced them aside.

"How long have you two been married?" Charlotte asked stiffly.

"Four years. We met at university. I was studying law. She was studying medicine."

"So she's a doctor?" Sabattini asked.

"No. She switched to psychology about two years into her medical degree."

"Where did your wife work?" Sabattini asked.

"She has...had her own counseling practice in Cronulla Plaza. She opened the doors a couple of years ago."

"Did she ever mention any patients she was having trouble with?" Charlotte asked.

"No, she never talked about her work. Patient confidentiality and all that. It was the same for me."

"Was there anything unusual about your wife's behavior in recent times?" Sabattini asked.

"What do you mean?"

"You know, strange phone calls, hang-ups, did she act like something was troubling her? Did you ever hear her arguing with someone over the phone?"

He averted his gaze and stared at the grass. "No, nothing like that."

Charlotte frowned. There was a subtle change in Thorpe's demeanor. A new tension around his mouth and his body had a tautness that hadn't been in evidence before. Charlotte flicked a glance toward her partner. The surreptitious movement of his head reassured her Sabattini had also noticed.

"Are you sure?" Charlotte asked.

Thorpe looked at her. "Yes, of course."

"What about the two of you?" Sabattini asked. "Any problems in your marriage?"

Charlotte's stomach somersaulted. She held her breath, waiting for Thorpe's response. He glanced at her briefly and then averted his gaze.

"Actually, we hadn't been getting on so good lately. Nothing I could put my finger on. She just seemed kind of... distant. We hadn't been intimate for months."

Charlotte eased out her breath. Until they had a time of death, she had to treat him like any other potential suspect. "Did the two of you fight?"

Thorpe shrugged. "I guess. Sometimes. Everyone fights."

"How often?" she asked.

"Not often."

"Did it ever get physical?" she asked.

His eyes flared with anger. "Never."

"What did you fight about?" Sabattini asked.

"I don't know. The usual stuff."

"Such as?" Sabattini persisted.

"Work, mainly."

"You said you didn't talk about your work with each other," Charlotte said.

"We didn't. What I meant was, we argued about how much time I spent at the office. That kind of thing." And then he looked at Sabattini, his eyes hard. "Am I a suspect, Detective?"

"Everyone's a suspect Mr Thorpe," Sabattini replied smoothly. "Surely you know those closest to the victim are the first ones we look at."

Thorpe gave a half-shrug in response.

"Do you have any children, Mr Thorpe?" Charlotte asked.

"No."

"Can't have any? Don't want any?"

"Neither. We... We haven't...hadn't gotten around to having that discussion, yet."

Charlotte blinked in surprise. "I'm sorry, how long did you say you've been married?"

Four years."

"Right. Four years. And in all that time you've never had a conversation with your wife about whether or not you want kids?"

Once again, his only response was a non-committal shrug.

"What time did you leave for work yesterday?" Sabattini asked.

"I was out the door by six o'clock. Same as every other day."

"You told one of our officers you arrived home about four this morning. Is that right?" Sabattini asked.

Thorpe drew in a deep breath and then released it on a sigh. "Yes."

Charlotte fixed her gaze on the ground, unable to look at Grayson. She braced herself for Sabattini's inevitable next line of questioning.

"That's a hell of a long day, Mr Thorpe. What time did you finish work?"

A flush stained Grayson's cheeks. "I... I left early. Just after three."

"I see. And where did you go?"

"I went to a bar."

"Until four this morning?"

"No. I'm not sure what time it was when I left the bar."

"Closing time?" Sabattini asked.

"No. Not that late. Maybe seven or eight."

"Where did you go then?" Sabattini asked.

Charlotte's breath caught in her throat.

I have to tell Sabattini… I have to come clean…

She tensed, waiting for Grayson's response.

"I met a woman in the bar. We went to a hotel. Afterwards, I went back to the bar and retrieved my car and drove home. That's when I found Lydia."

"Does this woman have a name?"

Grayson's gaze glanced off hers. Once again, Charlotte held her breath.

Grayson looked back at Sabattini and shook his head. "I guess. But we didn't exchange personal details."

Charlotte slowly eased out her breath and was immediately overcome with guilt.

I have to tell him… But I can hardly do it here…

"What about earlier? Where were you before you went to the bar?" Sabattini asked.

"I was at work."

"All day?"

"Well, I went out for lunch. About twelve. I got back to the office at two."

Charlotte forced herself back into the conversation before Sabattini wondered what was amiss. "That's a rather long lunch break," she said.

Grayson glanced again in her direction. "I had a few errands to run."

"Where did you go?" Sabattini asked.

Thorpe shrugged. "Does it matter?"

Sabattini gave him a hard look. "Don't piss me off, Mr Thorpe. Your wife's dead. Everything
matters."

A look of impatience crossed Grayson's face. Once again, he looked at Charlotte and then refocused his attention on her partner. "You're wasting time with all these questions. I didn't do it."

"Until we have a definitive time of death, we need to cover all bases," Charlotte replied.

Thorpe sighed. "I went to the mayor's office."

"In the city?" she asked.

"No. In...Sutherland."

"Your local council? You planning on doing some renovations?" Sabattini asked.

Thorpe flushed. "No. My meeting with the mayor was...of a personal nature."

"He a friend of yours?" Sabattini asked.

Thorpe's flush deepened. Charlotte caught a flash of anger in his eyes.

"No. We're not friends."

"What did you do afterwards?" Charlotte asked.

"I had a two o'clock appointment with a client in my office. I left again right afterwards. A bit after three. Ask my secretary. She'll confirm what I said."

"Oh, don't worry. We will." Sabattini shot him another hard look. "What time did you arrive at the bar last night?"

"About half-past three. I drove there straight from work."

"Three seems awfully early for a lawyer to be leaving work. Were you meeting someone?"

"No. I... I had a lot on my mind. I needed to get away for a while, to think."

So you went to a bar. Does this bar have a name?" Sabattini asked.

"The Brass Monkey. It's downstairs in Cronulla Plaza."

Sabattini's eyes narrowed. "Your wife had her office in the Cronulla Plaza, didn't she?"

Grayson's gaze remained steady on Sabattini's face. "Yes. So?"

"Nothing. Just a little curious that you'd go somewhere so close to wear your wife works. Especially when you were on the prowl for a little something on the side."

Anger flashed across Grayson's face. He glared at Sabattini. "First of all, it was half-past three when I got there. My wife's office closes at five. She normally does a Pilates class straight after work and then goes home. There was no chance of running into her. Secondly, I didn't go there to pick up a woman, Detective. I went

there to escape. Like I said, my wife had grown more and more distant and I didn't know what to do about it. I had a few drinks. Then I got talking to a woman. We had a drink. We danced. I didn't plan on sleeping with her, but it happened."

"I assume the bartender at the Brass Monkey will verify this?"

Grayson shrugged. "I don't know if he paid that much attention to us, but he should certainly remember I was there. He served me several times."

Charlotte took down the pertinent details, including Grayson's contact numbers. Then she handed him her business card. "We'll be in touch, Mr Thorpe. No doubt we'll have more questions. In the meantime, if you think of anything else, call me. By the way, we'll need you to stop by the station and make a formal statement. Sometime later today would be good. Oh, and don't go planning any trips out of town without telling us. Until we have an exact time of death and we've checked out alibis, we can't rule anyone out."

Grayson gave her an unreadable look and then slowly tucked the small piece of white cardboard into the pocket of his shirt. His eyes were still dazed with shock. Charlotte wished she could offer him some sympathy, but the truth was, she was also in a spin. Hell, for all she knew she was Grayson's alibi. Or not. Until they knew the time of death, anything was possible. She definitely needed to come clean with Sabattini. Now.

She turned toward her partner and braced herself for what needed to be done. Sabattini appeared oblivious to her inner turmoil. With casual movements, he tucked his notebook and pen back into his shirt pocket. Before she could open her mouth, he turned on his heel and headed toward the house. Charlotte's teeth snapped shut.

He didn't even bother to check if I was following him! Talk about rude and insufferable! We're meant to be partners...

Swallowing her irritation, she hurried after the senior detective. "Tony? Wait up. Tony? Could I have a word?"

To her consternation, he ignored her. Either that, or he didn't hear her. He continued passed two more officers and then into the house. Panting slightly from exertion, Charlotte came to a halt in the entryway.

The house was clean and modern. The overall color scheme was pale gray, including the tiled floor and soft furnishings. A massive wide-screen TV was mounted on one wall of the living room, complete with an impressive surround sound system. Whoever lived here liked watching movies, or sport, or whatever. The screen was big enough that it would almost feel like you were there on the set, or in the game.

The kitchen was a mixture of pale marble countertops and white cupboards. Like the rest of the house, it was also scrupulously clean. And then some of the uniformed officers moved aside and Charlotte caught a glimpse of the body. Her stomach clenched. Her breath came fast. With an effort, she kept herself calm. If she wanted to succeed as a homicide detective, she'd better get used to the sight of corpses.

Lydia Thorpe lay in a pool of blood on the tiles, not far from a large sectional sofa that took up a decent amount of the open plan living room. She was fully dressed in a tailored navy-blue suit and a pale pink silk blouse. The flash of a light bulb startled Charlotte. She blinked. The police photographer took another photo of the body and then moved a few steps away and took another one. Taking care not to step in any of the blood spatter, he continued to move cautiously around the perimeter of the crime scene, all the while preserving the gruesome images on his camera.

A bunch of crime scene technicians were also there processing the scene. Checking the place for fingerprints, bagging evidence and searching for pieces of the puzzle that would eventually come together to form a picture of what had happened there and who might be responsible. Charlotte caught sight of her partner talking to one of the uniforms.

"Any signs of forced entry?" Sabattini asked.

"No."

"Do we know if anything's missing?"

"I'm not sure. We haven't spoken to the husband about that yet, but the place is as neat as a pin. No cupboards left open. Nothing rummaged through. This doesn't look like a robbery to me."

Charlotte compressed her lips and stood there in silence. No signs of forced entry. No signs of a robbery. Whoever it was, it appeared Lydia Thorpe had invited the killer into her home, had possibly even known them.

"Have you found the murder weapon?" Sabattini asked the uniform.

"No. And there's nothing missing from the knife block we found in the kitchen."

Tony scratched at the bristles on his chin. "So the killer came prepared. That indicates premeditation."

"Certainly looks that way," the uniform replied.

A disturbance in the front doorway snagged Charlotte's attention. She turned around in time to see Doctor Samantha Wolfe, the state's chief forensic pathologist, enter the room, along with two morgue technicians who had a stretcher and body bag in tow. Samantha greeted those assembled with a brief smile and a wave and then went straight over to where Lydia lay. The photographer had finished and now took a step backwards to allow Samantha access to the body. She opened her black medical bag and began her examination.

Charlotte glanced at Sabattini. The uniform had since moved away. She couldn't put it off a moment longer. Dragging in a quick breath, she pulled Sabattini aside. Her stomach churned with nerves.

Sabattini frowned. "What is it, Barrington? You're looking a little queasy. Don't tell me you're going to lose it at your first homicide?"

With an effort, Charlotte forced herself to speak. "Of course not. It's nothing like that."

"Then what's the problem?"

She licked her dry lips and averted her gaze.

"Come on, Barrington. I don't have time for this. Spit it out."

He went to turn away and she reached out and grabbed his arm, stopping him. He frowned again.

"Tony... I'm sorry, but... I know him. Grayson Thorpe."

Tony's bushy eyebrows shot upwards. "You know him?"

Charlotte pulled a face. "Well, I don't *know* him.... The thing is, I..." She licked her lips again, and looked away, this time in embarrassment. "It was me. I was the woman he met in the Brass Monkey last night. I was the woman who went to a hotel with him."

Sabattini's eyes widened in shock. "Holy crap. You're kidding me?"

"I wish I was."

"So that's your thing, is it? Having sex with strangers?"

Charlotte tensed. "Not that it's any of your business, but no. It's not. I... I've never done that before."

Sabattini blew his breath out on a heavy sigh. "Hell. This complicates matters."

Charlotte grimaced. "You're telling me."

"We'll have to tell the boss. You won't be able to work on this case."

Her shoulders slumped on a sigh. "I thought you might say that."

He gave her an impatient look "What did you expect? It can't be any other way. You're off the case. As soon as we get back to the station, I'll bring Wendell up to speed. You can stay for now, but don't touch anything. I mean it. Stay the hell out of the way and for fuck's sake, don't go talking to anyone. Got it?"

His voice had turned as hard as his eyes. Charlotte nodded reluctantly. Inwardly, she cursed.

My first homicide case and I've managed to mess it up… Damn it!

Charlotte stood back and watched in silence as the morgue technicians zipped up a body bag around the corpse. They then lifted the body onto the stretcher and wheeled it away. With a sigh, she found a spot out of the way and hoped like crazy this wasn't the end of her incredibly short career in homicide.

Broken Promises is available for pre-order at all digital retailers. It is due for release on 30 November, 2021

Get a free book when you sign up for Chris Taylor's newsletter at: http://www.christaylorauthor.com.au

Other books by Chris Taylor

The Munro Family Series (in order)

The Profiler

The Investigator

The Predator

The Betrayal

The Deception

The Negotiator

The Christmas Vigil (A novella)

The Ransom

The Defendant

The Shooting

The Maker

The Sydney Harbour Hospital Series (in order)

The Perfect Husband

The Body Thief

The Baby Snatchers

The Final Bullet

The Debt Collector

The Lab Test

The Stolen Identity

The Cliff-top Killer

The Likeable Fraudster

The Sydney Legal Series
(in order)

An Accidental Murderer

At the Hand of her Father

A Woman Scorned

Lies and Deception

Ordinary Evil

The Ties that Bind

The Perfect Crime

A Toxic Inheritance

Malicious Love

The Craigdon Family Series

(in order)

Callum

Joel

Isabella

Nicholas

Sophia

Flynn

Noah

Logan

Elizabeth

The Barrington Family Series

(in order)

Broken Lives

Broken Promises

Broken Bonds

Broken Spirits

Broken Minds

Broken Vows

Broken Hearts

Broken Dreams

Broken Homes

The Fairfax Family Series

(in order)

A Cattleman in Disguise

A Cattleman's Quest

A Cattleman's Daughter

A Cattleman's Secret Baby

To Catch a Cattleman

The Doctor and the Cattleman

To Rescue a Cattleman

A Cattleman's Heart

For the Love of a Cattleman

Bachelors and Brides Series

(in order)

Matilda

Austin

Farrah

Benjamin

Verity

Denver

Ebony

Tyrone

Willow

Books by Chris Taylor

Writing as

Bella
Christian

This Is Where It Ends Series
(in order)

Jessie's Story

Ryan's Story

Holly's Story

Sarah's Story

Veronica's Story

366

Love audiobooks? Check out Chris Taylor Books on audio

iTunes   Amazon   Audible

Join Chris Taylor's Facebook reader group/fan page and be among the
first to receive news of book releases, cover reveals and other amazing offers.

Join Now!

Acknowledgments

As usual, no book comes into being without a lot of help and support by my friends and family. A world of thanks must go to my wonderful editor, Pat Thomas. Thank you for everything that you do to make my stories even more amazing than I could ever dare to dream. To former Detective Superintendent Michael Kilfoyle, thank you for lending my story credibility. Any mistakes are wholly my own.

To Justin Mendez and all of the team at 100 Covers, thank you for the fantastic book cover. To my sister, Nicole Guihot and to my friends, Ally Thomson and Sue Ricardo, thank you for your excellent editorial comments, proof reading skills and suggestions. I hope you like the final result.

To the fantastic writer organizations such as Romance Writers of Australia, Romance Writers of America and Romance Writers of New Zealand for all the help, support and encouragement they offer new and aspiring writers, including me.

To my readers, thank you for your support and love for my stories. Your encouragement and enjoyment make this journey all worthwhile.

And lastly, to my friends and family, especially my husband and children. Thank you for putting up with late dinners and even later conversations as I've emerged day after day from the sometimes scary but always enthralling world I've created on my computer.

About The Author

Chris Taylor grew up on a farm in north-west New South Wales, Australia. She always had a thirst for stories and recalls writing her first book at the ripe old age of eight. Always a lover of romance and happily-ever-afters, a career in criminal law sparked her interest in intrigue and suspense. For Chris to be able to combine romance with suspense in her books is a dream come true.

Chris is married to Linden and is the mother of five children. If not behind her computer, you can find her doing the school run, taxiing children to swimming lessons, football, ballet and cricket. In her spare time, Chris loves to read her favorite authors who include Richard North Patterson, Sandra Brown, Kathleen E Woodiwiss and Jude Devereaux.

You can find out more about Chris and get a free book when you sign up for her newsletter at her website:
http://www.christaylorauthor.com.au
Join Chris on Facebook at:

https://www.facebook.com/christaylorauthor/
Join Chris Taylor's reader/fan group on Facebook at:
https://www.facebook.com/groups/1758023621144744

9 781925 441000